The

TINKERER'S

DAUGHTER

By

Jamie Sedgwick

Published by Timber Hill Press

Look for these & other exciting titles by
Jamie Sedgwick:

Tinker's War, Book Two of the Tinkerer's Daughter

The Hank Mossberg, Private Ogre Mysteries

Aboard the Great Iron Horse (Steampunk Series)

Karma Crossed

The Shadow Born Trilogy

The Raven King's Chair

Now available, the thrilling conclusion to *Tinker's War:*

Blood & Steam!

Visit www.jamiesedgwick.com for more info!

Acknowledgements:

Special thanks to Tanja, Jeramiah, Mel, Jack, Lisa, Ian, Melissa, and all the others who've helped bring my stories to life.

Chapter 1

My only clear memory of my father is from the day he left me. That frosty autumn morning remains vivid in my memory as if I were there now watching the scene play out, though I can't seem to recall any other day before it.

Patches of frost glistened under the early morning sun and a cold wind howled across the southern plains, funneling up into the tiny valley around us. The trees blazed with fiery colors, painting the mountains in broad swaths of crimson and gold. Behind us, I could see the mouth of the valley and the plains spreading out, and beyond that, the narrow line of trees that sprouted up from the muddy banks of the Stillwater River.

I was riding in our old hay cart in tow behind my father's great stallion, bundled against the cold in a heavy wool blanket. I remember the uncomfortable shaking of the cart and the incessant squeaking of the rusty old leaf springs as we rattled up the mountainside.

Up ahead I saw the awkward shape of an old windmill rising up out of the hillside, and behind it a distant curl of chimney smoke drifting through the trees. The windmill blades were not spinning, despite the breeze.

Then, just as the trees began to close in around us, Father reined in his stallion and brought the cart to a shaking halt. I craned my neck around as he dismounted, and watched him walk towards me. He lifted me to his chest and I readily accepted his warm embrace. His skin was abrasive, his beard like steel wool against my cheek, but I pressed myself closer. I was afraid. I'd never been away from our tiny homestead before.

I glanced around and saw that we were at the edge of a broad clearing. The windmill stood behind us now, just down the road. Up ahead I saw a small cottage and, a stone's throw away, a crumbling old barn backed right up to the mountain.

Something I'd never seen before, a slow moving paddle-wheel, sprouted out of the west wall of the cottage. The lower half rested in a creek that gushed out of the woods behind the house. I would later learn that this wheel not only pumped a constant supply of fresh water into the house and garden, but also harnessed energy. To me, on that day, it was simply another oddity in a place filled with them.

Junk lay scattered from the cottage all the way down to the road. It sprouted up from the lawn in tall piles and stacks like the ruins of some ancient civilization on the verge of collapse. It was the oddest assortment of things I have ever seen. Rotting old wine barrels groaned under their burdens. Rusting hinges, nails, and pieces of scrap metal spilled out over the rims and lay scattered across the withering grass. Pipes and tubes, wooden crates, and metal boxes were strewn across the yard. I saw wheels, copper and brass pipes, gears and pulleys, and a hundred other things that were entirely foreign to me.

Out of the midst of it all, a man appeared. He was tall and thin, unshaven and dressed in filthy, oil-stained clothes. His hair was wildly unkempt and he had some sort of leather goggles wrapped across his forehead. He reeked of burnt oil and sulfur.

Though the man towered over my father in height, and they were of a similar age, I remember thinking that he looked very frail. My father was a broad-shouldered and sturdy veteran, hardened from years on the battlefield. At the time I didn't understand the difference between them, I only observed it, and it made the man seem that much stranger.

My father was the only human being I'd ever known. This man was so different, so unlike father that he hardly seemed human at all. I pulled closer, burying my face in Father's coat, but I kept an eye on the strange man in my peripheral vision.

"Good morning! Mr. Vale wasn't it?" the man said.

Father shook the man's hand and nodded. "Yes, Bran Vale. Good morning." There was hesitancy in his tone, but the stranger didn't know him as well as I did, and therefore didn't notice. I turned my face up to stare into Father's eyes. They were dark, and it was more than just the shadows of the trees.

"What have you brought me?" the man said. "Wagon wheels or horseshoes? Perhaps a clock?" His voice rose at this last word, and I glanced at him. His eyes were wide, excited. Nothing would have pleased him more than a broken clock.

"Not today, Tinkerman," my father said. His voice boomed out of his chest like a drum, and I could feel the reverberations inside me. "I've a much more precious trinket this time."

The Tinkerman scratched his head, and glanced at the empty cart. "I don't understand."

"They've called me back to the front," my father said. "I don't want to impose but I have no one else. Leaving her in town... was not an option."

I was wearing a cap, a light summer thing made from white fabric with a narrow brim. Father pulled it off and kissed my forehead. "Will you help me, Tinkerman? I can pay you well."

The Tinkerman fixed his stare on me, and I felt a shiver. I saw his glance stray to my ears, and suddenly felt very self-conscious. I look human mostly, but I got my ears from my mother. I didn't understand the difference then, but very soon I would know all too well.

My mother's people, the Tal'mar (often known as wood-folk among humans, or *elves* in the mythology of the age) have very light skin and long, pointed ears. Unlike humans, the Tal'mar have a strong way with magic and a distrust of all things mechanical.

Humans are exactly the opposite. Humans have little talent for magic and thus fear it, but they love the wonders of machines and chemistry. Their beliefs and cultures are as different as their appearances, and it has always been those differences that defined their war-torn relationship. As a child of both races, with a human father and a Tal-mar mother, I was doomed from the start.

The silence hung over us for a long time, until Tinker finally said in a cracking voice: "All right, then. Bring her up to the cottage." He led the way, and my father held me tightly as we navigated through piles of twisted metal and broken machinery.

Father had to turn sideways to fit his broad shoulders through the narrow cottage doorway. It was dark inside, until Tinker pulled a metal switch on the wall. A shower of sparks rained down from the ceiling, and a dim light flooded the room. I glanced up at the odd device and saw a glowing coil of metal attached to two thick wires. My father paid little attention to this gadget, but to me it may as well have been magic. I had never seen anything like it. Our small cabin had always been lit by candles and oil-burning lanterns. This was something new, something exciting!

Reluctantly, I pulled my eyes away to see what else the Tinker might have, and realized that the junk inside the cottage made the front yard look like a palace courtyard. Shelves lined the living room walls, straining against the weight of hundreds of glass jars, all filled with the oddest assortments of tiny metal objects and strangely colored liquids. Some of them had labels, or words painted on them, but I couldn't understand any of it. My father had taught me a bit of reading and writing, but Tinker's script was indecipherable to me.

At the far end of the building I saw a small fireplace and an old rocking chair. A ladder leaned against the wall, leading up to a sleeping loft. The floor area between the kitchen and the loft was a maze of books and papers, some stacked waist-high.

The kitchen was equally cluttered, most of the junk similarly unidentifiable. There was a small rectangular table with two benches pressed up against the back wall, and opposing that a small wood-burning cook stove. To the left, a small window gazed out over the yard.

"Would you like some tea?" Tinker said, and I pulled my eyes away from the mess. I'd almost forgotten where I was. He grabbed a metal dipper from a nearby shelf and started filling cups from a steaming pot on the stove. Father gave me a light nudge.

"The Tinkerman has some tea for you," he said.

"No!" I said in a muffled voice. I buried my face in his neck again. There was something happening here, something I didn't understand. I was frightened.

"I have sugar," Tinker said. "And some honey-cakes!"

Father took a small cake and offered it to me. I took it, but refused to take a bite. I held it in my hand and kept my face hidden.

Father stood there holding me like that for a while. He and the Tinkerman began to discuss the weather and such trivial things. The trick worked. After a few moments I started to feel more at ease, and shortly I began to eat the cake. It was small, and when I was finished, I raised my head to look for more.

"Ah, here we are," said the Tinker. "Would you like another?" I nodded.

"Here," father said. "You should sit at the table while you eat. It's polite." He settled me onto the bench, and Tinker served up a plate of cakes and a steaming cup of tea. I snatched up one of the cakes, and Father knelt down close to me as I started to eat. "I have to tell you something, Princess. I have to take a trip. I will be back soon, but while I'm gone, the Tinkerman will take care of you."

I had known something was coming; had been terrified of it from the moment we left our cabin. Now the weight of the truth seemed to squeeze the breath out of me. My chest tightened, my mind ran wild with visions of what might happen to me without my father.

I started to weep, and my father's eyes welled up with tears. He pulled me close. "Don't cry," he said. "I won't be gone long. And the Tinkerman has many interesting things to show you."

I felt a painful wrenching in my heart as Father gave me a final hug and then turned away. He paused in the doorway. "I'll leave her bag on the drive," he said to Tinker. "Take care of her. Don't let her get hurt by all this junk." Then he turned to me. "Be a good girl for the Tinkerman. I love you, Breeze."

That fast it was over, and he was gone. The pieces of my tiny world crumbled around me. My heart lurched in my chest and I felt sick to my stomach. Somehow, I think I knew even then that I would never see him again.

Chapter 2

A dark emptiness settled over me as I heard my father's cart rattling down the road. Everything I'd ever known was quite suddenly gone, and I found myself alone in that strange place.

Well, not alone... I cast a wary glance at the odd, very tall man who was shuffling around the kitchen.

"So your name is Breeze?" Tinker said. He settled down on the opposite bench and poured himself a cup of tea. I nodded. "That's a pretty name. How old are you?" I held up four fingers. "Four?" he exclaimed. He started to laugh. "Well that doesn't seem likely."

I must have looked much older to Tinker. What he didn't know was that my mother's people age very quickly in their youth. The Tal'mar grow in spurts as humans do, but our growth is much more rapid. Generally, by the age of five or six we have matured into our adult stage. At this point we have the appearance of a teenage human. I was young but on the verge of this final growth spurt and in a year or two, I'd look like a matured adult.

Part of this difference is due to the fact that we are physically smaller than humans. Tal'mar are several inches shorter than the average human. With less height and body mass, less growth is needed. Unlike humans however, the Tal'mar can live for several hundred years.

"Well what do you like to do?" Tinker asked. I knew that he was trying to comfort me, trying to distract me from the fact that my father was leaving. It was too much for me. I couldn't take it.

I jumped off the bench and ran to the front door, my heart drumming in my chest as I yanked back the latch. "Wait!" Tinker called out, but I was too fast for him to catch me.

I jerked the door open and raced headlong through that maze of junk, stopping only when I reached the edge of the homestead. I could see my father at the far end of the valley below, heading out across the plains.

I fell to my knees and started sobbing. I called out to him, but he didn't come back. I struggled to understand this unforgivable turn of events. He had abandoned me. I couldn't have understood that he was a soldier and that he had been called back to war. It wouldn't have meant anything to me, even if they had tried to explain it. All I knew was that my father had gone, that he had left me.

I called out to him, choking through my tears, straining my voice with volume. He never glanced back. I told myself that he couldn't hear me, even though I knew it wasn't true. Tinker found me and tried to comfort me, but it was a wasted effort. I refused to listen to him, or to move from the spot.

I fell silent eventually, but if the old man came near me I started wailing again. Finally, Tinker left me and went to see to some of his work. He returned later and found me quiet and still, lying on the ground. He hauled me back into the kitchen, where he fed me again and spoke to me in gentle reassuring tones. I ate silently with my head down. Dragging a response out of me was like wringing water from stone.

Eventually, after dinner, he took me to his bed in the loft. It was clear that he was unused to dealing with a child, and was uncomfortable in this new situation. He didn't tell me a story, and he didn't bother to tuck me in. He simply said, "Good night." Then he went back downstairs. I lay there in the darkness, staring at the ceiling for what seemed like hours.

When I woke the next morning, I found my doll in my arms. Tinker must have found her in my personal belongings after I'd gone to sleep. I squeezed her, and buried my face in her hair. That scent carried a wave of familiarity, and for a moment I was back in my father's cabin, sleeping in his bed. And then the moment passed, and I remembered just how alone I was. Father was gone. The only thing I had left was my doll.

I cried for a while, until the pain subsided and I noticed the smell of food drifting up from below. Then I dried my tears and climbed down the ladder. Tinker was outside working on some noisy project, but he had left me a plate of breakfast on the table. I clutched my doll in one hand and ate with the other. Only when my belly was filled did I finally venture outside the cottage.

It was another frosty morning in that shaded valley, though I could see the sunlight glistening on the plains to the south. The river was there, and the trees were just as breathtaking as they had been the day before. Somehow, I felt a little more at home.

I found Tinker behind the cottage, sawing and hammering, and I watched him for a while. He used a strange metal device and a string to measure and mark the lengths of wood. Then he cut them using a variety of handsaws and chisels. It was a long, mysterious process, which ultimately seemed to leave him with nothing but another stack of wood. Eventually I found the courage to ask what he was doing.

He paused and wiped the sweat from his brow across the back of his sleeve. "I'm making a surprise," he said with a wink.

I wasn't ready to trust him yet, but my heart did flutter a little. "What is it?"

"If I tell you, it won't be a surprise," he said. Then he went back to work.

I watched him for another thirty minutes, determined to figure out what the surprise was. It seemed to consist of nothing more than several stacks of oddly cut wood. Eventually I tired of this, and began to suspect that Tinker's "surprise" would not be nearly as spectacular as it had initially sounded. I went for a walk.

I followed the stream along the hillside, pausing here and there to take a closer look at the stuff scattered around the yard. I doubt there ever existed a stranger collection of miscellaneous junk. Two things became immediately apparent. The first –which was obvious from the start- was that the Tinkerman was a junk collector. While I could imagine some of the items being useful in some way, it was unlikely that they would ever be desperately needed, or irreplaceable. Most of it hardly seemed worth keeping.

The second thing I realized was that if the man ever did need anything, he would almost certainly never be able to find it. This became quite clear as I stood gazing at those misshapen piles. There needed to be some sort of order. The wood should not go with the metal. The black metal parts should not go with the yellow metals. The big pieces should not be piled up on top of the little ones.

Unfortunately, the mess was so expansive that I couldn't imagine how a person might ever get it organized. It seemed the best way would simply be to bury it all, or toss it over the mountainside and start all over again. Somehow, I suspected the Tinkerman would not be happy with that solution. I let my mind work on the problem as I wandered further downstream.

I located a small waterfall about halfway down the hillside and stopped there, listening to the sound of gurgling water and watching the shivering wind through the trees. My thoughts began to drift, and I gradually became aware of a low murmuring sound just at the edges of my perception. I glanced around, thinking at first that I'd heard a distant voice.

The sound came again, and I almost thought I heard a word. "Wind," it seemed to say. Another voice echoed the word. Then, a second later, I felt a chilly gust blow up the valley. The trees shook under the force of it for a few moments, and then it settled down into a gentle breeze.

I sat there for a long time, listening to the trees sigh and moan, certain that they were talking about the sun and the breeze and the creek. I was so lost in this study that I jumped when I heard the Tinkerman call my name. Reluctantly, I followed the sound of his voice back to the cottage.

"Dinner's ready," he announced as I entered. A bowl of soup and a slice of buttered bread were waiting for me at the table. I settled on the bench across from him, in the same place I'd sat on the previous day. I hadn't even realized it was getting dark outside, until I sat under that strange glowing creation on the ceiling and saw the darkness through the windows.

"You were gone for a long time," he said. "What were you doing?"

"Listening to the trees," I said.

He cocked his head. "Is that so? What were they saying?"

"I didn't understand everything," I said. "They seem to like the sun. I think the wind disturbs them. They seem very sleepy."

"No wonder," he said. "It's nearly winter. All sensible creatures know winter is a time of rest. Only we *civilized* beings are silly enough to work through the winter."

I smiled at that, and he smiled back. I think he was starting to enjoy having someone to talk to. "Well, next time you're listening to the trees, tell them we need some firewood. I haven't had time to stock up yet."

"I'll try," I promised.

I went to bed that night, cuddling with my doll, my head full of thoughts. I missed my father, and the thought of him brought tears to my eyes. Still, the feeling wasn't as bad as it had been before. I told myself that he would soon return, and that thought comforted me a bit. He had promised to come back. I held on to that, and it tempered my sadness.

Eventually my mind strayed to the trees, and in my half-sleeping state, I imagined that I was out there listening to them. "Wood Folk, here in the vale," one of them said. "Strange times these are."

"I'm not Wood Folk," I said.

There was a creaking and groaning among them. "What do you want with us?" another said.

I thought about it. "The Tinkerman needs firewood for the winter," I said. They murmured a response that I couldn't quite hear, and their voices seemed to drift away on the wind. Soon, I fell asleep, and lost myself in the dreams of a child.

The next day was much the same as the first. The Tinkerman went straight to work on his project, and I wandered down to the quiet end of the valley where I could listen to the trees and gaze out over the plains. Perhaps I thought that if I stared long enough, I'd see my father coming back across those fields. Or perhaps I feared he wouldn't, and found some small comfort in the beauty of nature around me. Either way, it wasn't long before I was lost in daydreams.

The trees started to murmur again as I wandered around, and I climbed the hill at the edge of the woods, thinking I might understand better if I was closer. Gradually, one word became clear to me.

"Fire," the voices said. I tilted my head, stepping closer. I didn't smell smoke, so it seemed odd that they should use that word. Then suddenly the trees all along the mountainside began to shake and shiver, and branches began to rain down around me. There was a lot of noise for a minute or two, and then suddenly it stopped. "Firewood," the voices murmured. "Fire. Wood."

I surveyed the hillside, hardly able to believe what had just happened. *I wasn't dreaming*, I realized. I had actually spoken to the trees... and they had given us firewood for the winter!

Then I glanced around and realized that they had given me more wood than I could carry. It was going to take a while to gather it all. I started picking up the smaller branches. I had an armload ready to take to the cottage when the Tinkerman appeared. He'd been running, and he was breathless.

"You're all right?" he said. "What was that noise?"

Then he noted my arms full of wood. His eyes widened as he glanced up the hillside. "Firewood," I said cheerfully. "The trees gave it to us."

His jaw dropped, and he watched in silence as I clambered up the slope towards the cottage, struggling with an armload of branches that must have weighed as much as I did. On my way back to the trees, he passed me on the trail with a load of his own.

We spent the whole afternoon clearing the hillside. As I gathered my last load, I paused to thank the trees. Tinker witnessed this and did the same, though his face reddened before he rushed up the hill ahead of me with his eyes downcast. The trees didn't seem to notice his embarrassment. They simply gave me a warm feeling and returned to their dreams.

It was on my third day that the trouble started.

Chapter 3

It was mid-morning. The weather was cool but not uncomfortable, and the sun was warm on my skin. I had gotten used to Tinker's routine, and though I wasn't by any means settled, there was a certain comfort that came with the sense of familiarity and the acceptance that my father was far away and that I wouldn't see him for a long time. This led me to seek other distractions. One thing had been weighing heavily on my mind since I arrived: what to do with all of Tinker's junk?

I hadn't quite settled on how to deal with Tinker's mess but clearly something had to be done, and clearly I was the person to do it. Not that Tinker had asked or in any way even hinted that he was unhappy with the situation, but it was obvious to me that he was too distracted by his work to even acknowledge that there was a problem. Therefore, I set my mind to it, determined that anything I came up with would be better than what he had.

The easiest –and in my opinion best- solution was to toss it all down the mountainside. I suspected Tinker might not approve, so I kept working on the problem. It occurred to me then that there might be room to store some of that junk in the barn. I decided to investigate. So far I'd only seen the barn from a distance, but it didn't look much different from my father's old barn. If anything it was slightly larger, but I suspected it would be much the same on the inside. I was wrong.

Strange odors assaulted me as I slid between the partially opened doors. I paused, suddenly reluctant, with my nostrils burning from the scent. It made my eyes water. I hesitated there, at the threshold of something new and potentially wonderful.

It wasn't grease or oil, I knew those scents well already. It was subtle, and yet in it's own way even more potent. It was the smell of the foundry; the smell of burnt coal and soot, and the acidic tinge of molten metal and cooked flux.

The barn's interior was dark, illuminated only by random beams of light that broke through the slats in the walls. As my eyes adjusted to the darkness, my courage began to build. I swept my gaze across the shadowy interior and saw tables and workbenches covered with miscellaneous parts of machinery and tools. Beneath the tables I saw more junk, packed into boxes and stacked as tightly as Tinker could fit them, and still more dangled from hooks and nails on the walls. The stuff was piled up in the corners right up to the rafters.

Tinker's clutter problem was ridiculous beyond belief. I was astounded. The cottage had been bad. The front yard was downright hazardous. The barn... Ah, the barn.

At some point, as I gazed across that minefield of chaos, my mission changed. I forgot my naïve idea of organizing the yard. I had found a new world to explore. It was a world of strange things: of gadgets, tools and trinkets from the far corners of the world. Somehow they had all landed here, and their mysteries beckoned to me.

I found myself drawn towards a workbench at the far wall. It was the tidiest area that I had seen since my arrival. Glass and stone beakers filled with colored liquids lined the back corner. One of these cast a pale glowing light across the tabletop. At the center of the table rested a small rectangular metal tray. It held a dozen balls of varying sizes, the largest being about the size of my fist and the smallest the size of my thumb. They all appeared to be made from some sort of stone. I picked up one of the smaller balls and felt its weight in my palm.

Like everything else in the room it gave off an odd scent, but it looked and felt just like a stone. I don't know what came over me, but for some reason I got the idea to test my aim. Perhaps it was because I had seen my father throw rocks to chase off rodents around my old home.

I took aim at a tin pot hanging on the far wall, and let it fly. I missed, and when the rock hit the wall, it exploded. The thundering *BOOM*! that followed tore a hole right through the side of the barn. It sent splinters and boards flying in every direction. The concussive shock threw me back against the table. The noise was so horrendous that it left my ears ringing. I could only barely hear myself screaming.

"Tinker!" I cried, as loud as I could. "TINKER!"

Sunlight filtered in through the enormous hole I'd made in the wall and smoke drifted in and out of the shadows. Tinker appeared in the doorway, horror-stricken. He eyed me up and down, making certain that I hadn't been damaged, and then snatched me up and hauled me back outside. He sat me down outside with an accusatory look.

"Don't ever, ever go in there child! That barn is dangerous, do you understand me?" I nodded. I was terrified, and I burst into tears.

"There now," he said, lifting me up. "I didn't mean to yell. You just frightened me, that's all."

I sobbed for a few moments and then lay there with my head resting against his shoulder. Tinker's shoulders were smaller than father's, and he was very bony. He wasn't comfortable the way Father was. It was comforting, however, to be held.

He carried me up to his work site behind the cottage, and set me down on a stump. I was surprised to find that his stacks of wood were nearly all used up. A large box-like structure with bare plank siding rose before me. The far end was attached to the back wall of the cottage. He reached for a hammer and then paused as he saw me staring.

"It's almost finished," he said. "Would you like to take a look inside?"

The shock of my previous experience faded instantly. Tinker saw my wide eyes and smiled. He turned and motioned for me to follow. We went inside the cottage, and he led the way to the back door. I'd never even realized there was a back door because it had been hidden behind shelves. Tinker had moved all of this aside, and now he opened the door into the newly-built room. It was little more than a box with plank floors and bare walls. He stepped inside and I followed.

"Well what do you think? It's going to be *your room!*"

I looked at him, uncertain as to what I should say. It didn't look terribly inviting, and I couldn't imagine what use I might have for a room.

He smiled. "We will paint it this evening, and tomorrow I'll make you your own bed. We can decorate it any way you want. And after it's painted, we'll put in some furniture of course. Where would you like the window?"

I was overwhelmed, but his excitement was contagious. I walked around the room for several minutes, imagining what I was supposed to do with such a place. I'd never had a private space of my own.

I finally decided I wanted a window on the western wall, closest to the trees. I also wanted a window on the roof, so that I could see the sky at night, and so the sun would shine in during the day.

"I'll have to think about that," he mumbled. "Ain't ever seen a window on a roof before."

Over the next few days my room became a quaint, cozy little space. Soon I had a bed and bookshelves just as Tinker had promised, and even a small writing desk. He offered to make one of his light-creations for my room, but I asked for candles. My little accident in the barn had left me with a new respect for Tinker's devices, and the thing's proclivity for throwing sparks made me nervous.

Chapter 4

This was the manner in which I came to know Tinker, and it wasn't the first time I would be surprised by his willingness to push everything aside just to make me comfortable or happy. That was Tinker's way. Despite his quiet, solitary nature, Tinker's heart was in everything he did, especially when it came to his friends. Not only that, Tinker was also the smartest person I ever met.

He was a quiet man, not given to boasting or showing off, and because of this most people never really knew him. If I hadn't seen the things that I witnessed in the days to come, I never would have guessed the true depth of Tinker's character. But even then, before I really knew anything about him, I learned something from him every single day. Tinker never withheld knowledge from me, and more importantly, he gave me the curiosity to seek it out myself. Without this curiosity, things never would have turned out like they did.

The weeks slipped quietly by, and over time Tinker and I became close friends. He began to teach me details about his work; about the mechanisms inside a clock or the way that iron could be turned to steel and made into things like blades and springs. He encouraged me to think of new ways to use the junk we had, and I found myself approaching the world from a decidedly *Tinkerish* perspective. The more I watched

Tinker and learned, the more I wanted to follow in his footsteps. Tinkering was fun!

Unfortunately, there was very little work that was safe for a child and I continued to spend much of my time wandering the woods around the cottage and listening to the quiet thoughts of the trees. I stayed far away from the barn and anything else that looked even remotely explosive.

Gradually, Tinker's little cottage became my home. There were still nights when I would lie in bed and think of my father –and on occasion I might shed a few tears- but for the most part I had gotten used to my new life. On those nights when I was sad and lonely, I would sneak up the ladder into Tinker's bed and curl up next to him.

It was a week after the first snow when Tinker announced that he must take a trip into town. "I have neglected my business," he said, "and we are low on supplies. I spent far too much time building that extra room, and now I must set things to right."

"Can I go?" I asked. "Please take me with you!"

He frowned. "It's not a good idea."

"Please, Tinker? I'll behave. I won't touch anything!"

He sighed and ran his hand through that rat's nest he called hair. "I suppose it's just as dangerous, leaving you here alone..." He disappeared into the loft and came back holding a knit wool cap. "You must wear this," he said. "You must promise me that you won't take it off, no matter what happens. You must not let anyone see your ears, or they might become angry."

"I promise," I said.

"Alright then, remember you must do whatever I say. We don't have money to spend so we won't be doing any shopping, and we won't be staying long, understand?"

"I understand."

I tried on my new hat as Tinker went behind the garage and pulled out an old wagon. It was a rusty, rickety thing that looked like it would rattle apart if someone sneezed. There was a long bench seat across the front, and an odd contraption rested just behind the seat. He crawled into the back of the wagon and built a fire inside the tall metal chamber.

I watched with growing curiosity, and soon enough the questions came bubbling out. "What is that thing, Tinker? What does it do? Will it keep us warm? How will we pull the wagon without a horse?"

He chuckled as the questions streamed out of me. "Aren't you the curious one today?" he said. I smiled. "Just be patient, child. All your questions will be answered soon enough." He lifted me onto the seat. "You wait here while I load the wagon."

I did as he instructed, eager to prove that I was worthy of his trust. He hauled a few boxes out of the barn and then climbed into the seat next to me. I felt warmth radiating off the contraption, and it felt good on that wintry morning.

"Hang on," Tinker said. He pulled back on a long metal bar that rose up in front of the bench (which I soon learned was the brake), and the cart started to move. I gasped, and he shot me a smile. "This is what we call steam locomotion," he said. "This is my *steamwagon*."

I bent over, trying to get a look at what was happening underneath us. He grabbed my coat by the collar and hauled me back. "I don't want you bouncing out," he said. "Last thing I need is you with a broken arm, or worse yet, a broken neck." I glanced around and saw steam exhausting out of the machine, and heard a loud hissing noise.

The wagon bounced happily down the road as I twisted left and right, searching for an understanding of this bizarre creation. It was slow-going as we traveled down the valley, but once we reached the flatlands, Tinker let it go. We easily doubled the speed of a horse-drawn carriage and in less than an hour, we rolled into town.

It was breathtaking.

Like Tinker, my father had lived in seclusion. I'd never been near a town in my life. I had never even dreamed of the wonders that now revealed themselves to me. The town of Riverfork was alive with festivity. The buildings were decorated with dancing skeletons and brilliant streamers of gold and red for the celebration of Sowen, the week of the dead.

Tinker explained that although the name of the holiday sounded morbid, it was actually a celebration of the seasonal harvest and the transition into winter. The citizens celebrated by hanging stick figures in the shape of skeletons and black cats from the street lamps and doors, and by placing pumpkins with angry faces carved into them on their porches to ward off the specter of death.

I absorbed this all in mute wonder. I was equally awed by the town itself. The buildings were tall, some as high as four stories, and their steep roofs cast shadows across the cobbled streets even in the middle of the day. I saw dozens of people on the streets, some pulling carts, others riding in wagons or, rarely, even in a carriage. Others strolled along the wooden boardwalks peering into shop windows and greeting one another with smiles and nods. Lamps rose up along the street every few yards, and Tinker was kind enough to explain their purpose as I stared in wide-eyed wonder.

Looking back now, I know that our town was really little more than a backwater village, but at that moment it was a city. I had never imagined so many people might exist in the whole world, much less in one place. I was so overwhelmed with excitement that I completely forgot who I was and why I was there. I just wanted to see it all.

We made several stops along the way and Tinker was cautious to warn me every time. "Stay put, and keep that hat on! I'll be back in a few moments."

He wandered into the first shop with a box of nuts and bolts, and other hand-made fasteners. He returned with saw blades, paint, and sandpaper. At another stop he traded knife blades and sharpening tools for a good supply of smoked meat. A peddler on the street gave us a pig and two chickens for a clock and a small supply of Tinker's explosive balls. Tinker delivered several boxes of those balls at the post office, and I was glad to see them gone.

We made several more stops like this, and our wagon slowly filled with the supplies that Tinker would need to get us through the winter. It wasn't until our last stop that things went bad.

It was late afternoon when we pulled up to the mercantile at the far end of town. The sun had already begun to set behind the mountains. A middle-aged man and his plump wife were standing on the long porch, greeting people on the street. They waved as we pulled up. "Evening, Tinkerman," said the man. "What can we do for you?"

Before Tinker could reply, the woman let out a squeal. "Oh, my, look at this dear child. Tell me this isn't one of your fabulous inventions!"

Tinker smiled and said, "This is my niece, Breeze. She's visiting for a few weeks while her family tends to matters with their farm in South Bronwyr." It was so well rehearsed that I almost believed it myself.

"Well, lucky for us!" said the woman. "Come, child, let's get you inside. I'll fetch you a piece of candy." Before I knew it, she was at my side, lifting me out of the wagon.

Tinker reached out but I was already gone. "I don't think... we don't really have time for-"

"Oh, nonsense. You men see about your business, while us ladies get acquainted."

Tinker gave me a helpless look as the woman hauled me away. Inside the store, she plopped me down on the counter. She bent over, and reappeared with a small, brightly colored stick. "Here we go, the best sweets in Riverfork." She handed it to me, and I thanked her. "Well now, we haven't been properly introduced. Your name is Breeze, yes? Well I'm Analyn Trader. My husband out there is Daran. This is our store. So tell me Breeze, how long will you be staying?"

"I don't know."

"I see. Tell me, what sort of education have you?"

"Education?"

"Yes, proper education I mean. Not tending sheep and chickens and the like, but writing and reading and math. Do you know these things?"

"Some," I said awkwardly. I wasn't sure where her train of questioning was leading, and I was afraid

Tinker was going to be angry with me. I didn't want to say the wrong thing.

"Some? Tell me, how long ago did you start school?"

I gave her a blank look.

"You haven't been to school?" she said. "Well this is a scandal! It's an outrage! I'm going to have a talk with that tinkerer." She was scowling, but she must have seen the terror in my eyes. Her face softened a bit and she decided to change the subject. "Ah well, later for that. You are a pretty little thing, do you know that? And look at those curls. Do you know what we call hair that color? Strawberry-blonde. It's almost pink in the sunlight, isn't it? Here, let's brush it out."

Before I even realized what was happening, she reached out and pulled off my hat. She didn't give me a second glance as she spun around and grabbed a brush off the counter behind her. I froze, terrified of what was about to happen, but powerless to stop it.

Then Analyn turned around. She saw my ears. She screamed.

Chapter 5

Analyn's brush hit the floor at the same instant the door flew open. Tinker and Daran burst in, their eyes searching for the cause of the outcry. Tinker saw me sitting on the counter and froze. He glanced at the cap and then back at me, and his eyebrows narrowed. Daran looked at his wife questioningly, and then followed her gaze to me and did a double take. His jaw dropped.

"What have you done, Tinkerman?" he said.

"Half-breed," Analyn hissed. "He's created an abomination."

I glanced back and forth between the three of them, my heart in my throat. I didn't know what an abomination was, or what the term "half-breed" meant, but Analyn's cold stare gave me a wrenching feeling in my gut.

Seconds ago she'd been such a sweet, kind woman... the change had been instantaneous. It was terrifying to see her change like that. I had no idea what I'd done wrong, or how I could have incited such venomous anger. I wanted to crawl down a hole and die.

"Breeze, put on your hat and go wait for me in the wagon." Tinker's voice was stiff and controlled, but I could hear the anger behind his words. The situation was so unfair, so hard to understand. I wanted to break down in tears.

"But Tinker..." I started to object. I wanted to explain that it wasn't my fault, that I hadn't done anything wrong.

"Do it, now," he said firmly. It was clear from his tone that I'd better do it. I grabbed my hat from the counter and yanked it over my head. I jumped down, and ran outside. Fortunately, I had the good sense to keep my fingers on that stick of candy.

I waited on the wagon, my heart thumping wildly and my eyes downcast so that no passing stranger might see my tears. A light snow had begun falling and the flakes drifted down around me, settling onto the padded bench beside me and onto the floor of the steamwagon, dusting everything in a thin layer of white. The steam engine in the back chugged along, idling and belching out clouds of hot vapor and releasing a loud hiss every few seconds.

I held out my hands, letting the flakes settle onto my palms where they dissipated almost instantly. I heard harsh voices drifting out through the mercantile doors, and I tried not to listen. I didn't want to hear any more. I didn't entirely understand what had happened, but I had enough sense to know that I was in trouble. And that, for reasons that were beyond my understanding, I was bad.

Eventually Tinker came out of the store. He was carrying canvas bags full of food which he carelessly tossed into the back of the wagon. He didn't say a word as he climbed into the driver's seat and released the brake. In fact, he didn't speak at all as we raced down the busy street, weaving a dangerous path through the traffic. He ignored the waves and angry shouts of people he'd nearly run over.

35

It wasn't until we were well out of town, speeding across the frozen ground with scarves wrapped around our faces to protect us from the icy snowflakes that I found the courage to speak. I did so reluctantly, uncertain of whether Tinker was still angry with me. I pulled my scarf down under my chin so I could speak.

"I'm sorry," I said. "I didn't mean to make you angry."

"I know," he gave me an understanding look. "All of this, this trouble, it's not your fault. It's not about you, not really."

"But those people... Analyn, she hated me." I said. "It's because of my ears, right? Because I look different?"

He gave me a sad look and paused before he replied, as if he were trying to find the right answer. When he finally spoke, it was a very unexpected question. "Do you know where your father is?" I shook my head. It had been a month since he left, and the memory was still painful. Until then, Tinker and I had never spoken of him.

"He went to war. Do you know what war is?" I nodded. I had heard the word, and was familiar with its meaning in a naïve sort of way. "Astatia, the kingdom of men," he continued, "has been at war with the Isle of Tal'mar for centuries."

"So my father went to fight the Tal'mar?" I asked. "Why?"

Tinker chuckled a little. "That's a very intelligent question," he said. "Too bad more people aren't smart enough to wonder the same thing. There are different reasons I suppose. Territorial disputes, vengeance killings, anger over past wrongs. It seems men can always find a reason to kill one another. But in truth, I doubt anybody remembers how it got started. Humans and Tal'mar are so different, maybe there's no greater reason than that. Maybe two peoples so different can never get along."

"But we get along," I argued, and he smiled.

"That we do. But we're both very, very smart." We both laughed at that.

We were quiet for a few minutes while I thought it over. Then I had an epiphany. "Analyn shouldn't hate me for being Tal'mar," I postulated, "because I'm human, too!" It seemed perfectly sensible to me that I should have friends on both sides of the conflict. After all, I was both sides. Human, Tal'mar... if anyone should have been able to get along with both races, it should've been me.

Tinker took a deep breath. "Analyn and the others don't hate you, Breeze. Not exactly, anyway. When a human looks at you, they see your ears. They don't care about who you are inside, because on the outside you look like Tal'mar. To them you are Tal'mar. That makes you the enemy, and possibly even a spy. So they fear you, and mistrust you.

"Unfortunately, the Tal'mar will do the same if you ever meet them. You may have their ears, but you've got the build and coloring of a human, so they won't trust you either."

It was a lot for a child my age to absorb. I considered what he'd said, and a thought occurred to me. It was a desperate thought, the sort of idea that only an innocent child could conceive. "What if the war was over, Tinker? Maybe then they wouldn't hate me." Tinker sadly shook his head.

"I'm afraid it's not that easy, Breeze. There's been talk of treaties and such over the years, but nothing ever came from it. The distrust runs too deep, and has been ingrained into peoples' minds for too long. The humans and Tal'mar hate each other. They always have, and they always will."

I shivered, not from the icy windborne snowflakes that cut into my face, but from the coldness that was growing inside of me. How could I have been born into a world so cruel? I'd started out knowing nothing about the world, and had found that the more I knew, the more I hated it.

I didn't like feeling that way. I didn't like the hopelessness that was gripping me, the promise of a future full of loneliness and rejection. Then something happened. It was a like a switch got flipped in my mind.

I'm going to change things, I decided. *I'm going to find a way to make them like me. I'm not going to live my whole life like a hermit in the mountains, even if Tinker says I will. Someday I'll be able to go to town, maybe even live there...*

And I was off, dreaming about changing the world in ways that no one with any sense would have ever bothered dreaming. Little did I know that in setting such high hopes, I was making my inevitable defeat even more painful. But I had the mind of a child, and the ability to hope and dream bigger than anyone. And why not? No one else stood to gain or lose as much as me, the half-breed.

I didn't bother telling Tinker of these thoughts because I knew he wouldn't agree. I just kept them hidden inside of me, sowing them like carefully tended seeds. I became convinced that someday, when I was smart enough, I could change things. Someday I wouldn't be Breeze the half-breed, I'd be just another person... just like everyone else.

I was wrong, of course. I could never, ever be just like everyone else.

Chapter 6

Back at the cottage, I went inside to make dinner while Tinker unloaded our winter supplies. When he came through the front door, I already had bread warming on the stove and the soup was boiling. "Breeze, that smells wonderful!" he said. He tossed his old coat and scarf on the hook by the door and came into the kitchen rubbing his hands. I smiled, but I was lost in thought.

I had been learning to cook because it gave Tinker more time to work and at the same time gave me something to do, especially since the weather was cold and my long walks outside were getting shorter by the day. There really wasn't much to do, other than reading from Tinker's collection of old books and journals. Unfortunately, these were almost all nonfiction sciency type stuff. The books were filled with words I didn't know, about things I didn't understand. Needless to say, none of it was very interesting.

It didn't take long to figure out that Tinker's home was just not designed for children, and especially not for a girl. I longed for things that I couldn't even begin to voice, and I knew Tinker wouldn't understand. Still, he did a lot for me, and I was grateful for everything I had. Without Tinker, I couldn't imagine what my world would have been like.

I was quiet as we sat down to eat. Thoughts of what happened that afternoon were still churning through my mind. "Breeze, I'm sorry to have told you all that I did," he said. "You're too young. I should not have been so blunt."

I disagreed, but I didn't bother to argue. I had other things on my mind. "Tinker, what is school?"

He stopped chewing with a piece of bread crust hanging out of his mouth. He looked me up and down, and then swallowed awkwardly. "Well, I don't really think you'd be interested in that. It's very hard, and very boring..."

"Does it make you smart?"

"Well..." he cleared his throat awkwardly. "I suppose it helps. Nature makes you smart, but knowledge is something you can use. But I really don't think you'd like it."

"Because I'm a half-breed?" I said. He froze, eyes darting around the room in search of an answer. There wasn't one, of course. It was an unfair question, designed to shut him up. It succeeded.

"Let me go to school," I said. "I'll cover my ears, I promise. No one will ever know. You have to let me go to school, Tinker. You have to let me learn!"

He leaned back, his eyes searching the ceiling. When he looked back at me, I saw anger on his face. "Don't ask me about this again," he said flatly. He rose from the table and stomped out the door, slamming it behind him. I stared hard at his half-eaten bowl of soup.

It didn't take much thinking to figure Tinker out. He was trying to protect me. He'd never spoken to me in real anger, not even when I almost blew up the barn. The fact that he'd become angry with me now just told me one thing: he really loved me, and he was terrified of what might happen if I went back into a public place.

Unfortunately, I didn't have it in me to live out my life as an uneducated hermit. I was going to learn, no matter what it took. I was going to get smart, and I was going to change the world. I was audacious enough to believe it, too. Fortunately it takes that kind of audacity to accomplish anything significant. Naturally, I started planning.

Over the next few days I showed a renewed interest in Tinker's work. It was a genuine interest, because I was truly fascinated by the mechanics of his trade. I was especially curious about two of the inventions I had already encountered. He refused to teach me about the exploding rocks, but he was more than happy to teach me about the steam engine.

He cleared a section in the barn and set up a large table where we could assemble a smaller version. This required a great deal of fabrication, and in the process I learned a lot about soldering and welding. By the time our project was finished, I was practically his apprentice.

Winter had blown in with a vengeance, leaving us more or less stranded in Tinker's little homestead. There was a well-trampled path between the cottage and the barn, but if I stepped off to the side I quickly sank up to my hips in the snow. My long walks in the woods were out of the question now, and not just because of the weather. Tinker told me of beasts that lived in the mountains to the north, about the winter wargs that came with the north wind, traveling in packs that would murder an entire herd of livestock in the night, leaving nothing but bloodstained snow to be found at dawn. And then there were the bears, great grizzled creatures that could swallow a man whole; and the trolls, the green-skinned wild men who raided villages and farms all along the borderlands every winter.

All of this talk was more than adequate to keep me within the confines of our homestead. In fact, it was enough to give me more than a few sleepless nights as well.

Fortunately, our steam engine project occupied so much of my time that I hardly even had a moment to worry about wargs and trolls. I had to keep the forge and foundry warm, I had to prep the molds and file the castings. In those days, everything was made at home, right down to the steel. The engine block, the pistons, even the piping was machined right there in Tinker's barn. And I helped, every step of the way.

All along, I continued to question Tinker about school. I did it subtly, with simple questions here and there when he was distracted by his work. I asked where the school was, and got the angry response that it was down by the river, but that I didn't need to know and not to ask about it again. I waited a few days before asking who the teacher was. To my surprise I learned that it was Analyn Trader, the woman who had discovered my secret. Suddenly I understood why she'd been so adamant that I should be in school. I wondered if she still felt that way, now that she knew I was a half-breed.

I went on like this for weeks, dropping my questions here and there, trying to wring information out of Tinker. I squeezed at least a little out of him every few days, but not much.

Gradually I got a feel for what school was and how it worked, but in the end I was no closer to getting there than I had been at the beginning. Then one day, news that would change my life forever came right to our doorstep. It came in a very surprising form.

We had completed the engine and we had it running on the table. It was our first test-run, and Tinker and I were observing it for any problems. It chugged away, occasionally hissing and puffing out little clouds of steam, but working exactly as it was supposed to. Tinker adjusted a gauge and then asked me to check a release valve. I reached for a screwdriver but froze as I heard an urgent whisper in the back of my mind. It confused me at first. It had been weeks since I'd spoken with the trees, and for a moment I doubted whether I'd really heard anything. Since the snow had started falling, the trees had all seemed to be sleeping.

The message came again, one word: "Warning!" It was an urgent whisper that seemed to tease at the edges of my perception. I stopped what I was doing, and let my mind reach out. The word came to me again, this time louder than before. "WARNING!" I raced over to peer out through the crack between the doors.

"Someone is coming," I whispered. I saw a slow moving, horse-drawn carriage coming up the trail. The two horses pulling the thing had worked up a froth getting to the top of the hill in the deep snow, and I felt sorry for them.

Tinker pushed past me and whispered, "Stay here!" He stomped out across the snow with a heavy wrench in his hand. It looked like he was prepared to use the thing as a weapon.

Then, as the carriage got closer, I was disturbed to recognize Analyn and her husband. I immediately began to panic. Had Analyn betrayed me? Had she brought others, perhaps a sheriff or even an angry mob? My mind went to the trees, asking them if they'd seen more people coming. The response was a lethargic drone that I couldn't understand. I persisted, trying to rouse the trees from their slumber and eventually got a "no," though I couldn't be sure if it was an answer to my questions or just an attempt to shut me up.

Analyn and Daran spoke to Tinker in hushed voices for several minutes. The tone of their conversation changed as they spoke, but I could scarcely hear a word of it. Their voices were somber at first, then after a few moments, they started to rise in anger. Then they got themselves under control, and managed a civil "farewell," before leaving. Then the carriage went rolling back down the hillside, and silence blanketed our homestead once again. Tinker came plodding back to the barn with his eyes downcast.

"What did they want?" I asked as he entered.

Tinker went over to the table, and slumped down on a stool. He sat there for some time, fiddling with our motor. He tightened up a few bolts with his wrench and polished the brass and copper pipes with an old rag. I asked him again, and still he ignored me. I was starting to get angry. "Why won't you tell me what they wanted?" I shouted. "Did they come to tell me to leave? Are they going to kill me?"

"No one's going to kill you," he said. He tossed the wrench down on the bench. He still wouldn't look me in the eyes. "Breeze, your father is dead. He was killed in an ambush six weeks ago."

Chapter 7

I felt a chill moving across my skin as I heard those words. It had been close to three months since I'd seen my father. In the life of a Tal'mar child, that might as well have been three years. I had grown in that time, enough that Tinker had started stitching together pieces of his old clothes to make dresses for me.

My father had been absent from my life for so long that I could hardly remember what he looked like. And yet, there wasn't a day that passed in which I didn't think of him, where I didn't dream of his return. I felt my chest tightening as Tinker spoke, and my breath caught in my throat. Tears came to my eyes and I tried to choke them back.

What did it mean, my father being gone? That I'd never go home? That possibility wasn't frightening, not anymore. I had learned to love Tinker's quiet little homestead. What it really meant was that Father would never be there. He'd never tuck me into bed and read me a story; he'd never hold me so tight that his beard made red marks on my face. Never, ever again.

No, it wasn't just that *he* was gone forever. *We* were gone. That magical spark between two people who love and understand one another explicitly was gone forever from my life, and it left me less than whole. My father, the only person I had in the world, was gone.

I realized suddenly that I was bawling. My body was shaking, my breath coming in short gasps as tears streamed down my face. I felt a painful twisting in my chest, like a knife inside of me, and I got the powerful feeling that I just wanted to die.

Tinker lifted me up and held me, and I pressed my face into his shoulder. He whispered to me quiet comforting words, but all I heard was the low drone of his voice. It helped, somewhat. It helped to know that he was there.

I cried for a long time, even after my voice fell to a whimper and my heaving sobs gave way to a slow, steady breathing. The tears came until it didn't seem there could possibly be more, and then they came again. I don't know how long that process went on, but eventually I fell asleep in Tinker's arms.

When I woke, I was lying on my bed. Tinker had thrown a light blanket over me and tucked my doll under my arm. I felt the warmth of the fireplace radiating through the doorway, washing over me. It felt good. I lay there for a while, staring at the thick layer of snow on top of my ceiling window, feeling not unlike I had on that very first morning after my father left. Not as alone, and not as afraid as I'd been then, but just as empty.

No, that wasn't true. As bad as I felt, it couldn't compare to those first days, when my father had been the only person in my world. I was older now and a little bit wiser, and not entirely alone. I had Tinker. I had our homestead, with my own little room, and a snow-covered window in my ceiling.

Tinker had eventually figured out how to make that window. He'd gotten it done just before the snow started. How many other things had he done for me? I couldn't even count them.

Strangest of all was the fact that Tinker was in no way obligated to me. The only reason my father had chosen him was that he was an outsider. He was a hermit that lived miles from town with no friends or family. It was the safest reasonable place to leave a young girl like me. Tinker had no duty to accept that responsibility. He could have sent us on our way and forgotten all about us. Why didn't he do that?

I knew the answer, of course. The Tinker was a good man. He wasn't wealthy or powerful, and at first glance he certainly didn't seem to be anyone special, but inside he truly was. He saw past our external differences. He saw me as a person, a child that needed love and guidance. At the time I had been wrapped up in all of my own emotions. How many other people would have accepted a half-breed into their homes, the way that Tinker had?

I gradually became aware of the smell of food and the gnawing of my stomach got the best of me. Tinker was not in the cottage, but he'd left a warm roast on the stove. I took advantage of the quiet time to think. When I was done eating and thinking, I ventured out into the darkness. I found Tinker in the barn. He was working at the bench against the far wall, the one where he produced the explosive stone balls. I approached him, but not close enough that I might disturb him.

"Feeling better?" he asked. He shot me a glance out of the corner of his eye, and then quickly went back to work. He was mixing powders in a large bowl.

"I want to go to school," I said.

He set the bowl aside and twisted on his stool to face me. "I thought we weren't going to talk about that anymore."

"I want to go to school." There didn't seem to be much else to say. I didn't want to argue about it. I didn't want to dance around the subject, the way we had been doing for weeks. I had reached a point of no return. I was going to get what I wanted, or I was going to leave. I'd been thinking about it for a long time, and the news of my father's death had made me realize something. If I didn't start working towards my dreams now, then I never would.

I think my determination was clear in my voice, and on my face. He didn't get angry the way he usually did.

"This spring," he said, a tone of resignation in his voice.

My eyebrows shot up. "What?"

"This spring. I spoke to Analyn and she agreed that you can start school this spring."

I was flabbergasted. I rushed over and threw my arms around him, almost knocking him off the stool. "Truly? You're going to let me go?"

"It doesn't seem the choice is mine," he said. "Analyn all but insisted when she came here this morning. She apologized for the way she treated you. She wants you to know that she is sorry. She says that a little girl is just that, no matter what ears she might have, and every little girl deserves an education."

I could hardly believe what I was hearing. My heart filled with joy at those words, and I found my old hopes resurging. People really could change. It was possible, in time, that I might even be accepted. I glanced at the engine sitting on our workbench.

"Teach me more," I said.

He looked down at me. "More what?"

"Tinkering. What else can we do?"

A broad smile crept over his face. "There is another project I've been thinking about..."

Chapter 8

We spent the next few weeks working on Tinker's newly invented *steamsleigh*. From the very beginning the idea seemed improbable to me. His design called for a custom built fan, which he called a "propeller." Supposedly this device would be able to push the sleigh and its occupants across the snow. I laughed when I saw his schematic.

"Just you wait," Tinker said determinedly. "It will work." I just smiled.

Despite my misgivings, I started helping him. I didn't have much else to do until the snow melted. Much of the parts we needed had to be found amidst Tinker's junk piles. Some of them had to be made. And then there were the others, stored in boxes high in the barn's rafters. Naturally, being young and small and nearly fearless, that adventure was mine.

On my fourth trip into the barn rafters, I stumbled over an old box and almost went crashing down to my death. I barely caught myself by throwing an arm out across a parallel beam. I grunted as my full weight hit the beam, and I found myself dangling there in midair, a good twenty feet above the floor.

"Hang on!" Tinker screamed as he went lurching for a ladder. By the time he had one, I had already pulled myself back up. He met me at the far wall, his eyes wild with panic. "Are you all right?"

"Of course," I said. I ignored the painful bruise forming around my shoulder. I turned over the box that had almost killed me, displaying its contents. It was a collection of old swords. I held one up for him to see. "Where did you get these?"

"Oh, I've collected them over the years. Sometimes people give me their old steel as payment for work. Usually its junk that I melt down or save, but I'm not one to waste good blacksmithing. Those are some fine weapons."

I lifted a short cutlass out of the pile, and pulled it from the scabbard. The brass hilt gleamed, and intricate patterns crawled up and down the blade. The weight and balance felt good in my hand. I felt like a heroine out of some old fairy tale, like I could slay dragons with that sword. "Can I have this one?" I said.

"I don't know much about swordplay," Tinker said. "A person's likely to get themselves killed, walking around with a weapon they don't know how to use."

Tinker clearly wasn't eager to let me have a dangerous weapon, but he also hadn't said "no." Not exactly, anyway. "I'll just bring it down," I said. "I'll leave it in the barn and we can practice when we're bored."

Tinker grunted but made no protest as I sheathed the weapon and brought it down with me. I hung it on a nail over the workbench. "What now,?" I said.

Tinker's foundry had been warming so that we could make some brackets and bolts, and he instructed me to work the bellows to warm his forge. While the molds warmed, Tinker scrounged up some iron and placed it in a clay pot. He covered the opening with straw and ash, and then set the whole thing deep into the embers of the forge.

"Pump now," he ordered. I started working the bellows. I lifted the handle and the contraption sucked in fresh air. Then I brought the handle back down, forcing the air into the forge, and fanning the coals to an incredible heat. Soon, the iron began to melt.

Tinker pulled it out twice to stir up the contents. Once he was satisfied that the mixture was ready, he told me to go stand by the door. "If there's even a slight bit of moisture left in these molds they will explode," he said, "and we'll have molten iron burning holes right through us."

I quickly moved over to the doorway. Actually, I stepped outside, and leaned in just far enough that I could see what was going on. I cringed as Tinker lifted the jar out of the fire with his tongs, and tipped it over the mold. I could hardly believe that the glowing orange liquid was actually metal.

Tinker patiently filled the molds, and then set the remainder aside. He shot me a smile. "Perfect," he said. "We'll just let that cool overnight. Now for the skis..."

That was when things got interesting.

Tinker and I cut two long strips of wood. He set one aside and clamped the other down on the table top, leaving about six inches hanging over the edge. He proceeded to explain that we could use steam to bend the wood, stretching the fibers. Then he wandered off to the house to retrieve some hot water, and I found myself alone.

I walked over to the end of the table, and touched the wood. It was very light and flexible, and it bent quite easily under the weight of my hand. I released it, and it sprang right back into shape. Something happened as I did this. I felt the movement of the wood react to something inside me. It was an instinctive thing, like a sixth sense that allowed me to feel what was going on inside the wood. I noted the shape and the grain of the wood, and I had the sense in my mind that I could actually see it from the inside out.

I closed my eyes and followed that vision. The internal structure became clear to me. I saw the overlapping strands of fiber, and the smaller cellular structures that made up the organic composition of the material. I could see it all. I moved my hands, bending the board down on the end. I felt the grain stretching on the outside, and compressing beneath. I sensed the change in these structures. As I did this, a thought occurred to me. Why was heat necessary to make this change? Why did the change have to be forced?

I reached into the wood with my mind, and began to systematically refine its structure. I can't explain how I did this, except to say that I could *touch* the wood with my mind. My consciousness flowed through my arms, and into the wood itself, as if I were actually somehow inside the wood.

I eased the pressure on the top, where the fibers were stretched from bending. I made them relax, I urged them to stretch and grow ever so slightly. Then I reached even deeper, down to where the compression was occurring. Mentally, I moved the fibers ever so delicately; just enough to ease that pressure and allow the wood to remain naturally in that position.

Tinker returned just as I finished. He stepped through the doors in a cloud of steam, and I could hardly see him until he set the pot aside. He glanced over at me. "We just need to hang some weights from that string," he said.

He came over to my side, and I pulled my hands away from the wood. Tinker furrowed his eyebrows as he stared at the shape. "What in the world?"

"Did I ruin it?" I said anxiously. "I'm sorry if I did it wrong. I can fix it, I think."

He tugged at the wood, but it remained frozen, bent in a graceful downward curve. "You did this?"

I nodded fearfully.

"How?"

"I don't know... I just touched it. I could see it in my mind, so I told the wood to stretch. I'm sorry, Tinker. Please don't be mad!"

He laughed. "I'm not angry, girl. I'm shocked. Do you think you can do it again?"

I nodded. "I think so."

"Excellent. Come over here, to the other end. Take it in your hands. Hold it just like you did before. Okay, are you ready?"

"Yes."

"No... Wait." He walked over to the wall and grabbed an iron bar. "Hold this," he said. I did as he instructed, holding the bar in one hand, and the wood in the other.

"I don't understand," I said. "What should I do with it?"

"Just hold it," he said. "Now. Bend the wood."

I closed my eyes, and reached out for that sensation. It was a bit more difficult, doing the process with one hand, but I managed. As before, I rearranged the structure of the wood, guiding the tiny fibers into the correct order to create the shape I wanted. When I was done, I stood back and examined my work. It was almost exactly same as the first. Tinker tugged at the wood, and it didn't budge.

"Unbelievable," he said. He took a couple awkward steps back and leaned up against a bench, all the while his eyes fixed on me.

I was uncomfortable, to say the least. It was clear to me now that this was something Tinker and his kind could not do. It was a skill of my mother's people. I didn't understand however, why he was so shocked that I had this ability.

"Did I do wrong?" I asked again.

The sound of my voice shook him out of his thoughts. "I'm sorry, I didn't mean to confuse you. It's just... how can I explain? I was always taught that when two different races combine, the offspring combines the worst traits of both. If you graft one plant with another, you get a plant that's susceptible to twice as many diseases. Or, in a case like this, a bi-racial child would have none of the magic possessed by the wood folk, and none of the strength and logic of humankind. I should have known better when you called the wood out of the trees last fall. I assumed that the forest was simply offering you respect. I didn't realize that you had actually commanded it..."

His voice trailed away, and he started getting that distant look in his eyes again. "I don't understand," I said. "If I have magic, is that bad?"

He raised an eyebrow. "Yes and no. First of all, it's absolutely wonderful that you have magic. You have a gift that is unique to the Tal'mar, and it has extraordinary use and purpose in this world. But I must temper that with this: never, ever let anyone see you use this magic. You've already seen how humans react when they see your ears. There's no telling what they might think if they witnessed something like this."

"I understand." I started to move, and became conscious of the iron bar in my hand. I raised it up between us. "What was this for?"

"Among your mother's kind, iron and steel are feared. There is something about the metal that destroys their power. It sucks the magic right out of them. I wanted to know if it affected you in the same manner."

"But it didn't," I said. "I didn't notice anything at all."

"Correct. As I said, it has always been believed that one such as you would possess all the weaknesses and none of the strengths of her parents. You, I believe, are quite the opposite. You have the strengths of both and, perhaps, none of the weaknesses."

Chapter 9

I didn't get to practice my newly discovered powers much. I had a few opportunities while we worked on the sleigh but Tinker warned me not to become accustomed to using magic. "If humans see you doing something they can't explain, they'll place you as a Tal'mar and possibly even kill you," he warned. "It's best that you learn to do things just as I do."

And so I did. I worked the bellows in the forge, I cut wood with a handsaw and chisels, I turned the bolts with a thread-cutter and a vice. I used hammers and screwdrivers and wrenches every day, so often that I could tell what size they were from across the room. I couldn't have been more human, except for my telltale ears.

In my heart I continued to hope that some day things would be different. I yearned to live in a world where I could live among humans like Tinker and my father and yet use magic any time I wanted. I wanted to live in a world where I could be complete, where I could be accepted for all the things I was, rather than trying to hide them. I even found myself wondering if -among the Tal'mar- things might be different. Perhaps they were more open, more accepting than humans. Maybe if I went to them, the Tal'mar would accept me.

I kept these thoughts to myself, but at one point I did ask Tinker about my mother. It was a turning point for me, because I'd never known my mother and had never really wondered about her. It was a sign of me growing up.

"I never knew your mother," he said. "I never even knew your father had married. That's not surprising, considering. If people knew he'd married a Tal'mar, heaven knows what they might have done."

"So you have no idea where she lives? You don't even know if she's alive?"

Tinker pursed his lips. Reluctantly, he spoke: "Do you have no memories of your mother?" he asked. I shook my head.

"I never saw her."

"She didn't live with you? She didn't visit? You never went to see her?"

"Not that I can remember," I said.

"And don't you think that's strange?" It was. I realized then that in truth, my mother was probably dead. That realization brought me pain. It wasn't the kind of pain that I'd had when my father left. This was different, a slow ache in my heart and a feeling of deep regret. I would never know her. I would never know what my mother had been like, or how she had come to be with my father.

Then one cloudy day, the steamsleigh was finished. Despite the fact that we'd been working on it for weeks, it seemed like it happened so suddenly. Tinker filled the water tank and fired up the small furnace. It was time to test the machine. I was terrified.

The steamsleigh sat just outside the barn doors, resting on several inches of packed snow and ice. It was a decent size, nearly as big as Tinker's wagon. The bench seat rested just in front of the steam engine. The space in front of that could be used for carrying goods. Tinker's giant fan rose up behind the engine at the back of the sleigh, a propeller with three long wooden arms, each about as tall as me.

The water tank had been warming all morning, and the steam engine told us, hissing at steady intervals, that it was ready to go. Tinker revved the throttle a bit, and the fan whipped up the snow in a flurry behind the sleigh. He waved me over.

"Get on!" he shouted. "Let's try it out!"

Reluctantly, I joined him on the driver's bench. I was a bit frightened of this noisy machine we had created, especially when I saw the speed at which the fan rotated. I twisted sideways, keeping a nervous eye on the thing as Tinker throttled it up.

The speed built slowly at first, as with all steam operated machines, but then the fan blades became a blur. Tinker's face was a mask of grim determination. I could see that he believed with every fiber of his being that this idea would work. As the throttle speed increased, I grew more skeptical, and increasingly nervous.

By this time, there was a good gust of wind blowing around us. The fan was truly pulling the air, and pushing it away behind us, but this simply was not a strong enough force to move our weight. I could easily imagine the fan blowing a small item, such as a scarf or a hat, but I could see that Tinker's dream was impossible. It simply could not be done. A fan could not move a whole sleigh.

Tinker set his jaw, clearly frustrated. He throttled the thing as far as it would go, and I had to wonder at that point if he was just trying to break it. Then, to our surprise, the sleigh moved a nudge forward. There was a slight jerking feeling as it pulled free of the ice. Then, incredibly, we started to move.

I let out a shriek as the sleigh jumped forward and Tinker yanked at the steering controls. We barely missed a pile of rusty wagon parts, sliding between that and an old wine barrel full of hinges. Tinker shot me a triumphant look as he guided our machine down the hillside.

In the summertime the hill is not a steep one, but on that sleigh, riding on the ice-covered snow, it may as well have been straight down. We took off like a rocket, plummeting down the valley so fast that the slightest over-steer could have thrown us into a tree and killed us both. The sleigh bounced along the uneven road, occasionally even taking flight as we hit the larger bumps.

Tinker and I held on to the bench for dear life. There was nothing else we could do, short of jumping off. When we landed, the sleigh bounced a bit, but the leaf springs saved us from jarring our spines.

Then, suddenly, we were clear of the valley. We shot out into the wide-open plains and Tinker gunned the throttle, letting out a triumphant shout as he did it. Snow billowed up in a great cloud behind us as we tore out across the fields.

We headed east, following the foothills of the mountains, until Tinker decided that we should have a look at the river. I didn't care where we went. I was in heaven with the wind blowing in my face and the land speeding by. My fear was gone, now replaced with unabashed exhilaration. I was thrilled. My faith in Tinker had been restored, and then some. I was in awe of the man's creative genius.

We turned south, cutting across that ocean of snow until we reached the tree line that marked the river. Here, Tinker stopped. We walked around for a few minutes, stretching our legs. Tinker showed me how thick the ice on the river was, by walking along the edge of the bank. "Tomorrow, we must come down here and do some ice fishing," he said.

Naturally, I didn't know what that was. When I asked, I received a well-detailed but rather boring explanation. I suppose some people find fishing thrilling, but I'm afraid I'm not one of them. I couldn't wait to get back on the sleigh and get the wind in my face. Finally, Tinker was ready to head back home.

"Your turn," he said. He climbed onto the bench and motioned for me to sit at the controls.

Chapter 10

I shook my head. "You can't be serious."

"Of course I am. You built this thing as much as I did. It's half yours, so you best learn how to drive it!"

I could see from the look on his face that he was not going to let me say no. "All right," I said. "But it's your fault if we crash and die."

He laughed at that. "Here, hold this stick. You swing it to the right or left to steer, like so… and this is your throttle control. If you twist it…" I twisted the grip as he said this, and the machine jumped forward. I let out a scream and he laughed. "Good, very good. Now steer, a little to the right. Good!"

I followed his instructions for the first few minutes, until I had the confidence that I knew what I was doing. Then I throttled up, and felt the machine respond. Emotions flooded though me. I was thrilled with this new sense of power and freedom, and I never wanted it to end. At the same time, I had thoughts of my father lingering in the back of my mind. It was sad that he couldn't have been there, that he couldn't have enjoyed this exciting new adventure with me.

I glanced sideways at Tinker and laughed at the crazy grin that split his face. I was grateful that my father had left me with this man. It was his last and perhaps greatest show of love, that he had taken the care to leave me in such capable hands. There was no longer any doubt in my mind that my father had known what he was doing. The Tinkerer's home wasn't just a safe place to hide me, it was a perfect place. It was *exactly* where I needed to be.

I had a sense then that perhaps my father was still watching out for me. That somewhere, in the spirit world -or whatever magical journey awaits us on the other side of death- he was watching over me and caring for me just as he always had.

I drove our sleigh across that smooth, sparkling plain and I felt warm and free, and alive! I felt like my cares were gone, as if there was nothing else in the world that mattered except this single moment.

As my mind went to this other, carefree place, my subconscious reached out into my environment. I felt the sleigh beneath me, sensed the stresses and changes in its shape as we plowed across the drifts. In my mind's eye, I saw the slight imperfections in our work, the areas upon which we could improve, and the flaws that might become dangerous if they were not tended.

I made mental notes of everything. I was anxious to tell Tinker what must be done to perfect this machine as soon as we got home. At some point, he tapped me on the shoulder and nodded in the direction of home, and I changed our course. By the time we arrived, the land was awash in pale blue evening twilight. We had spent the entire afternoon playing with our sleigh, and we had nearly run out of fuel. Tinker must have been watching the gauges, because I had been oblivious until he pointed it out.

We shared the chore of preparing dinner, laughing and giggling the entire time. All along, I had a fear in the back of my mind that something terrible was about to happen, that something would inevitably ruin this wonderful day for me.

It was only later, as I lay in bed that night, that I sorted out this feeling and examined it. I realized that since my father had left, I had not enjoyed a single carefree day. This had been the first time since his departure that I actually felt like a child.

It may sound like a sad thought, but in truth it was wonderful. It meant that I was moving forward, that I had found something new to embrace, something that could make me forget my anxiety about the outside world and my fear that I would never find my place. Suddenly I realized that I had found my place.

This thought process might have been part of the greater changes going on within me as well. Strange as it may sound, I was in fact becoming a woman during this time. As I've mentioned before, my mother's people age extremely fast. It had been about six months since my father left me with Tinker, and in that time, I had doubled in size. I had changed from a child of six or seven in appearance to a young woman, in human terms. I was, in all practicality, a teenager now.

This rapid growth brought with it certain internal changes, a metamorphosis of my internal organs and a surge of hormones. I didn't understand this at the time. These physiological changes bring about certain occurrences with human females. This is the time that marks the beginning of a young woman's cycle, the time that ushers her into womanhood.

Among the Tal'mar, these changes do not occur. Apparently, I was more Tal'mar than human in this aspect. I felt the changes within me, but did not experience the rest. I did not then and still do not fully understand the difference between our kinds, but this was one I was glad for. I would not have well adapted myself to this discipline of regularity. At least not at this age.

Tinker and I spent the next few weeks toying with and perfecting our sleigh. It was a pleasant distraction, and it was all too soon that we saw signs of warmer weather approaching. Patches of green appeared on the plains, and the snow that remained became too soft for our machine to be of practical use. Sadly, I helped Tinker push it back into the barn.

My mood lapsed briefly until I realized that at long last, the time had come for me to go to school. I asked Tinker about this at dinner one night. We had a fire burning in the fireplace, but the kitchen window was open and the air was sweet and cool in my lungs.

He looked me over, contemplating my question. "We have a few weeks still," he said. "I will take you then, when the snow has melted and the school reopens. But before that, you will need new clothes. And we'll have to get a bath. Young ladies are expected to be prim and proper."

"Prim and proper? What does that mean?"

"It means that you must be correct, both in appearance and behavior. You must be washed and well dressed, rightly mannered and well-spoken. Do you think you can do all this?"

"If you will show me how," I said.

Tinker smiled. "I know that you will. But what will we do about your ears?"

"I will wear a hat," I said. "I'll always wear it, every day."

"I know, I know. But we're going to need more than one hat. The one you've been wearing is good enough for winter, but what will happen when summer arrives? And what about the rest of those rags you wear? It won't do to have you wearing my old clothes." He made a great show of contemplating this problem, and then finally sighed. "Well, there is nothing else for it. I'm afraid we'll have to go shopping."

I felt a surge of conflicting emotions at those words. I truly and deeply wanted the new clothes of which he spoke, but the thought of returning to town terrified me. "I should wait here," I said.

"Nonsense. If you're to be in school every day, you might as well get used to the scrutiny. We'll go tomorrow."

That was the end of it.

Chapter 11

Tinker fired up his steamwagon early the next morning and drove us straight to the mercantile. Analyn was shocked to see me. "Goodness, look how you've grown!" she exclaimed. "You've become a young woman." I knew that any response would have taken our conversation into dangerous territory, so I just smiled politely.

"We need to see your catalog," Tinker said. "Breeze needs a new wardrobe, and some new hats."

"I see," Analyn said. She went into the back room and returned with a thick leather-bound book. She gave me a knowing smile as she thumped it down on the counter. "Here we go, all the latest fashions, direct from Avenston." She opened the book and started flipping through pages and pages of black and white sketches. "Ah, here's the young ladies' section." She flipped the book around so I could see it. She shot Tinker a look. "How much are we wanting to spend?"

Tinker pulled at his collar uncomfortably. "Well, she'll be needing school clothes, and hats. And something for home, too. She's outgrown everything we have."

"All right, then. Let's get some measurements. Breeze, if you'll follow me into the back room. Tinkerman, why don't you go for a walk? Come back in an hour."

Tinker sighed and disappeared through the front door. As promised, Analyn had me ready to go when he returned. She had a bill for Tinker. "I'll get this order posted this afternoon," she said. "It should be here by the end of the week. You won't be disappointed; the tailors in Avenston do incredible work."

"I hope they do," Tinker said as he signed the bill. "I'm gonna have to do a lot of incredible work myself, if I'm going to pay for this."

"Ah, but she's worth it," Analyn said with a twisted grin.

"That she is," Tinker smiled. He rubbed my head as if I were still the little girl my father had left in his care.

"Well, it seems we have some time to fill," Tinker said as we drove home. "Do you feel like starting another project?"

I glanced at him sideways. "What did you have in mind?"

He smiled, and nodded towards a hawk circling over the fields. I followed his gaze, and then shrugged. "I don't understand."

"What would you think of a machine that could do that?" he said.

My jaw dropped. "You want to build a machine that can fly like a bird? Is that possible?"

His grin widened. "Anything's possible, if you try hard enough."

I took a deep breath. I knew better than to second-guess Tinker. Regardless of how impossible the task appeared, if he thought it was possible, then it probably was. I watched the bird soaring on the breeze, paying special attention to the gentle movement of its wings. I wished I could observe more closely, but I could only guess as to most of what was going on.

"Do the wings work like a fan?" I said. Tinker didn't answer. I turned to him and realized that he was lost in thought. He hadn't even heard me. He was watching the bird.

Tinker spent the rest of the day in the barn. I could tell that his mind was in other places, so I just stayed out of his way. Later that evening I brought him some dinner, and stole a glance at his designs. I saw pages and pages of sketches scattered across his workbench. The general design seemed to be the same: two large wings attached to a long tail section. The details however, changed dramatically. The size and shape of the wings varied from a sharp triangular design to long, elegant bird-wing shapes.

Tinker also had pages and pages of calculations, probably regarding the weight of the wood in comparison with the size of the wings. I couldn't imagine how math could solve such a problem, but I left it in the Tinker's capable hands.

The next morning, he was ready to start. Tinker had put a lot of thought into the weight problem, and he had some interesting design ideas. Rather than carving the wings from solid wood, he wanted to build a frame that consisted of light wood reinforced with metal pipes. "Will it be strong enough?" I asked, as I saw the frame coming together.

"It will be strong enough to fly," Tinker answered. "It's the landing that I'm worried about."

I mused over this for a couple of days. I helped Tinker when I could, but unfortunately, much of the craftsmanship required was beyond my skills. Rather than injecting myself into an already complicated project, I mostly just busied myself fetching tools and supplies when he needed them. The thing was practically finished by the time I noticed the biggest problem of all.

"Tinker, where will you put the engine?"

He laughed. "This won't have an engine. That would be far too heavy."

"Then how will it fly?"

"We're going to *kite* it," he said.

"Kite?"

"Yes, like the toys they sell in the mercantile. We will tow it with the coach, until it catches wind. Then, perhaps it will fly."

My reservations grew with every passing hour as I saw the project coming together. It was bad enough that Tinker wanted to build a flying machine. The dangers there were obvious. Then I saw the thin, light frame, and I knew what would happen if the thing ever crashed. When I learned that the flying machine would travel without power, I felt like crying. I knew something bad was going to happen this time. I could feel it.

The day of our first flight was a cool, frosty morning. Tinkerman was dressed in his leather pants and jacket. He was padded with extra clothing beneath. His theory was that if he crashed, the additional layers would help absorb the impact. I could only shake my head at this thinking.

We carried the machine down to the field at sunrise, and by nine a.m. Tinker was ready to fly. I tried desperately to convince him that this was a mistake, but he refused to listen. "You just get me in the air," he said. "I'll take it from there."

I obediently took my place at the driver's seat and watched him with my head twisted around. Tinker crawled on top of the thing and strapped himself into position. When he gave me the signal, I held my breath and gunned the engine.

As soon as we started to move, the glider's tail lifted into the air and it leveled out. Suddenly I could see Tinker's face. He was wearing his leather goggles, the ones that he had been wearing on the day we met, and his eyes were hidden behind the dark glass.

The glider bounced along on its metal wheels, and it looked rather painful. Then it bounced into the air and, to my surprise, did not come down. The glider lifted into the sky. I could feel it tugging against the steamwagon. Tinker disengaged the rope, and flew free.

I engaged the brakes and sat there watching him for at least fifteen minutes. Tinker flew down to the end of the field, and then made a slow arc across the river and headed west towards where we had started. I spun slowly on the seat, my attention riveted on Tinker's virgin flight.

He came back in my direction and then made another broad circle. He did this several times. As I watched, I noted that he seemed to lose altitude fastest over the river, but he quickly regained it when he flew out across the fields.

Eventually, he came in for a landing and I took the wagon to go meet him. He gradually lost altitude, until his wheels were just inches off the ground. Then he set down. To my horror, the wings snapped. The glider spun sideways and then flipped, turning over three full times before it finally landed in a wrecked heap.

Chapter 12

I sped across the field to the crash site and ran over to the debris. I located him off to the side, lying on his back, still strapped to a section of wing.

"Tinker! Tinker, can you hear me? Are you alive?" My heart thudded in my chest. I was terrified.

He raised his head and chuckled. "Did you see that flight?"

"I saw, Tinker. It almost got you killed." I knelt down to help him get the straps off.

"Yes, but she flew, Breeze. Did you see? It was amazing. I could have stayed up there for hours. Until sunset, at least."

"Yes, wonderful," I said angrily. "Except that your glider is destroyed."

He glanced around the wreckage. "Ah, yes... slight miscalculation there. But I know how to fix it!"

I turned away and stomped angrily back towards the coach.

"Wait, Breeze. Wait!"

"What is it?"

"Umm. I don't think I can walk. I think my leg's broken."

The doctor in town took a look at Tinker's leg and proclaimed that it had, in fact, been broken. Just below his hip. Oddly, the treatment for this involved pulling it straight, which appeared to be ungodly painful, and then securing the leg to a long brace.

He gave me explicit instructions about keeping the leg straight, and not allowing Tinker to walk on it. I promised to do all I could, though I knew that the instructions wouldn't sit well with Tinker. He was not the sort of man to spend a dozen weeks lying around the house.

The doctor also gave us a small bottle of medicine. A teaspoon of it he said would kill Tinker's pain. Tinker took a swig of it on the way home, and by the time we arrived, he was in a stupor. I didn't have the strength to carry him up to the loft, so I tucked him into my bed and I slept in his.

As I drifted to sleep, it occurred to me that we had somehow switched roles. For months now Tinker had been looking out for me and protecting me. Now, strangely, I found myself acting as the responsible party. How had that happened? I was too exhausted to give it much thought. I told myself that in the morning everything would be back to normal, and went to sleep.

It must have been three a.m. when Tinker's scream woke me from a dead sleep. I flew down the ladder and found him on the floor next to my bed. Apparently, he had been tossing and turning, and managed to knock himself out of bed. I rushed to his side. "Shh, calm down. Take a deep breath, Tinker. What happened?"

He was sweating and his breath came in gasps. "My leg is on fire," he said. "Something's wrong." He clenched his teeth as another spasm of pain racked his body, and a loud cry escaped from his lips. I put my hand on his forehead. He was burning up.

"You have a fever," I said. "We've got to get you back into bed. Can you help me?"

He nodded, and I grabbed him by the shoulders. I had him halfway up before I realized it may have been a mistake. The pain was killing him. Unfortunately, by that time it was too late. I heaved again, and he pushed just enough to get his torso back up.

Slowly and delicately I lifted the broken leg back into place. He howled as the brace that should have been holding it straight came loose. "I'm going to get your medicine," I said. "I'll be right back."

I returned a moment later with the bottle, and poured some of the foul smelling liquid down his throat. Tinker's cries died away immediately, and he fell to moaning and panting while I sat there. I put a cool rag over his forehead.

"Tinker, I wish I knew what to do," I said. "I wish I knew how to fix you."

"Just do it," he mumbled incoherently. I looked at him sideways.

"Just do what?"

His only response was a grunt. I thought about it, wondering what he'd meant. Was he talking about what I'd done with the sleigh? Was that what he wanted from me? To reach into his body with my mind, and try to mend him? I wasn't even sure such a thing was possible. Still, it seemed worth a try. I would have done anything to relieve his pain.

I placed my hands on Tinker's thigh and closed my eyes. Instantly I heard his heartbeat, and felt the rhythmic pulse of his blood. I expanded my awareness and felt rather than saw the tiny sparks of electricity shooting through his body. I saw the bones and the way the skeletal system lined up with the internal organs and the muscles. My mind drew the connections between these different systems and I saw how they worked together as one. There was magic there, I realized. More magic than I had ever seen or imagined.

I pulled my attention down to Tinker's leg, and immediately discerned the problem. The bone had not only been separated, but fine fragments were now floating freely inside his body. I saw the gush of uncontained blood and fluids, and knew that this had already started to become infected. I started by directing my thoughts towards the bone.

I pulled with my hands, separating the bone and getting it into a proper alignment. Then I mentally urged the tiny fragments to dissolve. I watched them liquify, and guided Tinker's body to absorb the calcium and other minerals, and then to utilize these materials in rebuilding the bone. I didn't know of course that this was calcium, I simply *felt* what it was, and how it could be used.

I caused the bone to move and stretch in some places, just enough to build a solid bridge across the break, so that I could remove the pressure from my hands. Once this was done, I was able to give my full concentration to the healing process.

Tinker's body knew what to do for the most part. It was up to me to urge it forward, to increase the speed of healing. During this process, I had to look to other sources for building supplies. The body needed energy, and it needed the building blocks of bone and sinew. I borrowed sparingly from the rest of his body, leaving the instructions that these areas should be rebuilt as soon as Tinker started ingesting food again.

The bone was not complete at the end of the process, but it was serviceable, and I knew it would be fully healed within a few weeks. Tinker still had the immediate issue of an infection, but I had removed the initial cause of the problem. It was now up to his body to clear the toxins from his bloodstream. There was nothing more that I could do.

Chapter 13

Tinker wasn't quite his old self the next morning, but he was a far sight better than the previous night. He ate a full plate for breakfast. Then he asked for another, and he drank nearly a full pot of tea. I could tell that his body was working hard to replenish the resources I'd used in repairing his bone. I was concerned for him, and I desperately wanted to check the status of those repairs, but I was uncertain as to how to broach the subject.

What I had done to Tinker was an extremely personal thing. I knew that he was an open-minded and sensible man, but I wasn't sure if I had crossed a line. Using magic to help build a machine is rather different than using it to go inside someone's body. Especially since I didn't have Tinker's permission. Not in so many words, anyway. His unconscious babbling certainly didn't grant me the right to do what I'd done.

I eventually determined that the best course was one of silence. If he noted what I had done, or asked about it, then we would discuss it. If not, then there was no point in bringing it up. This didn't do anything to ease my nagging concern about the healing process, but I forced myself to believe that the healing would continue naturally, without further intervention. If I was wrong, I hoped I would see signs and be able to correct the problems before it was too late.

I managed to keep Tinker in bed for that first day, but thereafter he would have none of it. "I'm not going to lie around like an invalid!" he said. "Better to crawl into a cave and die than to live like that. Help me up or get out of my way, woman!"

It was a rare tone for Tinker, this condescending masculine attitude. I knew that it meant he was compensating for his fear and sense of inadequacy. He felt that his injury made him less of a man, that his need to rely on someone made him appear weak.

This realization shed new light on Tinker's personality and in a way, on my father's as well. Both men were proudly independent, and their lifestyles reflected their masculinity. They lived in remote areas where they wouldn't be bothered with the trivialities of "civilized folk." They ignored the inherent dangers that came with such a choice. It was important to them to be free of those societal constraints.

Strangely, I knew exactly how they felt. I would have hated to have someone watching and inspecting everything I did. I was more like them than I had ever realized.

I took this study to heart, and I gave Tinker all the space he wanted. I helped him get around once he was out of bed, until he built himself a pair of crutches. Then he was mostly on his own. I never strayed far enough that I wouldn't hear if he cried out, or needed me to fetch something from some awkward place, but beyond that I let him have his privacy.

Meanwhile, I set out to get the yard organized. I had to do something to keep my mind from the fact that school was just days away. The yard seemed like an appropriate task. It had been on my mind for months, and finally I felt ready to take it on.

The piles shrank almost magically as I found proper places for the massive amounts of junk. The wood went behind the barn into carefully organized stacks. The metals went on the sides of the barn, steel and iron on the south side, brass and copper on the north.

I used some of the wood to build shelves on the outside walls, and then I moved the barrels, buckets, and other assorted containers into their respective areas. By the end of the week, the yard was starting to actually look like a yard. There were only a few spots of green here and there, but it was a start.

Saturday morning, while I was working outside, I caught a whisper on the breeze. It was the trees, and they warned of an approaching carriage. I found Tinker in the barn, and warned him that company was approaching. He left me there, and I stole a peek at his designs. He was still working on the glider.

I saw three different versions, all of which looked like vast improvements over the original. Their wings were broader and sturdier, their frames longer and more refined. The steering controls were entirely redesigned, using a wire system that actually controlled aileron flaps at the back of the wings. And on one of them, attached to the front, I saw a fan.

There was no explanation as to how Tinker planned on powering this new glider, but the direction in which he was headed was clear. The next version was to be powered.

I heard voices outside, and pulled myself away from the workbench to go peer through the cracks in the barn doors. It was Analyn, and she had packages! I ran outside, and she met me with a smile.

"Ah, just the young lady I was looking for!" she said. "Tinker, we'll need some privacy so she can try these things on."

Tinker nodded. "If you need me, I'll be in the barn."

The afternoon flew by. As Analyn dressed me up in my new clothes, she taught me about the customs of human women. I learned about hairstyles and perfumes, and about manners and social status. She was very concerned that I should use all the proper mannerisms of a young human girl.

"This is most important," she said. "You are an attractive enough girl, but you have the look of your mother's people. You must give no one reason to doubt that you are who you say you are."

"I understand," I said.

"Good. Remember, the children in our school have known each other for all their lives. You will already be a stranger to them. Therefore you must be just like them, in every way. The sooner they accept you, the better off we are."

"I'll do my best," I promised.

"I know you will. You're a smart child."

Analyn left that afternoon with a stern reminder that school would begin at eight a.m. sharp, Monday morning. I was useless for the rest of the weekend. I was a nervous wreck. My heart soared with hopes and fantasies, but my mind was full of uncertainty and fear.

I had wanted this so badly for so long. It wasn't until now that I began to think about all the things that could potentially go wrong. Ironically, it was Tinker that calmed this fear in me.

I was pacing across the front yard Sunday afternoon. I had gone out there with the intent of clearing my mind with some good, hard work. Instead I ended up wandering around the yard all morning with my head in a daze.

"Stop worrying," he said.

I halted mid-step. I hadn't even seen him watching me. "I can't," I said. "What if they find out? What if I do or say something wrong?"

"What if the moon falls out of the sky?" he said. "There are millions of things that could go wrong every day, from the time we get up in the morning to the time we hit the pillow at night. We can't live our lives worrying about what-ifs. We have to focus on doing the best we can, and making the most of what we've got."

I knew the truth of his words, but my stomach was a jumble of knots and I would not be calmed so easily. "I'm going to screw things up," I said. "I just know it."

He took my hand and we started walking along the creek. "Yes, there's a chance that will happen. I won't lie. We do our best to avoid mistakes but they happen, and then we fix them. Take my glider, for example. It didn't work out well the first time..."

"Didn't work out well? It almost killed you!"

"Exactly. But I survived. And now I can perfect it. I can deal with the flaws in the original design, and make it better."

I couldn't mention the fact that he might have died if I hadn't intervened. But that didn't matter. I knew what he meant, and I understood the emotion behind his argument. I decided to change the subject.

"I saw your designs," I said. "Did you figure out how to put an engine on the glider?"

"Unfortunately, no. I'm going to have to come up with some new kind of power. The engine is too cumbersome. Even if I could make it work without the water tank and burner, it still might be too heavy. I've been racking my brain trying to figure out what else I can do."

I thought it over. "I don't know enough about your inventions," I said. "I know how the steam engine works, but that's no help... what about the light in the kitchen? How does that work?"

"The water wheel turns a magnet inside a coil of copper wire. It creates *electricity*. It's like a sort of harnessed lightning. There's no way we could make use of that."

"What about your clocks?" I said. "What makes them keep working?"

"They have to be wound. They don't have a power source, they merely store power... by God, you've done it!"

We stopped in our tracks. "What did I do?"

"You solved the problem! The glider doesn't need an engine. It needs a spring, and a gearbox! Don't you see? The gearbox controls the spring, only releasing a bit of the energy at a time. What we need is a powerful spring. Something larger than anything I've made before. It's going to require a lot of steel."

I could see him disappearing into that place in his mind. I didn't understand half of what he was saying, but that didn't matter. Tinker was already designing the thing. At times like that, it was always best just to stay out of his way.

He mumbled for a few more minutes about tension and carbon content, and then he went wandering towards the barn. I settled down on a rock next to the creek, lost in my own thoughts. Tinker's problem had been solved. Mine couldn't be solved. All I could do was wait and see what happened in the morning.

Chapter 14

School turned out to be both everything I'd hoped, and everything I'd feared. Analyn, or Mrs. Trader as we called her in class, was a powerfully intelligent woman. Not only was she well read, but she seemed to have memorized every book she'd ever touched. This knowledge came bubbling out of her so fast that at times, it seemed a waste of time to try to remember any of it. She had particular interest in some subjects, one of these being the war. We discussed this subject at the end of my first week. It was in the afternoon.

"Class, I must apologize to some of you regarding this next subject. You in particular, Breeze. I know that your father was recently killed in combat, and you should know we're all very proud of him." All eyes turned to me, and I shriveled.

I suppose it was Analyn's way of trying to help break the ice. The fact that my father had sacrificed himself in the war effort was likely to earn me some respect from my peers. I don't know if the ploy worked or not.

"As you all know we have been at war with the Tal'mar for centuries. Can anyone tell me how this started? Yes, Jesha?"

Jesha Miller was Mrs. Trader's darling. She had bright blue eyes and perfect blonde hair, and she knew every subject so extensively that it was sickening. I was certain that Jesha would someday take Mrs. Trader's place as the town's teacher.

"No one knows how it started. Some people say that there was an agreement between the humans and the Tal'mar, and that the Tal'mar betrayed that agreement. Others say that the Tal'mar were involved in a civil war, and humans sent supplies to one faction but not the other."

"Very good," said Mrs. Trader. "In fact, these theories might both be true... or they could both be legends. You see, whatever the original dispute was, the animosity between our peoples has been passed down for centuries. At times the tensions die down, and it almost seems that we have peace. Then something happens, and it all starts up again."

"Like the battle of Brell Creek?" Robie said. He was the oldest child in the school by a full year, but usually acted the youngest. For some reason, several of the girls liked him, but I simply could not understand it. He was immature and boorish, and generally quite full of himself.

Mrs. Trader frequently caught him breaking the rules, and when he wasn't in trouble he was usually making jokes at her expense. It was beyond me why anyone would give him a second thought. Nonetheless, several of my female peers adored him.

"Yes, Brell Creek is our most recent example. A Tal'mar hunting party went missing and their bodies were found upriver, near a human settlement there. The Tal'mar assumed these men had been killed by humans from the nearby town of Brell Creek, and they attacked leaving no one alive."

"How horrible," said Terra Cooper. She was one of the nicer girls, a dark haired farmer's daughter with big blue eyes. Of the five girls in my school, Terra was the only one who ever gave me a smile.

"Indeed, especially for the families of those murdered. And now, we have had several skirmishes with the Tal'mar, and the situation is escalating rapidly. At any moment we could be engaged in full-out war once again." Mrs. Trader glanced at the clock. "It's time to go children. Have a wonderful weekend, and stay out of trouble! Breeze, would you please stay for a moment?"

Robie couldn't resist teasing me as he and the other students filed out of the room. He obviously assumed I was being held after class because I was in trouble. "What did you do Breeze?" he laughed.

"Mind your own business, Robie," Analyn said. She shooed him off with a gesture, and he pranced out the door, laughing. The rest of the group disappeared behind him. As the door closed, Analyn turned her attention to me.

"How was your first week?"

"It was fun," I said. "I've learned a lot."

"I'm glad you think so. I've seen a huge improvement in your work already. Breeze, I'm sorry if I upset you by bringing up your father, but I thought it might help the other kids to warm up to you."

"I understand. Actually, the more I learn about what he did, the more I feel like I know him."

"I'm glad to hear it. I wish I could tell you more about him, but I never really knew your father. He came to the mercantile a few times for supplies, but he never had much to say. He mostly kept to himself. I do know that he wasn't from this area."

"Really?"

87

"Yes. He moved here a few years ago, probably just after you were born." I realized as she spoke that my past was a dizzying black hole. Having been so steadily distracted by Tinker's projects, and having matured so rapidly, I hadn't had much time to wonder about my own origins. Suddenly these thoughts came flooding into me, and I felt a rush of apprehension as I realized I knew nothing about my past.

I had always assumed I'd been born and raised in the Riverfork area, and that my mother had probably died in childbirth or fallen ill. This revelation that my father was a foreigner opened up a whole new path of questioning.

"Do you know where he came from?" I asked. My heart was thumping. Who was my father? How had we ended up here, and without my mother?

"I believe he came from the Borderlands, the part of the kingdom that borders the Crimson Strait."

"The Borderlands? That's where the war is, isn't it?"

"Mostly, yes. The Strait is a narrow channel of water that separates the land of Astatia from the Isle of Tal'mar, the home of your mother's people. That's where most of the fighting has taken place over the centuries. Legends say that during great battles, the water has turned the color of blood. Hence the name."

I shivered at the appalling thought. How many people had died to spill that much blood? It was no wonder that the humans and Tal'mar hated each other so. All they'd ever done was slaughter one another. I hated to think that my father had been a part of that.

"Why do you think my father was from the Borderlands?"

"First of all, he had the coloring and build of a Northman, and being that close to the border, it wouldn't be unlikely that a human and Tal'mar might cross paths. I'm guessing you got your hair from your father's side of the family, because Tal'mar hair is usually either violet or green."

"Violet and green? Truly?"

"Yes. Bear in mind that the Tal'mar are not humans, child. They may resemble us in certain ways, but they are most certainly a different species. In fact, I'm surprised that you exist at all, to be honest. I had thought such a mating would be impossible."

Chapter 15

In the span of a few sentences Analyn had gone from acting as if I were completely human to talking about me like some sort of unnatural experiment. I ignored the pain that her statement brought to me, because I knew she didn't mean it. I could tell from her face that it was totally unintentional. It was just a surfacing of deep, unexplored feelings that she'd never questioned. Even though she had chosen to treat me as a friend –as one of her kind- she still couldn't forget the duality of my nature. It would always be there, no matter what happened.

If it was impossible for a woman like Analyn Trader to forget our differences, then how likely was it that other, less open-minded people might act? Had I been deluding myself, thinking that people might change that much?

"I suppose it's just as well, since they're both dead," I said bluntly. "Once I die, everything can go back to normal."

Analyn's eyebrows shot up. Her face changed, and I saw then that she realized the grief she had given me. "Oh dear," she said, throwing her arms around me. "Breeze, I'm sorry for everything that's happened to you. I'm sorry that things are the way they are." She let me go and saw that I had tears in my eyes. She handed me a handkerchief.

"Why did they do it?"

Analyn smiled. "Love," she said gently. "What else could it be? Who would enter into such a tragic relationship for any other reason? It's quite romantic really, if you think about it. The two of them, forbidden lovers from two separate worlds, no hope that they could ever truly unite. It must have been exhilarating and frightening all at once. They certainly must have known that if anyone found out there would be trouble. Your father would have likely been jailed and hanged as a traitor."

"My father was *not* a traitor!" I said.

"Calmly, Breeze. I didn't say that he was. I only meant that people would suspect. Humans are simple that way. Once they get a thought in their heads, there's no changing it. Anyway, there is another reason that I brought all this up. I have friends and family up north. I was considering asking them if they knew your father, or had heard of him. I didn't want to do it without your permission."

My heart skipped. "You would do that?" I said.

"Of course. I'll mention your father as a friend, and I'll tell them I'd like to contact his family. Nothing more than that. That way we can discreetly find out if you have any more family, and hopefully learn more about your father, possibly even your mother. How does that sound?"

I was crying again. I didn't even have the words to thank Analyn for what she was doing. I threw my arms around her and wept, and she held me as if I were a human.

How can I describe what it's like, not knowing anything about your parents, or your heritage? A large part of me, the biggest part of me, was a mystery. *What if I did have more family?* Would they accept me, or chase me away? I hardly dared to wonder.

"I'll compose a letter this weekend. Perhaps in a week or two, we'll know more."

"Thank you," I said. "Thank you so much."

She patted me on the back. "You're welcome, Breeze. Don't worry. In time, all will be known." She held me at arms length and gave me a wink. "Run along now, I hear the Tinkerman and that rattletrap contraption of his outside."

I thanked her again as I left, and she waved me off. On the way home, I told Tinker of our conversation. He too, was touched by Analyn's generosity. "I never knew your father well, either," he admitted. "I traded some horseshoes to him once, and some nails another time. He never had much to say. I guess he wasn't too anxious to make friends. Now we all know why, don't we?"

The next few weeks flew by. Between my studies and Tinker's glider, I hardly had a moment to think. In school, I didn't make friends as quickly as I had hoped. The other children didn't seem to suspect me, but they weren't opening their arms to me either. I was learning however, and that was the important thing.

Analyn had a library in the school room, and she readily let me borrow anything that I wanted. Needless to say, I spent many late nights reading by candlelight in my room. I had a voracious thirst for knowledge, and at last I had a taste of what I'd been craving.

I studied the history of my world, and the history of the war. More than anything else, it seemed to be a study of fear, paranoia, and racism. Humans thought

Tal'mar were arrogant and devious. Tal'mar believed humans to be inferior and barbaric. The generations of mistrust bred hatred and fear. The two people, it seemed, would never find common ground.

I learned of another race of men who lived to the south, in the barren desert that was officially named Kantraya. Commonly, it was known as the Badlands. The men who lived there were wild, nomadic barbarians who worshipped dark gods and practiced a strange, mystical religion. There was little solid information regarding these peoples, but plenty of conjecture.

It was said they used black magic, and that they practiced human sacrifice and cannibalism. The stories said the Kantrayans, or Kanters, were descended from giants, and that the smallest of them were twice the size of the largest humans.

They conducted raids along the borders from time to time, but they seemed to have little use for logic or organization. The only thing that saved the northern lands from the Kanters invading was the fact that they were too unorganized to form a real army. As a result, they were generally presumed to be too stupid to teach and too powerful to train as slaves.

I found the lack of good information about the Kanters to be troubling. Humans had determined that Kanters were too stupid to be a threat, and therefore simply ignored them. I shouldn't have been too surprised by this. The humans focused their attention on the greater danger, the Tal'mar. Ultimately, this complacency could have destroyed us all.

Chapter 16

Tinker's project moved steadily forward. I helped him when time allowed, but not nearly so much as I had before school started. The new fuselage was larger and sturdier than the first, and Tinker asked me to see to the shaping of the wood. I did what I could. The thing was little more than a hollow shell.

It was three weeks after the crash that this new glider, now called an "airplane" by Tinker, had its virgin flight. I walked around the aircraft the night before, searching it with my mind. There was no doubt that this vehicle was superior in every way to its predecessor. The wood and steel were meshed, acting as one. The wings were flexible to allow for increased lift and changes in wind resistance, but they had spines like bones to keep them from breaking. In all, I was quite proud of the job we had done.

"She's beautiful, isn't she?" Tinker stood behind me. He was smoking a cigar, as he did on rare occasions, and the bittersweet smell of tobacco drifted through the air around us, drowning out the aromas of lilac and grease that defined our homestead.

"I don't think you should fly it," I said. I turned to face him, gauging his reaction. He immediately became defensive.

"It won't crash this time!" he insisted. "I've got it right now. You can see that, can't you? It's a hundred times better than the first one."

"I know, Tinker," I said calmly. "I didn't say it wouldn't fly. I just said you shouldn't fly it. Your leg is still healing, and I'm afraid it might not be as strong as it used to be."

"You want to fly it?" he said. I heard so many things in his voice: disbelief, reluctance, fear. Everything except the acceptance I wanted. "Absolutely not! I won't even think of it. I won't allow you to risk your neck on this crazy thing."

I grinned. "And yet I should let you?"

His eyes were wide and they searched for an answer in the night around us. "Breeze, that's crazy. You don't know what you're asking."

"I do know, Tinker. I know exactly. I'm asking you to let me do this. Imagine what would happen if something happened to you. I'd be as good as dead. I would have nowhere to go. On the other hand, if anything happened to me, nobody would even care."

"That's not true."

"Besides you, I mean. Not only that, but the truth is I want to do it. I want to go up there in the sky, to feel the freedom that you felt when you flew. Do you know what that would be like for me? All I've ever seen of this world is this valley, and I can barely hope to see more. But up there, up in the sky..."

I could see my words affecting him. A change came over his face. He'd been worried and defensive, but he was starting to see it now. He was realizing what it would mean to me.

He looked at our craft. It was stronger now. It was better. More stable, more controllable. "You won't take off right away," he said. "You'll taxi around the field. You'll learn the controls; test the aircraft's weakness..."

I rushed into his arms. "Thank you, Tinker."

95

The next morning I stood next to our aircraft, watching as Tinker hooked it up to the steamwagon to wind the spring. There was something comforting about the familiar *chort-chort* of the steam engine, and the vague but ever-present smell of burning coal. It calmed my soul, if only a little. I don't know why I was so apprehensive. I had explicit instructions about safety, and I knew that I might not even get into the air. Still, there was an anxious feeling in the pit of my stomach. It was almost as if I knew how important this moment was, in the grand scheme of my life.

I could tell from the heat of the sun that it would be sweltering by noon. I was dressed in leathers and had a pair of goggles strapped to my forehead. Tinker had insisted on all these safety measures, but as the sun beat down, I was sorely tempted to start tearing it all off. At last, he gave me the signal, and I climbed aboard.

The airframe was designed in such a way that the pilot had to lay across it, face down and facing forward. Guidance controls were located to my left and right, and the throttle control was near my right handgrip. My arms and legs slid into metal hoops that would hold me down, should the craft tilt too far or spin upside down. Tinker had thought of everything.

He pulled the steamwagon around the craft and drove up ahead to my right. He started shouting about all of his safety rules, and I waved him off. Grudgingly, he gave me the go-ahead. I released the brake and slowly throttled up. I felt a rush of wind on my face, and the hum of the propeller filled my ears. The blades became a blur.

The plane was at three-quarters throttle before it started to move. The wheels broke free of the dusty ground and I went bouncing across the field, a broad grin plastered across my face. It was a rough ride, far more uncomfortable than the sleigh had been. But still, it made me want to laugh out loud. I made a full circle around the field, which was about three miles long. By the time I got back to my starting point, my body was aching from all the bouncing. Tinker gave me an approving smile. I nodded, and continued on, increasing the throttle slightly.

I immediately noticed a smoothing of the ride at this higher speed. Encouraged, I gave it a bit more power. The transition was notable. The ride went from jerking and painful to rolling, and then suddenly to perfectly smooth. This was the only indication I had that I was off the ground. When I realized what had happened, I shot a worried glance back at Tinker. He stood on the steamwagon, his hands shielding the sun over his eyes, riveted on me.

I had a choice to make then. Should I try to land, risking a return to that rough, rocky plain? Or should I give it a bit more throttle, and get the machine safely high enough to test the controls? Naturally, the latter seemed more scientifically prudent. And my bruised body begged me not to return to the ground. I pulled back on the flight controls, raised the throttle, and the plane started to climb.

Chapter 17

I knew that Tinker would be furious that I had lifted off, but what else could I do? At that point, it seemed safer to continue flying than to return and face his wrath. Besides, now that the thing was in the air, there was no reason not to continue. It had proven itself capable. I was aware of the danger, but at that moment, I didn't even care. I was *flying*. I was completely free. Words can't even describe the liberation that I felt.

I used my ability to feel the wood. I let my consciousness stretch out, joining with the machine beneath me. What I found was encouraging. The airframe was sturdy; it was completely unaffected by the change in gravitational forces and wind shear. The wings were strong. Their design was superior, and they flexed easily with the movement of the wind. In all, the entire plane was quite sound, and under very little stress. I was certain that there was nothing to worry about.

I let my attention wane, just enough that I could focus on the actual flying. I circled the field six or seven times, my heart pounding wildly and my breath coming in sputtering gasps against the wind. The land below me changed as I climbed in altitude. The river became a narrow blue snake, and the trees looked no larger than a man. To the northwest, I saw the buildings of Riverfork rising up out of the prairie. It was marvelous.

I turned and swept down between the trees along the banks of the river. I flew upstream, the belly of the plane barely scratching the surface of the water. The cool spray flashed up around me, leaving icy droplets on my skin and a vaporous cloud in my wake. Then I pulled back and roared up into the sky.

I don't know how long it went on. I completely lost track of time. I didn't come back down until the spring ran out of energy and I suddenly realized that the fan had stopped. Naturally, I panicked. I knew that below a certain speed, the craft would drop from the sky like a rock. I had no idea what speed that was, and even if I had, there was no way to gauge it. So I circled around as quickly as I could, and brought the thing down to ground level. I was going quite fast at that point, too fast to land, so I glided along the ground for a while.

Eventually the craft burned off its speed, and the wheels settled onto the ground. My smooth flight instantly became a bone-jarring, tooth-rattling hellride. I hit the brakes, and in a cloud of dust, rolled to a stop. I was barely out of the safety straps when Tinker got there.

I braced myself as I heard the steamwagon roll up. I was certain that I was about to be receive a long lecture. Instead, Tinker raced over and threw his arms around me. "That was beautiful!" he exclaimed. "Absolutely beautiful. How was it? Did you feel the heat thermals? Did the wings respond to the change in airspeed? How did it steer?" He asked this and about a dozen more questions before I could even catch my breath. When he finally stopped, I just took a second to stare into his wild, maniacal eyes.

"What?" he said. "What's wrong?"

I pulled my goggles off, and started laughing hysterically. I laughed so hard that I leaned back against the plane and doubled over. I think he was starting to get concerned by the time I finally caught my breath. "There's nothing wrong, Tinker. It was absolutely perfect. The thing hardly even noticed it was flying. In fact, the worst part of it was running on the field. Do you know how far I went?"

He shook his head. His eyes were huge, his face a mask of blank expectation. "How far? Where did you go?"

I told him, and the memory of it was so thrilling that I actually started to cry. I described going up over the mountains and feeling the turbulent rush of air. I told him about cruising up the river and watching the water spray up behind me. I described flying so high in the sky that Riverfork looked like a child's toy down below, and the people became completely invisible. By the time I was done, he had tears in his eyes, too.

Tinker was silent for a while as he listened, and then he began to question me. He wanted to know about the wind currents, and about how the plane responded to atmospheric changes. He wanted to know how far I thought it could fly, and how much weight it could bear. I did my best to answer all these questions, but I quickly became distracted. Finally, I interrupted him in mid-sentence: "Tinker, wind it back up."

He paused for a second and then glanced around, as if just then realizing that we were standing around in broad daylight in the middle of a field. "Right," he said.

I made three complete flights that day, and the plane performed spectacularly. At the end of the day, there wasn't a single sign of weakness or wear. Aside from the thick layer of dust on the fuselage, it looked like new. Tinker questioned me relentlessly for the rest of the evening.

"There must be something," he said as we were eating dinner, "some way to improve it. The machine cannot simply be perfect."

"It was perfect," I argued. "If it wasn't for the spring winding down, I could have flown for days."

"There was nothing else?" he said. I thought it over.

"There was one moment, the first time I landed." He leaned closer, his eyes wide, begging for more. "The fan stopped while I was still flying. I had no way of knowing when the power would run out."

"Ahh!" he said. "Of course! We need some measurement, some gauge. I'll start on it tomorrow. What else? Was there nothing else?"

"In fact there was one more thing," I said. I had completely forgotten about it, until just then. "I couldn't tell how fast I was going. It didn't seem important until the fan stopped, and I realized that if I went too slow I could crash."

"I see." Tinker's eyes got that distant look, and he wandered out to the barn. I went to bed. As I lay there, staring through my ceiling window, I almost felt like I was still flying.

I drifted into a light sleep, my dreams filled with thoughts of soaring through the clouds. I flew over strange and distant lands, and the whole world stretched out before me. Then, at some point, my dreams began to change. The clouds became dark, and lightning arced across the sky. The wind whipped at my face, and rain came hurtling down, angrily beating into my face.

There was a flash of light and thunder shook the mountainside. My eyes snapped open, and I looked up through my window in my ceiling. The darkened figure of a man's head was staring back at me. Lightning flashed and I saw a face. His skin was dark and covered with tattoos. His eyes were yellow, and his teeth had been sharpened into fangs. I screamed.

Chapter 18

It wasn't two seconds before Tinker was at my side. I pointed at the window. "A face!" I said. I was shaking and terrified, almost crying. "There was a face in the window!"

Tinker went into the kitchen and reappeared a moment later holding a knife. "Lock this door," he ordered. "Don't open it until I come back."

"No!" I shouted. "Don't leave me! Please, Tinker, don't go out there!"

Tinker stared at me for a minute before he finally took pity on me, and came back to my side. He set his knife on my sideboard, within easy reach. Then he held my head in his arms, and stroked my hair back from my eyes. He started talking, telling me about how amazing I was, and about how well I'd flown his plane. He mumbled about the changes he wanted to make, and about the difficulties of measuring wind speed.

My head was lost in this random series of images and calculations, and his voice, along with the sound of the wind and rain outside, lulled me back into a pleasant, dreamy state. I began to wonder if the terrifying face I'd seen was no more than a dream. I *had* been sleeping. I'd been having a nightmare, because of the storm that was raging outside. Maybe that was all it was, just a dream...

Tinker spoke no more of this. When I woke the next morning, he had breakfast ready on the table, and he announced that we were going for a drive.

"No flying today?" I said, my voice tinged with regret.

"I'm afraid not. The storm flooded our field. Besides, it might not be safe. If the wind or lightning start up again, who knows what might happen?"

"Then where are we going?" I said.

He shot me a wink. "It's a surprise."

What I didn't know was that Tinker had already been outside. He'd seen the tracks in the yard, and he knew that my nightmare had been more than a dream. This was the reason for our drive. Only he didn't tell me, and it wasn't until much later that I realized what had really happened.

Tinker drove us down to the river and then turned west, following the banks towards town. We passed several small farms, and eventually stopped at one of them. It was a quaint little homestead brimming with livestock. I saw Terra Cooper working with a horse in the corral. She waved as we pulled up. A man I assumed to be her father came over to greet us. I was wearing my cap, of course. I always wore something on my head those days, even around home. In fact, when I took my hat off at night, it still felt like I was wearing one.

"Tinkerman, how have you been?" The man said.

"Doing well, Thom," Tinker said. "I don't believe you've met my niece, Breeze." We had decided it was best to stick with that original story, that I was his niece from South Bronwyr. Though the children in school knew my father had died in battle, they didn't know much else about me, so we were free to fabricate as much of my past as we needed.

Thom nodded and smiled at me. "My pleasure, Breeze. Terra has told me a lot about you. Quick as a whip, she says."

"It's nice to meet you, sir," I said. I accepted his handshake.

"That's my Breeze," said Tinker. "There's not much she can't do once she puts her mind to it. Before we know it she'll be doing the Tinkering and I'll have to retire. So how's life been treating you?"

"Fair enough, up until this morning. Found my prize bull slaughtered down by the creek." Tinker's eyebrows shot up.

"Is that so?"

"Yep. Wasn't pretty, either. Them blasted wood-folk are up to their business again." His face twisted up as he said *wood-folk*, and he practically spit the word out. My ears started burning. I wanted to argue, to defend my mother's people, but I was afraid too. The anger, the hatred that I saw in his eyes was something beyond reason.

Tinker must have seen me stiffen up because he put a reassuring hand on my shoulder. "How do you know it was them?" he said.

"Who else would it be?" Tinker shrugged.

"Did you see any tracks?"

Thom's anger faded, and a sheepish look came over him. "Well, I don't remember seeing any tracks. I suppose there weren't any."

Tinker gave him a weak smile. "Sure. At any rate, that's not the point of my visit. Rumor has it you're looking to sell some pups."

"That I am. Got quite a few. Litter's a few weeks old now. They're all good, smart cattle dogs." He gestured for us to follow him. We climbed off the wagon and walked towards the barn. I was looking at Tinker quizzically, wondering what he was up to, but he ignored my stare.

"I don't have any cattle," Tinker said, "but I would like a little extra company around the house. Some companionship for Breeze." We stepped inside, and my heart leapt as I saw the tiny, furry pups. They were curled up with their mother on an old blanket in the corner. She was a medium-sized dog, with a beautiful dark blue coat. I knelt down and started petting them.

"Well," said Thom, "If you don't want to work 'em, I'd recommend a female. The males are the best heelers, so they'll fetch a higher price. And the females are good, loyal dogs. They're smart, too."

My heart and mind went out to the tiny creatures as I stroked their impossibly soft coats, and I couldn't help hearing their thoughts. It was all incoherent of course, just a blur of emotions. I sensed that one was tired, another afraid, and another hungry. I immediately got a sense of their personalities, and one in particular caught my attention. It was a female, and she came right for me. I sensed a curiosity in her, and a complete lack of fear. She wanted to know who I was. I lifted her up to my face, and looked into her squinting eyes. She licked me.

"I want this one," I told Tinker. He smiled. "All right then. She looks good enough to me. Go wait outside."

He started working out the deal with Thom, and I wandered back to the steamwagon to wait for him. I crawled into the seat, my attention completely taken with my new companion.

I didn't even notice Terra until she was standing next to me. "That's a good choice," she said. I yanked my eyes up, and nearly jumped out of the seat. She laughed. "Sorry, I didn't mean to scare you."

"I didn't hear you come over," I said. I giggled at my own nervousness.

"What I meant is, you chose a good pup. We've been calling that one Cinder, because of her reddish coat. That coloration is pretty rare. You can call her whatever you want, of course."

I held her up and examined her coat in the light. I hadn't even noticed it in the barn, she was in fact very reddish in color, almost orange. "I like Cinder," I said. "It fits her. I think she likes it, too."

Terra smiled. "Keep an eye on her, she's a curious one. She'll get into trouble if you don't watch her."

"Thanks, I'll do that."

"Breeze, there's something you should know..." the tone of Terra's voice changed, and I instinctively glanced around to see if anyone was listening. We appeared to be alone.

"What do you mean?"

"It's about school. Some of the other girls... they have a bit of a problem with you."

My chest tightened up, and my mouth went dry. Problems at school were the last thing I needed. "What are you talking about?"

She glanced around, and then leaned in closer. Her voice was a whisper. "Some of them have noticed that Robie seems to have a liking for you."

"Robie?" I said. I laughed. "That's ridiculous."

"Well you may not have noticed it, but the girls have. Especially Shue. She thinks you're after him."

My mind raced, trying to figure out why this was so important. I wanted nothing to do with Robie. I didn't even like him. And even if I did, such a thing simply wouldn't be possible. I shook my head. "Terra, I don't like Robie. I mean, I *really* don't like him. He's annoying."

She laughed. "That's what I thought. But the thing with Robie is, his dad is Baron Par'Tishan. He owns most of town, and a lot of the land around here. He's also King Ryshan's first cousin."

"That's what it's all about? They're jealous because he likes me? And they like him because he's noble?" It was more a revelation than a question.

"And because he's rich," she said.

I heard voices and glanced up to see Tinker and Thom exiting the barn. "Well, tell them they have nothing to worry about," I whispered.

She nodded. "I'll try, but I don't know if they'll believe me. Anyway, I thought you should know."

"Thanks."

"Did you and Terra have an interesting conversation?" Tinker asked on the way home.

"Oh, we were just talking about school," I said. Half of me wanted to tell Tinker all about it, but the other half knew I shouldn't. If he saw it as a sign of trouble, he just might pull me out of school. That was the last thing I wanted. So I kept this little problem to myself and changed the subject by asking Tinker about our plane.

He said he had a few ideas, but nothing concrete enough to discuss it. He promised that by the end of the week, we would have another test flight. I was disappointed. I wanted to get back in the air right away, even if it wasn't practical. I couldn't wait to experience that feeling again.

Chapter 19

Over the days and weeks that followed, Cinder and I quickly became best friends. She slept on my chest from the very first night, and followed me everywhere during the day. I found I had a sense for when she was getting into trouble, even when I couldn't see her. All I had to do was think of her and she would come running. It was a type of companionship that I hadn't known before. Cinder didn't care if I was human or Tal'mar; she didn't even know the difference. Unfortunately, not all of my relationships were progressing so perfectly.

After my conversation with Terra, my attention at school was distracted, to say the least. She showed no outward sign that we had ever spoken, of course. I wasn't surprised by this, but I was disappointed. It had almost seemed that she wanted to be friends. The truth was that she had not sought me out with her warning. She only brought it to me at a time when it was safe and convenient. I had to wonder if she ever would have said anything if I hadn't appeared at her family's farm.

I stole glances at Jesha Miller and Shue Tanin, trying to discern if there was any truth behind what I had been told. To my dismay, I soon realized that it was all true. Several times I caught the older girls whispering and staring at me. I also began to notice the way that Robie smiled at me when I glanced at him, and the way he always seemed to be putting on a show.

I began to wonder if his abrasive personality was really his way of trying to get attention. *To get my attention.*

All of this made me understandably apprehensive, this palpable tension building between my classmates and me, but I kept the problem to myself. I feared that Tinker might yank me out of school at the first sign of trouble. I feared it so much, that I didn't even talk to Mrs. Trader about the situation. Instead, I forced my fears to take a backseat to my studies, and told myself that eventually the problem would go away. Unfortunately, I was wrong.

As the weight of my social problems settled on my shoulders, my mood started slipping. There were two thoughts that kept me going during those moments, when I was sitting at my desk, wishing to be anywhere else. The first was the thought of my lovely pup, who would be waiting for me at the end of the day. The latter was a promise Tinker had made to me. On Saturday, I would fly again. I found myself waiting and wishing for that moment, as if my escaping into the skies would solve all of my earthly problems. I was jolted back down to earth on Thursday when Analyn told me she had received a response to her letter.

It was another of those embarrassing, uncomfortable moments. Analyn called me aside as we were filing out at the end of the day. Robie shot me a glance but refrained from teasing for once. Shue and Jesha gave me toothy grins as they shoved past. They must have been thrilled, thinking that I was in trouble. After we were alone, Analyn showed me the letter.

"I'm afraid it's not much help," she said. "My relatives didn't know your father personally, but they knew of him. They were as saddened as everyone else to hear of his death. They don't know of him having any close family in the Borderlands, but they promised to ask around."

My heart sank. I was crushed by this news. I thanked Analyn and left in a dark mood. On the way home Tinker asked what the matter was and I hardly had the strength to tell him. I wasn't crying or emotional, though. It was more like I was broken, like I had nothing left. I had to force every word to come out, and I had to force every breath into my lungs. For the moment, I could hardly think of a reason to go on.

When we got home, I went to bed without dinner. I trudged through the next day as if I were a mindless zombie. I was so disheartened that I didn't even care about the fact that Jesha and Shue were now openly taunting and teasing me. Whatever they were doing or thinking seemed totally unimportant. As did everything else.

Then the weekend came and, to my dismay, I realized quite suddenly that I was glad to be *away* from school. How had that happened? My greatest dream was slowly turning into my worst nightmare, not because of anything that had happened, but because of my fears of what *might* happen.

Making friends was not something I'd have thought impossible. How wrong I was. Now I found myself watching my back constantly, with no way of knowing what those girls might be capable of. That distracted me from my studies, and my waning attention led to other difficulties with my performance. I realized for the first time that I didn't even care about going back to school.

It was a quiet thought in the back of my head; something I didn't fully realize until I was enjoying the rush of wind in my face and the unbroken aerial view that seemed to go on forever. I was zooming back and forth along the plains, straying ever further from the safety of my little valley. Cinder was tucked into my jacket, with her tiny nose poking out into the wind. I knew it was dangerous, bringing her with me, but she had refused to stay on the ground.

I tried to leave her with Tinker, but she kept wriggling out of his arms and jumping onto the plane with me. Ultimately, I decided to take a short ride with her, hoping it would frighten her. To the contrary, Cinder was perfectly happy riding along with me, even when the ride was painfully rough. So I took to the skies with my pup companion tucked safely into my jacket.

I circled the field at the mouth of Tinker's valley a few times and then made a broad arc, reaching several miles to the east. I went so far so fast that I didn't even realize how far I'd gone, until I looked for Tinker and found I could no longer see him. That set my heart to thumping, so I headed back in his direction.

Ten minutes later, I was back over familiar territory. I waved at Tinker as I passed overhead. My confidence grew as I flew. According to the meter Tinker had installed next to the controls, I had only used a fraction of the plane's power.

Tinker had gone through an extensive redesign of the power system. The controls still worked much the same as the original version, but the plane was no longer powered by one large spring. It was powered by four. Tinker had realized that he had overbuilt the original spring, making it heavier than necessary. The new, lighter version was not only more efficient; it also consumed less space and required no extra reinforcement.

Ultimately, the plane had more power and was capable of traveling much greater distances. If necessary, Tinker said I could even shut the fan down and glide for miles at a time.

I tested my flying abilities a little as I became more confident. I went into steep dives and then forced the plane to climb almost straight into the air. I paid close attention to the gravitational forces as they pulled on the airframe, and I made careful note of the effect of the wind changes against the wings. Ultimately, I was quite thrilled with the results. The plane seemed capable of some very daring maneuvers. Things I wouldn't dare try.

The higher I climbed, the more exhilarating the ride became. The air was cool up there, and I could see for hundreds of miles. I had long been tempted to fly over town, but I had resisted for fear that I might be recognized. Eventually, I realized this was not a danger. I was so high in the air that even if someone noticed me, they would not be able to tell me from a distant bird. As it was, Tinker's valley and the river to the south were hardly specks in my vision.

So I began to explore new territory. I flew to the north and the west, following the river until it disappeared into the northern forests known as Riverwood. A city grew out of that forest, a place that I would later learn was called Anora. It was several times the size of Riverfork, though I couldn't tell that from my vantage.

I headed east, and felt the gusting winds at the base of the Blackrock Mountains lifting me ever higher. Soon I was looking down across hundreds of miles of mountain tops. It was then, with Cinder tucked warmly into my jacket and the icy mountain winds blowing across my face, that my mind began to wander, and I realized I had made a mistake by going to school.

I had been so anxious, so eager to learn and so convinced that the knowledge I received there would help me change the world, that I didn't see the foolishness of that dream. It wasn't until I had my conversation with Terra that I started to realize the challenges that faced me. I couldn't even make friends with girls that thought I was human. How would I ever convince them to love a half-breed?

More important was the realization that I didn't even care. Looking down on the world as I was, I knew that I had complete and total freedom. There was no place I could not go; there was no one who could stop me. I had greater power and freedom than the mightiest king. In a few hours I could travel the span of an entire kingdom, a trip that could take days on horseback. I could see the entire world! What was school compared with that? What more could I ever learn from a book?

Unfortunately, this realization came too late.

Chapter 20

It was late summer. I had been going to school for almost six months, and still hadn't made friends in any significant way. I was still taking advantage of the opportunity to learn as best I could, but my studies were increasingly difficult as I faced growing animosity from the girls. I did my best to avoid Robie, but he persisted in trying to win my attention. This led the girls, Shue in particular, to become increasingly cruel towards me.

They began to make jokes at my expense, to talk loudly about me when they knew I could hear, and to play practical jokes on me. I sat down at my desk one day, only to find the chair had been unscrewed. I landed on the floor in a pile of books and notes. A few days later, I found a dead rat in my book bag.

This sort of thing went on for weeks before the situation finally came to a head. Ironically, the girls weren't my undoing in the end. I was.

It was Monday morning. I had spent the weekend flying, of course. Tinker had made a few more improvements to the plane, the most notable of which was a self-winding mechanism. He had determined that it was not practical to require a steam engine to wind the springs on the aircraft, so Tinker devised a clever braking mechanism to perform this function. Whenever I landed the plane, I simply had to activate the braking gearbox. This series of gears would then manually rewind the springs. After some practice it was possible, if I landed with enough speed, to completely reset the springs.

After a pleasant weekend in the air, I was quite depressed to be back in school. I had finally accepted the fact that inevitably, I was going to have to leave school. The only thing that prevented me from doing this immediately was my fear of disappointing Tinker and Analyn. I ultimately decided to finish out the year, and simply not return in the spring. Fate it seemed, had other plans for me.

The children were all outside for our midmorning break when it happened. It was a pleasant day. The air was still cool with the morning breeze, and the schoolyard was filled with the sounds of children playing. Robie and the other boys were engaged in a ball game they called "Hunter." The person with the ball was the Hunter, and it was his job to throw the ball and hit someone else. If he succeeded, that person was removed from the game. However, if the target caught the ball, then he became the Hunter and the previous Hunter was discharged from the game. Obviously, the last person with the ball was the winner.

The girls watched safely from the sidelines, cheering on their favorites and laughing at the boys who fell down and skinned their knees. In those days and in that culture, young ladies did not engage in that sort of activity. Judging from what I knew of them, it was probably for the best. Shue and Jesha would not have made good Hunters, nor would their fancy skirts have long withstood the rigors of such a game. I would have liked to try it myself, but I knew better than to push my luck.

At any rate, the boys were playing, and the girls were on the sidelines dishing out their moral support and mockery with equal aptitude. Naturally, Shue cheered loudest for Robie, while he kept stealing glances at me to be sure I was watching. I was not, of course. I was sitting alone on the school steps, reading.

Mrs. Trader came outside and blew her whistle, indicating that it was time to come inside. The children rushed over to the well for a quick drink of water before returning to their studies. Robie, being the largest and most obnoxious child in school, was naturally first in line. I didn't pay any notice to any of this, until I heard Jesha's scream. I put my book down and saw the children forming a circle next to the well. At their feet, I saw Robie's body.

Mrs. Trader and I both broke into a run, and I arrived just ahead of her. I pushed through the crowd. Robie was lying on his back, foaming at the mouth. His skin had turned blue.

"Get back, everyone!" Mrs. Trader shouted. "Get back, give me room!" She knelt down, and felt Robie's forehead. She looked at me. "He's cool. There's no fever."

Robie's body shook like he had hypothermia. I touched his neck, searching for a pulse. It was very weak. His skin was cool and clammy, and I could tell from the bluish color that he was starved for oxygen. I could feel something else, too. I could feel something inside of him.

I closed my eyes, and searched the images that went flashing through my mind. I saw Robie's heart, straining against the poison in his veins. I saw his lungs filling with liquid, his internal organs seizing as the poison took hold. I didn't even think about what I was doing. It was totally instinctive, just like when I had fixed Tinker's leg.

I worked quickly. I had to get the poison out of Robie's system before the damage became permanent. I ordered his pores to open, and I pulled at the toxin, commanding it out of his bloodstream. Green sweat poured out of him. I heard gasping all around me, but I wasn't done yet. His stomach was full of the stuff, and it had to get out fast.

"Turn him over!" I said.

I yanked at his shoulders. Mrs. Trader stared at me in disbelief. "Turn him over!" I shouted again. She nodded, and then helped me get him off his back. Immediately Robie started to vomit.

I closed my eyes again, and silently urged his body to rid itself of the poison by any means possible. It came out his pores, in his vomit, and through his urine. Robie was a mess. But thankfully, he was alive.

"We need to get him inside," I said. I rose and stared into a sea of blank faces. "We need to get him out of the sun, and he needs water. Good water. Don't drink from the well, it's been poisoned."

"Keenan, run down to the river," said Mrs. Trader. "Get us some water." Keenan was one of the younger boys, about ten years old. He gave me a strange look and then grabbed the water pail and went running across the field.

"Come on then," Mrs. Trader said. "Everyone lift!"

I bent over, only then realizing that my hat was lying at my feet. Somehow, in the excitement, it had gotten knocked off.

Shock settled over me as I glanced at their faces. They were all staring. I saw surprise, horror, and disdain. I saw everything except understanding. It didn't matter to these children that I had just saved Robie. All they saw was a Tal'mar. *Half-breed.* I could see it etched in their faces, written in their eyes.

The weight of what I had done settled over me as we lifted Robie and carried him inside. They had seen my ears. I had let them see me do magic...

My life was over.

We laid Robie across Mrs. Trader's desk and then I backed away, afraid of what might happen next. "He looks better," she said. "His breathing is steady now." All eyes turned on me.

"What did you do, witch?" That was Shue. Naturally she would be the first to attack.

"I didn't do anything!" I said. "I helped him. I made the poison come out of him!"

"Right," said Jesha. "Robie just happened to be poisoned, and you just happen to be Tal'mar. Just trying to cover for yourself, more likely."

"She's no witch, she's an assassin," Shue said. "Who else were you going to kill, Breeze? Were we all supposed to drink that water?"

I started back towards the door, my hands raised in protest. "I didn't do it!" I breathlessly protested. I was terrified.

"Girls, STOP THAT!" shouted Mrs. Trader. "Breeze just saved Robie's life. Why would she do that if she were an assassin?"

They faltered, but I didn't wait to hear any more. I turned and ran.

Chapter 21

The trees spoke to me in whispers as I raced up the hillside towards home. They sensed my anguish I think, and they tried to comfort me, but I withdrew. I couldn't think straight. I didn't know what to do. I was angry and frightened. I was heartbroken.

My head filled with images of the horrified faces of my classmates. I imagined them racing home to tell their parents. I imagined their parents, furious as they learned of a Tal'mar half-breed in their schools. I had no idea what to expect now that my secret was out.

I was so terror-stricken that I was sick, and I actually stopped to vomit at one point. I knew very well that in a few hours they might be coming for me; that they might drive me away, imprison me, or even kill me.

I didn't have the maturity to deal with it. As I said, I may have been physically and mentally mature, but emotionally I was only a child. I'd like to say that I calmly awaited my fate, or that I did something courageous and brilliant, but in truth I handled the situation in the only manner I could. I shut myself off. I went to my room and started to read as if nothing at all had happened. As if by ignoring it, the problem might go away.

Tinker didn't even realize that I had returned. He fired up the steamwagon and left at the usual time, headed to school to pick me up. I heard him leaving, but by that time it was too late to catch him. I didn't really feel like trying, either. I was so emotionally detached at that point that I wasn't really thinking about anything at all. I was a prisoner already, in my mind. I was just waiting for the executioner to carry out the sentence.

I was still in a daze when Tinker returned a half hour later. He burst into the cottage with Cinder at his heels. "Breeze! Breeze are you in here?"

Cinder ran into my room, jumped up on the bed and started licking my face. I glanced up as Tinker appeared in the doorway. "We have to get you out of here," he said. He started yanking open the dresser drawers. "Grab some clothes. You'll need food..." Tinker's desperation shook me out of my state, and I leapt to my feet. "There's a bag in the kitchen," he said. "Take bread, meat, whatever you can carry."

I followed his orders, and began stuffing all that I could into the bag. Tinker had a good supply of dried fruits and meats, and I took a lot of these, knowing that they wouldn't rot. I also took some sugar and tea, and whatever else I could find that seemed like it would last.

A few minutes later we crashed through the front door with my bags. "The plane's in the barn," he said.

"I'm taking the plane?"

"It's the only way we can be sure they won't follow. My maps are in your bag, and a few coins..."

Tinker threw open the barn door, and I caught my breath. "Tinker, what did you do?"

He shot me a cocky grin. "Do you like it?"

Tinker had been coming to me recently, asking me to bend a piece of wood, or secure a metal attachment in such a way that it wouldn't come loose. I thought he'd been working on the plane, making minor improvements here and there. I'd been so distracted by my problems and my schoolwork that I never even realized what he'd actually been up to.

Now, I saw that he'd actually built *another* plane. He'd cleared out the barn to make room for it. All the tables were stacked up against the back wall. Our old plane was pushed up tightly against the mess. The new one took up the remaining space.

"Third time's a charm," he said. "This one has all the previous improvements, and a couple more that I think you'll like. The most obvious of course, is this..." He gestured to the open cockpit, and the seat that rested within.

Tinker had cut open the top of the fuselage and installed a seat between the gearbox and the springs. "I thought it would be more comfortable," he said. "Especially since we can't seem to keep that mutt of yours on the ground. She's getting too big to fit in your jacket." He opened the storage compartment at the back of the fuselage and shoved the bags in there. "The controls are the same, but I've moved them back, so they'll be easy to reach..."

"*Trouble*," a voice murmured in the back of my mind. I reached out, and found all the trees echoing that word up and down the mountainside. I ran to the barn doors, and saw a wagon and a group of men on horseback coming up the valley. Tinker appeared beside me.

"Blast it!" he said. "Run around the back. Head up the hillside while I stall them!"

"It's too late Tinker." I put a hand on his arm. I could see him calculating the distance, the time it would take for me to get up the hillside and out of range. I could see that no matter what he did, it would be impossible. They had horses and weapons. If I tried to run, I'd probably just get myself killed.

I could see it tearing him apart. He knew what they might do to me, and he was willing to sacrifice anything, even his own life, to save me. "It's okay, Tinker. It's my fault. I wanted to go to school. I insisted on it. I knew it was a mistake even before today, but I didn't want to tell you."

His eyes started watering up, and I could hardly look at him. "You don't understand," he said. "You don't know what they will do. You have to get out of here! RUN! I'll stop them!"

I shook my head. "They'd never stop chasing me, Tinker."

"For pity's sake, child! You don't know what you're saying." I stepped past him, into the yard, and he followed me out. Cinder started yapping like crazy and running in circles around my feet.

A dozen armed horsemen and a black carriage roll-ed into the homestead. When the dust had settled, I saw several crossbows and one rusty musket pointed at me. "Breeze Tinkerman?" one of the men said. He stepped off the horse and walked up to me. He was tall and thick; a bit too thick to chase me down if I ran, but he was well muscled for his age. He looked to be in his late forties or early fifties. He wore a broad-brimmed hat that was filthy with sweat and dust, and he had a long brown beard that reached to the middle of his chest. A bronze badge on his dirty shirt proclaimed the word: *Peacekeeper*. A cutlass dangled from his belt.

"You're under arrest for suspicion of treason and attempted murder." He grabbed me by the arm and hauled me back to the coach. The door swung open and I saw a younger man, a deputy, waiting within. "Get in," the peacekeeper said.

They put heavy steel cuffs on my wrists and ankles, and then locked the door from the outside. The deputy stayed inside with me. He had short black hair, bright blue eyes, and a clean-shaven face. He couldn't have been more than eighteen, but he did his best to look mean. If it hadn't been for the circumstances, he might even have been cute.

It got very dark after the door closed. There were no windows, only a few stray beams of light that found their way through the cracks in the paneling. The deputy reached up and uncovered a lantern.

"Don't try anything," he said. "I've heard about the witchcraft your kind uses, but you're not faster than steel." He drew a long, thin-bladed dagger and held it tightly in his fist. I turned away from him, unable to face that cruel, senseless hatred.

I half expected him to reach across the coach and stab me in the chest, but he didn't. He just sat there staring at me with that cold, unblinking stare. I almost wished he would do it. It would be easier than going through the next few hours, waiting to learn my fate.

I heard Tinker arguing with the men outside. He started to shout, and then I heard a loud cracking sound. Tinker went silent, and I knew that he'd been knocked out. I reached out with my mind and commanded Cinder to stay with him, to make sure that he was safe. She obeyed, but she barked wildly as the carriage rolled away.

Chapter 22

We drove to the jail in town. An angry mob surrounded the carriage as I arrived, and the peacekeeper had to warn them back as he took me inside. "Judge Brooks will be here tomorrow afternoon. Until then you all need to go home and wait for justice to take its course!"

I heard people shouting for my head, shouting that they wanted to hang me, but the peacekeeper silenced them. "If anyone touches this jail, my men have been ordered to shoot to kill!" The crowd settled down after that.

The jail was a small building with a desk, two chairs, and a stove in the corner. There were two cells against the back wall, both empty except for the cots. The peacekeeper guided me into one. He paused to give me a hard stare as he turned the key in the lock. His eyes were cold and his face was hidden behind that scraggly beard. I couldn't imagine what he might be thinking, but I wasn't going to allow myself to feel guilty, regardless of how shameful he looked at me.

"I didn't do it," I said. "I didn't hurt anyone."

I saw a flash of something in his eyes, and he turned away. Was it surprise? Disbelief? I honestly couldn't tell. I slumped down on the cot and felt a wave of hopelessness wash over me. All I could do now was await my inevitable fate.

I'd been there for about an hour when someone started pounding on the door. "Go away!" the peacekeeper shouted. "The judge will be here tomorrow!"

I heard a woman's voice shouting but I couldn't understand the words, and then the pounding resumed. The peacekeeper pulled a blunderbuss out of his desk and walked up to the door. When he opened it, Analyn Trader came storming in, followed by a man I didn't recognize. He was tall and dark-haired, with broad shoulders and a strong jaw. He wore the fancy clothes of a merchant, and the purple cloak of royalty. A broadsword hung at his side.

"What in the world do you think you're doing, Shem?" Analyn demanded.

"You know the charges," he said. "She poisoned the well."

"Don't be ridiculous! I was there, I saw it all. If it hadn't been for that girl, Robie would be dead."

"Tell it to the judge."

"Judge Brooks?" Analyn hissed. "You know exactly what he'll say. That man is dumb as a rock and he has nothing but hate for Tal'mar. He only got to be a judge because he bribed his way into the position, and everyone knows he's crooked as snakewood!"

The stranger stepped forward. "If I may?"

Shem settled onto the edge of his desk, and laid the gun down. "I know what you're going to say, Devan. There's nothing I can do. It's not like I want to see the girl hanged, but the law is the law."

"I'm not asking you to do anything," said Devan. "Just hear me out. My boy almost died today, and other children would have, too. That girl saved their lives.

She may be a half-breed but she's no more murderer than you or I."

"Maybe she is, maybe she's not..."

"Stop it!" Devan interrupted him. "I'm not asking you to do anything. Just listen. Think about this: I have an audience with my cousin, King Ryshan next week. I understand your daughter is coming of age this year..."

"Are you bribing me?"

"It's not a bribe. If you happened to be asleep at midnight tonight, well there wouldn't be much anyone could say about that. And if the girl escaped, really what's the harm? You need to proceed with the investigation anyway. You need to find out who's really behind this. And if the king should happen to find room in his court next spring for your daughter, who could possibly suspect anything there? I hear she is highly talented, and beautiful as well."

The peacekeeper took a deep breath. "That's a tempting offer, but I take pride in my honesty. If word of something like this ever got out..."

"There will be none of that," said Devan. "I will personally see to it. And a man of your honor is certainly due some recognition. How would you like to be a baron?"

I could hardly believe what I was hearing. Robie's father was going to do all that, just to get me out? I was shocked just to learn that he was on my side. I glanced at Analyn and she shot me a wink.

The offer was too much to refuse, even for the sheriff. He settled into his chair and shook his head. He looked at me. "You better be worth all this trouble, girl."

A short while later Shem called his deputy into the building and told him to fetch us some food. When he returned, the peacekeeper sent everyone home. "I'll take the night watch, Wil," he said.

"Are you sure? I can handle her." The deputy was anxious to prove himself.

"Not this time. I need you up bright and early for crowd control."

"Yes, sir."

I had a lot of time to think things over that afternoon, and I had a lot to think about. After listening to Analyn's conversation with Peacekeeper Shem, I began to realize just how dire my situation was. I'd known that I might be killed, of course. I had just refused to believe it. I kept telling myself that deep down inside, everyone is a good person. After hearing Analyn's description of Judge Brooks, I had to wonder. Could a person really be that soulless and mean? Would he sentence me to die just because I was Tal'mar?

Who was I kidding? Half the people in town were ready to do that. They had asked Shem to hang me. They had yelled at me and threatened me. They didn't even know me. Tinker had been right about the way they would treat me; the way they would hate me. They didn't have any justifiable reason for any of it. Something bad had happened, and it was easier to blame me than it was to find out what was really going on.

I remembered the way Analyn had acted the first time she saw my ears. This was not that different. Except that she had thought about it, and then apologized. If the townsfolk got their way, I wouldn't be alive to accept any apologies later.

After deputy Wil went home, darkness fell across the town and I started to feel anxious. About an hour later, I heard a knock on the door. I remember thinking that it was too early for Analyn to be back. Shem opened the door and Deputy Wil burst in.

"We're under attack," he said.

"What the devil are you talking about?"

"It's the Kanters. They came up the river in flatboats and they're burning and killing everything in their path!"

"Kanters? Are you sure?"

"Yes, sir. There's a steady stream of evacuees coming into town right now. They're all raving about tattooed giants."

"That doesn't make any sense. Why would the Kanters be attacking us? They don't even have the brains to build a fence, much less a boat..."

"Maybe they're smarter than we thought."

"How long till they get here?"

"Two hours. Maybe less."

"Sound the alarm. We need every able-bodied man we can find." Shem shot me a glance and then disappeared out the door.

Chapter 23

I had read about Kanters, and I should have recognized the one I had seen staring through my window for what he was. I could have kicked myself as I realized it now. There may have been a small party of them that came in advance of the attack. They probably grouped up and camped near the Coopers' farm. That was why they slaughtered the cow.

I shuddered as I thought of that night. What if Tinker had gone out there? What if he'd gone after the man, only to find a giant waiting for him? Surely we would have both died that night.

It seemed that the humans had underestimated the Kanters. According to everything I'd read about them, they weren't smart enough to make the simplest of weapons. Apparently they were smarter than they'd been given credit. Perhaps they'd just been waiting for the right time. The Kanters must have been planning this for a long time, I realized. I wondered how many more wells had been poisoned ahead of their advance.

As I sat there in my cell, it slowly dawned on me how much danger I might be in. Locked in there and alone, I was a sitting duck. If the Kanters broke through the town's defenses, it would only be a matter of time until they found me. Unless I got lucky and the building caught fire. Then I'd just be burned alive. From what I'd read, that was better than being captured by the Kanters.

The history books had claimed the Kanters were cannibals. I'd taken that with a grain of salt, until now. I had seen the scout. I had seen his teeth.

Another thought occurred to me as all this flashed through my mind. The Kanters knew about our valley. If they were working north, they would almost certainly go there to steal supplies. If they found Tinker, the Kanters would kill him... and possibly eat him. I felt panic rising inside me.

I settled down on the cot and tried to calm myself. If I was going to get out of there, I'd need to use my head. I took a deep breath and surveyed my surroundings. At first glance, the jail seemed very well built. The outside walls were stone and the roof was timber. The two cells were iron cages that extended into the walls and floor, making it impossible to move or detach individual bars.

Fortunately, I had a unique ability that allowed me to find and exploit weaknesses no human would ever see. I steadied my breathing and then reached out with my mind, using my powers to study the cage around me. The iron bars extended into the stone in the back wall, but they were only secured by bolts on the outside of the building. There were no bars inside the stone.

I also learned that though the back wall was built of stone, it was constructed around a timber frame. I suspected that if I could cause the timbers to warp enough, they just might break the stones loose.

I closed my eyes and went into a meditative state. In my mind's eye, I reached out to the wood. I touched it, felt it, and examined it. There was very little moisture inside the wall. That was going to make it harder. I decided that my best chance was to cause the timbers to pull away from each other, straining against the masonry. In that manner, the aging structure might give.

I pushed and pulled, warping the boards out in both directions. I heard the timbers creaking, and cracking sounds came from the wall. I opened my eyes and stepped back, and saw that the wall was actually moving. It seemed to be ready to topple, but it wasn't clear which way it might fall. If it fell into the jail, I would be crushed!

I closed my eyes again, and forced myself to concentrate. There was one post at the center of the wall. I compressed the outside layer of fibers, causing it to bend outward. I was trying to use gravity to help pull at the weight of the wall, to make sure it would topple outward. It moved slightly in that direction, but not far enough.

I ran up to it and pushed, straining against the cold stone with everything I had. It didn't budge. I was about to give up, when I heard a loud groan inside, and it started to move. The timbers and posts inside the wall snapped like old dry toothpicks as the entire wall collapsed into the street.

I caught a few perplexed looks as I crawled over the rubble, but everyone was too busy to take much note of me. The women were gathering up their children and running for the safety of their homes. Unorganized groups of men were racing towards the edge of town carrying rusted old swords and muskets. I joined them, hoping they would be too distracted to realize who I was. I guess the last thing they were looking for was a Tal'mar, because no one even gave me a second glance.

When I reached the edge of town I saw that they had formed a defensive line at the river. The stronger men were busy piling stones and logs along the river banks to build a defensible wall. The younger boys were frantically loading muskets and getting the weapons ready for battle. I saw Robie there, and paused for a moment to watch him.

He took one of Tinker's small explosive balls and jammed it down the barrel of a musket. Then he grabbed a metal ball and jammed it down on top. He used a long wooden rod to hammer them tightly into place. Then he set the gun aside and started loading another. That was when he saw me.

"Breeze!" he shouted. He ran over and threw his arms around me.

"Robie," I said awkwardly.

He squeezed me and stepped back, his face reddening. "I'm... I just wanted to say thanks. For saving me, I mean."

I smiled. "You're welcome."

He held out a musket. "Here, you wanna help me load?"

"I can't," I said. "I have to find Tinker."

"Oh. Well be careful."

"Thanks, I will."

I wandered into the line of men and, before anyone could grab me, I ran across the bridge. "Girl, get back here!" someone shouted.

"Stop her," someone else yelled. "They'll kill you!"

I stopped and turned around, just long enough to shout, "So will you!" Then I turned and ran for all I was worth.

Chapter 24

There are a few unique things about Tal'mar which separate them from humans. Obviously, there are the physical differences that I have already described. Then there is the use of what humans call magic. To Tal'mar, using magic is no more "magical" than using your legs to walk. It's simply part of us. That's why, even though I didn't have any training, I still managed to learn to use my abilities. They came as naturally to me as breathing. Communicating with trees, healing Tinker's leg, and bending the wood on our airplane were all part of this very natural and simple process.

That's why, out there in the windswept fields and under the light of the waning crescent moon, I was able to see the enemy front advancing towards me. I had never observed this phenomenon before because I had never been outside in the woods at night. Most Tal'mar children would have known this almost from birth. Like most things, I had to discover this ability by accident.

In retrospect, I remember that I had been able to see my way around Tinker's house when I awoke in the night and made my way to his loft, but in that half-wakened state I didn't even notice the subtle changes in my vision. Now as I stood alone in that field, facing the front line of an advancing army, I fully realized what my eyes could do. Somehow my vision had adjusted to the shifting light, allowing me to see the body heat of the approaching enemies.

They had taken great pains to paint the steel on their swords and spears, to darken the colors of their clothing and skin, and yet I still saw them. I could see the heat emanating from their bodies. On that cool night, it was like a wall of fire moving towards me.

"Hide," said the voices of the trees. *"Come up into our branches."*

I obeyed. I turned to my left and went tearing up into the mountains. As I ran the, trees reached down to scoop me up in their branches. You might think I would have been scratched and bruised, but I was not. The trees touched me as gently as a mother cradling her infant.

I continued to run, even as the trees lifted me higher into the air. Incredibly, I found I could not miss a step. I hurtled forward without giving a thought to where my feet would land, but always there was a foothold. The branches moved and twisted, swung around to build a path for me as I raced along the mountainside. The land flew by beneath me, and to my breathless wonder, I became one with the trees.

To my right, I saw that great wall of heat pushing ever forward. Now that I understood what it was, I focused on looking for other signs of heat around me. I saw a handful of Kanter scouts moving through the trees here and there, but I passed by overhead without a sound. It wasn't long until I reached Tinker's little valley. Nothing could have prepared me for the horrors I found there.

The cottage was on fire. Three giant Kantrayan men were ambling about the yard, barking out in some crude language. Past them, up the hill beyond the barn, I saw Tinker's familiar body shape as a dim red glow.

He held Cinder in his arms, and Analyn Trader was kneeling in the bushes next to him.

A man's body lay strewn across the path in front of the barn. It was Daran Trader. He still clutched an old sword in his hand. I could tell even from that distance that there wasn't much life left in him. Obviously, he had confronted the Kanters, probably trying to distract them so Tinker and Analyn could escape. His heroic act very well might have cost him his life.

I spoke to the trees, my thoughts a rising wave of emotion and panic. I told them about the men in the clearing, that they were evil and that I had to save my friends. The trees quickly grasped the meaning of my thoughts, but their response was not altogether clear. Some told me to run, others to hide, but none offered a realistic solution to the problem.

Frustrated, I started making my way up the hillside and around to Tinker's position. My arrival was announced by little more than the sound of a breeze through the branches (if you'll pardon the pun). I came up near them, overhead, and whispered down, "Tinker!"

Analyn clutched at her heart and nearly screamed. Even the sound of her gasp was too much. I glanced up to see the Kanters staring in our direction. I commanded the tree I was in to bend its branch low, and I motioned for Analyn and Tinker to follow me into the trees. They did so awkwardly climbing among the branches and creating more than a bit of noise.

The branch returned to its normal position just as the Kanters appeared below us. They stomped around, grunting and thrashing around in the darkness. I quietly motioned for Tinker and Analyn to follow me. We disappeared into the treetops and didn't stop until we were halfway up the mountain. There, the trees gently settled us to the ground.

"My husband's down there," Analyn said. "He's dying!"

"Stay here!" I said. I went back up into the branches and disappeared, leaving the two of them safe but mystified. After all, they had been planning on *rescuing me*. My arrival must have been quite a shock to them.

By the time I got back down to the barn, I knew what I had to do. I dropped to the ground and crept up to the containers and barrels of junk behind the barn. I hid myself there in the shadows, and then asked the trees to start making noise. One of them shook, and dropped a few branches.

All three Kanters shouted and went running. Another tree, a bit further down the hillside did exactly what the first had done. The Kanters took off in that direction, hot on the trail of what they thought to be the escaping humans.

I ran around the barn and knelt down at Daran's side. His pulse was weak, almost nonexistent. I closed my eyes and touched his skin, searching his body for the wound. I was horrified to find that his neck had been broken.

I fought the urge to vomit as I surveyed the damage. I had to divide my attention between keeping his heart beating and repairing the damage to his spine. Spinal fluid had begun to seep out, and I caused the muscles to convulse and force it back towards the bone.

I set the bone to mending and then used my hands to stretch his neck out, lining everything up as straight as I could. Somehow, I managed to keep his spine intact as I did it. Without my Tal'mar abilities, this would have killed him.

Once his neck was set and the spinal column was sufficiently healed, I directed his body to use what resources it could, much the same way that I had with Tinker. There was no infection or sickness in Daran's blood, just an abundance of adrenaline.

His pulse strengthened quickly. After a few moments, I was sure that he would survive. It would be some time however, before he regained consciousness. Which left me in the unfortunate situation of having saved a man who would immediately be killed when the Kanters returned. I had to get him out of there, but I couldn't imagine how to do that without injuring him or attracting their attention.

Reluctantly I left him there and went back up the hill. I found Tinker and Analyn just where I had left them. "We have to go back," I said.

"Is he alive?" Analyn was frantic. Her face was streaked with tears.

"Yes, but we have to get him off the ground. We need to put him in the barn."

"But the Kanters," Tinker said. "They'll come back and kill us!"

I sent a thought out to the trees, describing my situation. Daran could not leave the valley for at least a few days. The only way to save him –to save all of us– was to make sure the Kanters wouldn't return. The trees acknowledged my request with a solemn confirmation.

"They won't be back," I said flatly. "Come on, we need to hurry."

The sound of the Kanters' screams echoed up the hillside as we made our way back to the barn. I pretended not to notice as Analyn and Tinker exchanged an uncomfortable look.

Chapter 25

We got Daran into the barn and settled into a position where I could work on him some more. "He's going to lose a couple toes," I told Analyn.

She gave me a mystified look. "What do you mean?"

"I need materials to repair his neck. The broken bones can't mend correctly otherwise."

"Do what you have to do," she said. "Just keep him alive."

I nodded and closed my eyes. I could have taken his fingers, but since Daran's work involved using his hands, it seemed more important to his livelihood that I use his toes instead. I hoped he could forgive me. His toes could never be replaced.

Unfortunately, there was nothing else I could do. Even if he were conscious and could eat, his body couldn't absorb the nutrients from food fast enough. Reluctantly, I proceeded with my work.

I had been leaning over his body for over two hours when I finally stepped back. "It's done," I said. I was exhausted.

Analyn's eyes misted with tears. "He'll be okay? He'll be able to walk?"

"He will be fine," I said. "He'll need to rest a few days, and he needs lots of food to eat."

"There's plenty in the cellar for now," Tinker said. He glanced through the open barn doors at the burning cottage. "I might have to do some digging to get to it. Are you sure the Kanters won't return?"

"Those three won't," I said. I followed his gaze and felt warm tears streaming down my cheeks. That cottage was the only home I'd ever known. I could remember watching him build my room.

Tinker sighed, and pulled his eyes away. "I don't know what to think of all this. It's not what I would have expected from the Kanters."

"Me either." If even half of what I'd read about them was true, they simply weren't capable of planning this invasion. "Do you think they made an alliance with the Tal'mar?" It was a blunt question, and Tinker wasn't prepared for it. He must have been thinking it, though. How could he not? Humans and Tal'mar had been enemies for generations.

He took a deep breath, and shook his head. "None of it makes sense. They sent out scouts in advance... they poisoned wells. Is it possible that we underestimated them so completely? I'm actually starting to wonder if the war between us has been perpetuated by the Kanters all along. I just can't figure out why they would do it."

The suggestion was so unexpected that I almost fell over. "You think the Kanters have been causing the war?"

"Think about it, Breeze. Every time we have a treaty something happens. The Tal'mar accuse us of raiding a village, or we accuse them of poisoning a well... that all looks quite a bit different now, doesn't it? We know the Kanters poisoned the school well. It had to be them. And if the same thing has been happening on the other side, then the Tal'mar certainly aren't their allies."

"But why would they do all that? Why not just invade, if that's what they were planning?"

"I don't know. I suppose they could have been trying to weaken us. Perhaps they knew we would out-number them. Or perhaps they feared an alliance between the human and the Tal'mar."

I thought about it for a few moments. Tinker's suggestion made sense. It was hard to believe that the Kanters could have been so misunderstood, and yet how else could their invasion been so carefully planned? They had long allowed the rest of the world to assume that they were mindless barbarians, barely even human, yet all along they had been scheming and planning.

I realized then that we knew far too little about the Kanters. "We should have been spying on them," I said. "We should have been watching them all along."

"Indeed. It seems we've been focused on the wrong war. And now, all of our troops are stationed in the Borderlands. By the time they get word of what's happened, it will already be too late. Half the kingdom will be gone."

"Not if I tell them," I said. He gave me a long look, and I could see the argument forming behind his eyes. I cut him off before he could start. "We have the plane ready to go, Tinker. It will take days for the message to reach them on horseback. I can get to the army in a matter of hours."

"What good would it do, Breeze? They won't trust you. They'll lock you up, just like what happened here."

"No they won't," Analyn said. "They'll do whatever you say, if you show them this."

She tossed me an object, and I caught it. It was a ring. It was a thick gold band with a silver crest of a gryphon inlaid on the face. It was far too large to be worn comfortably, even by a large man. "What is it?"

"It's the king's seal," said Tinker. "A seal entrusted only to the most noble of families. One might wonder how a simple school teacher might have acquired such a trinket."

"One might," Analyn said with a grim smile. "Fly to the Borderlands, Breeze. Get as close to the front as you can. Show that ring to a commander, or better yet, General Corsan if you can find him. Show him that ring, and he'll listen."

I shoved the ring into my pocket. "Then I guess I'd better be going."

"Wait!" said Tinker. "Before you go, let me paint the plane."

"Tinker, that's ridiculous. Why would you want to do that?"

"Because I want you to come back," he interrupted. "If you get yourself killed you won't do us much good, will you? Besides, you need to get a few hours of rest. The plane is already packed and ready to go. It won't take long."

I shook my head unable to understand Tinker's reasoning. "I don't understand."

"Don't worry. Just get some rest."

"Tinker, the house is burned down." He opened one of the cabinets and tossed me an old wool blanket. "There's a bench in the windmill. It should be comfortable enough."

I stumbled outside and made my way to the windmill. Strangely, it was the one place in Tinker's homestead I'd never explored. Spider webs snapped and dust motes swirled around me as I pulled the door open. There wasn't much too see.

The floor was thick with dust and rat's nests, and there was a hole in the ceiling where the mill used to be. The only furnishing in the room was the old bench that Tinker had told me about. I curled up and went to sleep, too tired to worry about the dust or the spiders that were no doubt scurrying around me. I was instantly asleep.

I woke to the sound of squeaking hinges, and looked up to see Tinker standing in the doorway. "It's ready," he said. I followed him outside, and saw the plane parked in the yard. The choice of colors was strikingly odd at first, until I thought about it. Only then did I understand what Tinker had meant. The top half of the plane was a chaotic mixture of yellow, green, and brown. The bottom half was dark blue with irregular streaks of misty white and gray.

"It's disguised," I said.

"Exactly. From the ground it will blend with the sky, but when landed, it can easily be hidden amongst the trees, or even in an open field. It will be perfectly camouflaged."

"You're too clever, Tinker." I was distracted by the sound of the barn door, and I turned to see Analyn walking out. She was wrapped in a shawl. Her eyes looked fatigued, her careworn face exhausted, but she managed a smile.

"How is Daran?" I said.

"He's doing well, thanks to you," she said. "Still sleeping soundly."

"He might not awaken for another day," I warned her. "His body will take time..."

"I understand. I just want to thank you, Breeze. Words can't even say. If there's any way I can repay you, please tell me."

I smiled. "I only want your friendship." She threw her arms around me.

"That, I can easily promise."

Chapter 26

The predawn sky was red with the light of a thousand fires as we pulled the plane to the mouth of the valley. The air was thick with smoke, and the horizon was so black it might have been painted. The very stars were choked out of existence.

Even in that dim twilight I could see the destruct-tion that the Kanters had left in their wake. Hundreds of homes and farms across the countryside lay in ruins. To the northwest, Riverfork was burning.

I was anxious to get flying, to get ahead of the Kanters and warn of their advance, but Tinker had to show me how to fly the plane with its new controls. I settled into the pilot's seat and Cinder curled up on the floor between my legs. I had Tinker's old sword in there with my supplies. I never really had learned how to use it, but I figured it might be better to have one than not.

"This lever is your throttle," Tinker said, pointing to the right. "The one in the middle controls your steering, and the one on the left is your brakes. Pull it down like so," he reached in and moved the lever. "Remember to land at high speed, because the brakes are tied in to the gear box. If you don't keep those springs wound, you won't get far."

"I can't believe you did all this when I was in school. Why?"

147

"I knew you would be leaving," he said. His voice was distant, sad. "I didn't think it would be like this, but I knew you wouldn't stay here forever."

"Tinker, I wouldn't leave!" I felt defensive, as if I had somehow hurt him without realizing it.

"Oh yes you would, and there's nothing wrong with that. I'm old, and I'm content to stay here in my little corner of the world, but that doesn't mean you should. Your future is more than that. You've got a whole world to see, and a life of your own to live. There's nothing wrong with going out there and finding your own destiny. I just wanted to make sure you would be safe... and that you'd come back here once in a while."

I threw my arms around him and fought back tears as he squeezed me. "Oh, Tinker. You know I couldn't stay away. You... you're like a father to me." Tinker held me even tighter when I said that.

"I never expected to have a family," he said. "But now I can't imagine life without you. Be careful, Breeze. Come back to me."

"I promise."

Tinker jogged out ahead of me, making sure the path was clear of dangerous holes or obstacles, and then waved me off. I sighed and pulled back on the throttle. As the ground slipped away and the darkness closed in around me, I knew that things would never be the same. The world had changed, and I had changed along with it. This was something new, a different stage of life. Tinker had hoped I would seek out my destiny. Now it seemed my destiny had found me. Strangely, I wasn't afraid. It seemed that Tinker knew more about me than I knew about myself.

A few minutes later, I passed over Riverfork. There wasn't much left of our little town. The buildings that had once evoked such awe in me were now little more than smoking timbers. The townspeople were gone, either in hiding or driven to the north by the invading force. A few miles ahead, the Kanter army pressed on, driving a wave of refugees before them. Even the animals fled before that cruel force.

I passed over them and saw hundreds of people crowded into wagons and on horseback, racing ahead of the invaders. I felt like weeping for those poor families, jammed into wagons, their homes, livestock, and belongings left to the fires of the Kanter horde. I thought of Terra Cooper and her family's farm, and I thought of the last time I'd seen Robie, jamming powder charges into muskets. I hoped they too, had survived. I could only take heart from the fact that so many had escaped with their lives, and wish for the best.

A few minutes later I saw deputy Wil riding a horse at a full gallop, with another unburdened steed in tow. Shem must have sent him ahead to warn the citizens of Anora, which was one hundred and fifty miles north of Riverfork. It was comforting to know that they would have time to prepare. Anora was a large enough city that it might even hold the Kanters back, at least for a time. Even so, I was sure they would still need the reinforcement of the king's army.

The smoke at that altitude was choking, so I pulled up, hoping to rise above it. It got thicker at first, and I pulled my scarf up over my face. Then suddenly I broke through the ceiling, and the brilliant starry sky stretched over me. The smoke was an ocean below; rolling black waves that were frozen in time as I slipped across the surface.

I located the bare sliver of moon overhead, and oriented myself accordingly. From that point on, I stayed above the clouds as much as possible.

I kept a close eye on my gauges. I had to land just after sunrise to rewind the springs, and again about two hours later. Part of this was due to the fact that I was going fast rather than conserving energy. I was about to land for a third time when, just after noon, I finally saw my destination.

The ocean had been visible to the west for some time. Now the land closed in, forming the narrow channel known as the Crimson Strait. A massive wall of fog hovered right along the edge of the coast. The land along the coast had been clear-cut, leaving miles of scarred land stretching from the sea to the mountains. It was obvious that the humans had done this in fear of the Tal'mar. The humans knew that the Tal'mar had a unique relationship with the woods, and so to protect themselves, they cut down all of the trees.

A sprawling military encampment rested at the eastern end of this strip of land, nestled in the foothills at the base of the Blackrock Mountains. Behind the camp rose a castle, its rough-hewn stone walls sprouting out of the granite cliffs.

I circled the area a few times, looking for a safe place to land, and decided on a wagon trail on the eastern end of the plain just below the castle. Had I the choice I would have preferred a more inconspicuous landing, but deep grass and rotting stumps covered the land. Even if I could have found a landing strip between the stumps, there was no telling what hazards the grass might conceal. I had no choice but to land in plain view of the entire army.

I nervously patted Cinder on the head as I came in. "Here we go, pup," I said. She whined and buried her head behind my legs.

When I touched down, the wheels threw a cloud of dust into the air. I hit the brakes and rolled to a stop directly between the castle and encampment. When the dust cleared, I saw a group of soldiers coming my way. I glanced up the hill and saw more soldiers gathering on the castle wall. I had certainly gotten everyone's attention.

I held my hands up in the air as they approached. I wanted to show that I wasn't armed, and that I was there for peaceful purposes. "I have a message for the general," I said, remembering Analyn's instructions. *General Corsan*, she had said. I was to show him the royal seal, and warn him of the Kanters' attack.

They encircled me, swords and spears at the ready. A larger group was gathering behind them. They were awestricken, having witnessed the landing of this strange machine. They had probably thought it some sort of prehistoric bird until they got closer. I also saw hostility in their faces. For some reason, I had neglected to put on my flying cap before I landed. I don't know if it was simple exhaustion or a subconscious decision I had made. Whatever the reason, my secret was out. I could only guess as to what must have been going through their minds. They were certainly awed by this incredibly flying machine, but they were equally baffled by its pilot.

I was tempted to reach into my pocket and hold the seal up in front of them, but I waited. I didn't want to play my only card too soon. I was hoping their leader would present himself. I didn't have to wait long.

There was a bustling among the crowd, and the bodies partied to make way for a tall, broad shouldered man with a scar across his left eye. The eye was gone and the lid had been sewn shut. His hair and beard were long and unkempt. He had the look of a man who had been living in a tent for a long, long time.

Still, there was something about the man that reminded me of my father. Perhaps it was his broad shoulders, or the way his arms bulged under the half-sleeves of his tunic. It was unlikely that they had been related, but they were clearly of the same stock.

He stepped onto the road and made a quick circle around the plane. "What is this... machine?"

"It's called a plane," I said. "An airplane."

"Plane?"

"Yes, because the wings plane across the air. Like the hull of a ship across water."

He studied the wings for a moment, and then reached out to feel the smooth finish of the wood. "This is your *plane*?"

"Yes. I helped Tinker build it."

"Tinker," the man echoed. A weak grin played at the corners of his mouth. "Who are you?"

"My name is Breeze Tinkerman. I've come with a message for your general." I purposely used Tinker's name, not only because he had basically become a father to me, but also because I didn't know how these men felt about my birth father. It was altogether possible that they considered him a traitor.

"Tinkerman? You're the Tinkerman's daughter?" He stared hard at my ears, and I felt my face going flush.

"Yes, but not by birth. He adopted me after my father died." The crowd livened at that. I heard voices muttering all around me, until the man waved them to silence.

"And what sort of a message do you have for me?"

It was at this point that I produced the ring. I held it up, and his eyebrows narrowed. "Where did you get that?"

"The Kanters have attacked Riverfork," I said. "They are moving north, killing everything in their path." He snatched the ring out of my hand, and rolled it over.

"This is the King's seal, where did you get this Tal'mar?"

"My teacher gave it to me." There was a round of laughter at this, and the man rolled his eyes... his eye, I should say.

"What teacher?"

"Analyn Trader." The smile vanished from his face.

"Come with me. Sergeant, get this thing off my road!"

Chapter 27

I hopped down and followed the man up the hill towards the castle. Cinder was right at my heels. I kept a wary eye on the soldiers moving my plane, until I was satisfied that they had just moved it off the road and no further. My plane was my life. The only certain safety I had was in the skies. On the ground, everyone was a potential enemy.

The only point of entry through the castle wall was a guarded portcullis. It was just large enough for a wagon to pass through. Now it was open, and the guards nodded as I followed the man inside. The courtyard was a pandemonium. To my right I saw a group of young men exercising horses near the stables. To my left, a dozen blacksmiths were working steadily, adding to piles of horseshoes, swords, and shields that were stacked up on tables along the wall. No one paid any heed to us as the man led me inside the keep.

As we entered, I immediately became aware of the sparse décor. The floors and walls were cold chiseled stone, and the only light streamed in through un-shuttered windows high on the wall. A few threadbare rugs and tapestries lent minimal warmth to the interior, and I saw only the barest of furnishings.

The man led me into a small chamber off the main hall, and motioned for me to close the door as he settled down at his desk. He nodded towards a chair, and I sat down opposite him. He tossed Analyn's ring out in front of me.

"Tell me the truth now, girl, and be quick about it. Where did you get that ring?"

"Are you the general?" At that point it was a stupid question, but I still waited for his nod. "I told you, it was given to me by Analyn Trader, my schoolteacher. She said I should give it to General Corsan, and he would know my words were true."

"This is your proof then? This is proof that Kanters have invaded our territories? The same mindless barbarians who've spent their entire history living like dogs and consuming the flesh of their own dead?"

"They aren't mindless! They've been manipulating the humans and the Tal'mar all along. They have been draining our resources on purpose!"

He settled back into his chair. His face was a mask of serenity; not even his eyes betrayed his thoughts. I had no idea what was going on in that calculating military mind. "How do I know that you're not a Tal'mar spy? Or an assassin? You could have easily stolen that ring from one of your victims."

I smiled ever so slightly. His argument was clearly flawed. "If I were an assassin, I wouldn't go to so much trouble. I'd simply climb the wall in the night and find you. And then I would slit your throat while you slept."

Still nothing. His eyes were so emotionless that he might as well have been dead. "And let's suppose that this message you bring is true, that the Kanters have invaded Astatia. What then would you expect me to do?"

"You have to move your forces to the south," I said. "You've got to meet them head on."

"Ah, there's the rub. You see, what you propose would leave the Borderlands unguarded and ripe for the plucking. The Tal'mar would stream across the strait and wipe us out. With our flank exposed, they would roll right over us."

This was a defining moment for me. I could have accepted the general's argument and left. It was, after all, a sound argument. He had every reason to believe what he said. And how could I convince him that the Tal'mar wouldn't attack? The truth was, they probably would.

That was when a plan came to me... a plan so ridiculous and unlikely that it just might work. I found myself speaking words that I hardly believed were coming out of my mouth.

"Give me a treaty. I'll take it to the Tal'mar and have it back, signed, in twenty-four hours."

Even as I said it, I knew how mad it must sound. I almost wanted him to laugh at me and chase me off, because I knew I was promising more than I could give. But I had to do something. I had to give some show of confidence, something that would convince him to move his troops. It was the only card I had to play.

For the first time, his eyes actually lit up. "You are an ambitious girl, aren't you? Don't you know that I've signed a dozen pacts and treaties with the Tal'mar over the years? Their treaties mean nothing. Their word isn't worth spit."

"But they were tricked!" I argued. I could hear my voice rising, and I knew that I was losing control of myself, but I couldn't help it. "They were fooled by the Kanters, just like you were. The Kanters raided villages and poisoned wells... they poisoned the well at my school just a few days ago. The people of Riverfork were going to hang me for it, until the Kanters attacked, and I was freed." That last part was a stretch, but I didn't figure the whole truth would have set very well with him.

"You're a lot like your father," he said. My jaw dropped open.

Chapter 28

I was speechless for a moment, staring at him, wondering. He stared back at me with his good eye.

"You knew my father?" I said, my voice barely a whisper.

He smiled grimly and rose from his chair. He went to the window, and gazed out across the courtyard as he spoke to me. "Your father was as much diplomat as soldier, did you know that?"

I shook my head. "I barely knew my father. I hardly remember him."

"That's a shame. He was a great man. I suppose you can blame me for that."

"You? Then you're the reason he went back to war?"

"Who else? I am the general, you know. I'm the one who makes the hard decisions. I send men out to battle, knowing that they might come back in pieces or, like your father, they might not come back at all."

A heavy uncomfortable silence descended over the room, and suddenly I could hear every sound in the castle around us. I glanced over the general's shoulder, and saw the young men training in the courtyard. What was he thinking? That he might send them out to die, too?

He spoke, interrupting my thoughts. "I believed this last treaty was going to be the one. I wanted your father to deliver it personally, because he had a history with the Tal'mar."

That was a loaded statement. Questions flooded my mind, and I could hardly think straight enough to sort them out. I asked the obvious one: "What kind of history?"

He twisted his head and shot me a sly look. "Diplomatic," he said. "Though I see now that his interests were more than professional." My ears reddened as he said this, but he ignored me. "How can I describe what your father did? You see, he was a large man. He was the kind of man that inspired loyalty and fear all at once -the kind of man that troops would follow into any battle, regardless of the odds. But at the same time he had a way with words like I've never seen before. He could speak the Tal'mar language. He could use their own tongue to charm them as if they were schoolgirls at a barn dance."

It warmed my heart to hear my father described like that. I could remember looking into his eyes, and the feeling of being in his arms. I knew that every woman would fall in love with him, human or Tal'mar. I knew the kind of charm he'd had, even though I'd never seen him use it. "What happened to the treaty?"

"Your father left with our offer, and then he disappeared. We didn't hear from him for almost two weeks. Then the Tal'mar delivered his body to us with the message that he had been waylaid by bandits. Needless to say, we didn't believe a word of it."

"It was the Kanters," I interrupted. I knew it just as surely as I knew they'd poisoned the well at school. They had killed my father to keep the treaty from reaching the Tal'mar. But how could they have known? Did they have spies? They must have. I suddenly felt sick to my stomach. I dropped into a chair and put my head in my hands.

I hardly heard the general move before I saw him in front of me. He knelt down and pulled my hands away from my face. He wiped the tears from my cheeks. "This is not the time for that," he said. "If you truly are your father's daughter, prove it to me now."

"How?"

He rose up, and I looked up into that grim, leathery face. "I'm inclined to believe you girl. I'm sure my men suspect you're a spy, but they don't understand people the way I do. You're no spy, I'd wager my good eye on that. I have another draft of that treaty in my desk. If you can have it back here tomorrow, as you say you can, then I will move my men."

He moved over to his desk and shoved all the papers aside, revealing a map of the Borderlands. "You are here, at Relian Keep," he said, pointing to a small castle. It was sitting on the side of the mountain. He drew his finger directly to the west, and settled at a large circle with two towers rising up from the center. "Silverspire is approximately three hundred miles to the west. It takes nearly a week to make that trip on horseback. How fast can you get there?"

"I left Riverfork at dawn," I said.

"Then you can be there by nightfall. Deliver your message and come back here as fast as you can. I will not move the troops until I have the treaty. Even then, it won't be easy."

"The Kanters will have a full day to march," I argued. "Do you know how many people could die?"

"It's not all my decision, girl. I have to convince Prince Sheldon that this must be done. After what's happened in the last few years, that will be no easy task. One day is the best I can offer."

I accepted that without further argument, instead determining to make the flight even faster, if such a thing were possible. The general threw open a desk drawer and produced the treaty. He signed it, and gave it an official seal. When it was finished, he handed it over. "Keep that safe, and don't let anyone see it," he warned. "There are those among us who no longer desire a peaceful accord."

I nodded, and tucked the letter into my jacket. Then he escorted me out of the castle and back to my plane. As we exited, I saw some sort of commotion at the bottom of the hill. Several soldiers were standing around the plane, and one of them was arguing with a man on horseback. As we got closer, I saw that his cloak was the deep purple of royalty.

"Is that Prince Sheldon?"

"Unfortunately."

"Really? So he's going to be king some day?"

"No, thank God. His older brother will. Sergeant! What's going on here?"

The two men dropped their argument, and turned to face us. The prince's eyebrows shot up as he saw me. "Tal'mar!" he hissed. "Arrest this woman!"

"Belay that," said the general. "This woman is a messenger, an ambassador. She was just leaving."

"Not with this machine!" said the prince. "I'm commandeering it."

"That's insane. What could you possibly need with this machine?"

"Watch your tongue, General Corsan. Don't forget your place. I plan to use this machine to spy on the

Tal'mar. Once we know the locations of their bases, we can finally end this war."

"Your highness, with all due respect..." Corsan's words were cold and calculated. He didn't use the title with respect, but rather with a vague threat. "Your regrettable decision in this matter belies an unacceptable inefficiency in the chain of communications. I'll see to this matter as soon as I debrief you personally, on certain events which have recently unfolded."

"Nonsense! Nothing could be as important as this. With this machine, we will win the war!" There were a few cheers from the guards standing around him.

I was starting to understand the general's distaste for the prince. The man was more stubborn than I could have imagined. His mind seemed to be completely distracted with the thought of his coming victory over the Tal'mar, so much so that he was unwilling to listen to information that would later paint him as an ignorant fool.

"Your highness, I really think it would be best if you came up to the keep. I have some very important information to relay. Sergeant, get this plane back on the road!"

"Halt!" The prince shouted. "Guards, commandeer this vehicle."

I held my breath as the prince's guards came forward, their hands on their sword hilts. The sergeant shot the general a look. General Corsan nodded, and the sergeant shouted, "Men, at arms!"

Chapter 29

General Corsan waved me back, and I happily complied. I paused on the far side of the road and turned to watch. Cinder whined at my feet as the air filled with the sound of sword blades being drawn from their sheaths. Cold, silvery steel glinted in the sunlight.

I glanced at the prince and saw him -still on horseback- calculating the situation. He was surrounded by at least three hundred men, and had less than a dozen guards. He wasn't beaten yet, though.

"Treason!" he shouted. "Sergeant, arrest this man for treason!"

It didn't take half a second to determine where the sergeant's loyalties lay. He turned his back on the prince. "Men, you heard the general! Get this machine back on the road!"

A handful of soldiers sheathed their swords and started pulling my plane back up to the wagon trail. The prince's hand strayed towards the hilt of his sword, but then he thought better of it. He heeled his horse up next to the general and stooped down.

"The king will hear of this!" he hissed. Then he sat back upright and shouted it out so that everyone could hear. "THE KING WILL HEAR OF THIS TREASON!" He heeled his horse and went tearing up the hillside towards the castle, with his guards running along behind.

I glanced nervously at the general, and he gave me a reassuring smile. "He's hard to get to know."

I laughed a little. "I guess so."

"Don't worry about the prince. He'll get drunk tonight, by tomorrow he won't remember a thing. By the time you're back he'll be right as rain."

I raised my eyebrows, hardly believing it was true. Even if it was, General Corsan had still taken a considerable risk. "Thank you," I said. I climbed into the seat and Cinder jumped onto my lap.

"No thanks are necessary. I want this war over as badly as you." He paused for a moment, as if trying to decide what he should say next. I gave him a quizzical look. "Before you go, I'd like to ask one thing. It will take you a bit out of your way, but it will buy us time. It may even save lives."

I couldn't imagine what he was talking about, but I certainly couldn't refuse his request. "All right. What do you want me to do?"

He gestured to one of the soldiers, and the man stepped forward carrying a small crate. He set it on the plane next to me and I peered inside. It was full of balls... Tinker's explosive charges. These were the larger ones, about the size of a man's fist.

"These are cannon charges. Do you know what these do?" he said. I nodded, my eyes wide. After my traumatic childhood experience, I was nervous just being near those things. "Good. This is what I want you to do: Fly back towards Riverfork and find the Kanters. Look for supply wagons and war machines. If you see any, drop a few of these on them. That should slow them down."

I nodded solemnly. "What if I don't see anything like that?"

"Then drop 'em on the Kanters." I accepted the box, setting it on my lap. Cinder curled up at my feet with a distasteful grunt. She wasn't at all happy about the invasion of her space.

"I'll be back as soon as I can. Get your men ready to move."

"Don't worry about that," he said. "They'll be ready."

"Thanks again for all that you've done."

"Don't thank me yet. Just get back here safely."

"I will."

"Good, because we're not done with you yet."

I left with that cryptic remark ringing in my ears.

Chapter 30

I must have been at three thousand feet before I felt like I could breathe again. The air was cold, as it always is at that altitude, but it was welcome after that suffocating tension. I wedged the box down on the floor between my legs and let Cinder jump onto my lap. She licked my neck and my chin, and then nuzzled into my collar and fell asleep.

I had worries. I had put myself to the hazard by promising the general something that I had no way to accomplish. If I failed, I could not only end up imprisoned or dead, but thousands of innocent lives would be lost. And I was afraid that even if I was successful at recruiting the cooperation of the Tal'mar, something could still go wrong.

The prince, for instance. He seemed like a disaster waiting to happen. The general didn't seem to have much control over him, and the prince appeared eager to cause trouble. And then there were the Kanters. They were the wild card. I could only guess as to what their ultimate objective might be. Were they trying to eradicate humans entirely? If they succeeded, would they then pursue the same goal with the Tal'mar?

But even with all these worries hanging over me, there was one thing that was even more prominent in my thoughts: my father. The general's praise still rang in my ears, and brought a smile to my face. I was jealous because I could never know my father the way the general had, but I was giddy over the things I was learning about him. My father had been all things to all men, it seemed. He was a man's man on the battlefield, a natural born leader. And he was a silver-tongued poet as well, and not only in the ways of politics.

It made sense of course, though I had never thought of it before. My father had managed to secure the interests of a Tal'mar woman. How many humans could claim that? I was a living testament to his charm. The very thought made me laugh.

Until that day I had always believed my father had been recalled as a soldier. It seemed logical enough, him being so large and strong, but now I knew he'd gone back as an ambassador. He'd gone back to ensure the success of this treaty. I was certain that he could have refused to do this, but he hadn't. The reason for that now struck me like a boot to the forehead. He'd been trying to create a world that was safe for me. Not by going to war, but by delivering treaties. By using his natural leadership qualities, he had been trying to bring our people together. And he died for it. He died so that the Kanters could keep the war going.

And suddenly I was angry.

My mind filled with thoughts that were new and strange to me. Thoughts of hatred and revenge. I glanced at the crate of explosives and realized that I might actually enjoy dropping a few of those on the Kanters. I had never felt that way before, and I hardly knew what to think of myself. Did it make me a bad person, wanting to avenge my father's death?

I knew that some people killed as a matter of routine. Soldiers spent every waking moment perfecting that ability. If they could march into battle on a simple command, couldn't I do the same in the name of my father?

Later, I realized that I was already doing the best thing I could. I was using my own unique gifts and station in life to fight for what I believed. I wasn't on a battlefield with a sword and shield; I was delivering a treaty that could bring the humans and Tal'mar together in the fight against a common enemy.

I also realized that I had somehow just filled my father's shoes, that I had followed in his footsteps and taken up his cause. Fortunately, the thought didn't occur to me at the time. If it had, I probably would have been too terrified to do anything but turn around and go home.

The Kanters had been marching steadily for the entire day, and it was late afternoon when I found them. They were fifty miles north of Riverfork. They had burned or crushed everything in their path, and left the land dead and blackened in their wake. I didn't see as many refugees in their path, and I assumed that most of those people had already made it to Anora. The Kanters were still less than halfway there.

I flew over them, scanning their ranks. It wasn't long until I found what I was looking for. The Kanters were moving like a well-organized army. They had scouts out front, followed by archers on foot and then a large infantry. Behind this, I saw the war machines General Corsan had warned me about.

Not all that I'd read about the Kanters was exaggeration. The largest of them were giants. I estimated their height to be about fifteen feet. A dozen of these creatures were pulling cannons and catapults with thick, braided ropes. Further back, I saw what could only have been the supply wagons. These would have been carrying the materials that the army needed to keep moving: clothing, building materials, weapons, and especially food. Then I saw the two large wagons filled with bodies. Human bodies. This, I realized with a sick feeling, must have been their food.

My stomach churned. I'd long since known that the Kanters practiced cannibalism, but it was one thing to read about it, and another to see it. Was it possible that they had actually lifted the bodies of their victims from the battlefield so that they could later eat them? I knew it to be true, and it made me want to vomit. I clenched my teeth and silently promised myself that the Kanters wouldn't touch any of those bodies.

I swept around behind them and came up from the rear. I waited until I saw the bodies, and then I started bombing. The Kanters must have thought the wrath of God was raining down on their heads. I took out the wagons first, making sure to cripple their movement and destroy their food supplies. I didn't like the idea of blowing up those bodies, but it was sure better than letting the Kanters eat them. A chill crept up my spine as I thought of it.

I swept back around and started bombing the war machines next. The Kanters had no choice but to break and run as I buzzed overhead, throwing those charges with increasing accuracy. The few who had the courage to stay with the cannons were doomed. They couldn't aim the weapons high enough to shoot at me, and even if they could it would have been impossible to train them on my fast moving plane.

Within minutes the Kanter army fell into disarray. Their cannons and catapults were lying in ruins, and their wagons were overturned and burning. I could have turned back then, but I chose not to. I had a few charges left. So I circled overhead, throwing them down at random, sending those monsters scurrying like insects across the ground. I don't know if I actually hit any of them, but it was worth it to see them fleeing in terror.

In some small way, I had my revenge. When I was done, I threw the crate down and turned back to the north. The sun had already set, and I still had hours to fly

Chapter 31

It was well past midnight when I flew past Relian Keep and crossed the Crimson Strait. It took all of ten minutes to cross the Strait, which appeared as no more than a wide river from my vantage. I passed over the churning black waters and a narrow strip of sandy beach, which immediately gave way to thick, impenetrable forest. The treetops formed a sort of green, bubbly landscape beneath me, rising and falling with the gentle roll of the hills. Flying over this strange expanse, I realized that I could see the curve of the earth at the horizon.

It was common knowledge that the world was round in those days, but according to Analyn, nothing existed beyond the known lands of Astatia and the Isle of Tal'mar. All the rest of the world was ocean. The best seafarers had set out to prove this wrong, and had either returned starved or more likely never returned at all. Of course, no one had ever had a plane before. No one had ever been able to go so far, or to see so much from a single vantage. Perhaps someday I could test my own luck...

I could see why Prince Sheldon had taken such an interest in my plane. Unlike the steamwagon, which was generally considered noisy and impractical, the plane was different. It had obvious potential for military applications. I doubted however that the prince perceived the other possibilities. I knew the plane could bring great changes to civilization. It could be a tool for explorers and adventurers, and a manner of trade and shipping as well. I could already see wealthy kings and merchants building fleets of planes that were larger and faster than mine.

Oddly, none of this had occurred to me while Tinker and I were building the thing. It was simply a distraction. I had never really seen any practical application for the machine until later, when I needed to carry Analyn's message to the general. I suspected that Tinker hadn't given much thought to this potential either.

When he'd designed the plane, I think he just wanted to prove that it could work. He wanted to test his theory about building a machine that could fly. In the process, he'd created a machine that was going to change our entire world. I wondered if he understood that yet.

As I flew, I tried reaching out to the trees to speak to them. I thought that perhaps they could help me. I was hoping at least to learn if I was heading in the right direction. In response, I heard only silence. Was it possible that the trees here didn't speak? I doubted that. More likely they were not so friendly as the trees in my valley. To these trees, I was an outsider, a potential enemy. Here, even the trees mistrusted me. I wondered if they would betray my approach? That was a chilling thought.

Finally, just before dawn, I saw the shimmering glow of my destination. Silverspire is the human name for the city, a rough translation of its Tal'mar name, Resha Lazenta, which means *The City of the Silver Spires*. An apt name I realized, as I saw the gleaming towers of the palace reaching into the clouds. Likewise, many of the buildings were tall and cylindrical in shape, and they all had that silvery luminescent surface.

The sight made me wonder if the Tal'mar actually had metalsmiths among them. I had been told that they hated metal, and yet those shining towers looked like they must have been made from silver, or at least polished steel.

I eventually learned that the color of the spires came from a unique type of glass. The Tal'mar had a technique of blending certain sands to create a glass that was both beautiful and resilient. This blend could be poured while it was hot, and was often used to coat stone or wood. After cooling, the glass became hard as stone, and its surface took on a reflective sheen.

The homes were different. While mostly silver or white in color, they were much closer in physical appearance to the buildings I'd seen in Riverfork. They stood three or four stories in height at most, and they all had the same steep roofs. Many of the buildings were connected by bridges because, as I later learned, the Tal'mar dread setting foot on soil. They believe it lowers them to the status of humans, whom many of them feel are little more than hairless apes.

I didn't know any of this at the time, of course. All I knew was that I had a message to deliver to the Tal'mar queen, a woman named Tarsa Salamenta. I was to allow no one to see the treaty except the queen herself. In order to make this happen, the general had given me the signed documents of a Royal Ambassador. I had no idea how the Tal'mar would receive me, but I was hopeful. After all, my father had apparently had great relations with them. Perhaps they would recognize me as his kin, just as General Corsan had.

I set the plane down on the road outside the city walls, and found guards already waiting for me. Sure enough, the trees had warned them I was coming. I should have known, since the trees at home had so faithfully done the same for me. The Tal'mar had probably known I was coming from the second I crossed the Crimson Strait.

I sensed rather than saw the eyes watching me in the branches overhead. I knew that there were at least a dozen archers ready to take me out in the blink of an eye. Cinder knew it too. She jumped onto my lap and started barking at the trees. A Tal'mar man stepped forward. Judging by his manner and uniform, he appeared to be some sort of peacekeeper or city official. He clearly didn't approve of my plane, or me.

"What is the meaning of this... this abomination?"

Abomination. Hadn't I been called that before? But he wasn't talking about me. It was my plane that bothered him, because of the Tal'mar aversion to metals. Clearly, he didn't approve of the way Tinker and I had melded wood and steel. He stood two yards away from me and almost seemed afraid to come closer. I put my hands in the air to show that I wasn't armed, and climbed out of the plane.

"I've come with a message for the queen," I said.

I still had my flying cap on, so my ears were covered, but I could tell that he could sense the Tal'mar in me. He frowned deeply and muttered something in his own language, which I could only assume meant "half-breed." The meaning was clear enough from the look on his face. I ignored this, and pulled the ambassador papers from my jacket. "I must have an audience with the queen."

He snatched the papers out of my hand and looked them over. "We no longer honor treaties with humans," he said. "Get back on that *thing* and pray we don't shoot you down before you're out of sight."

I glanced at the other guards standing behind him, and saw that he had their support. I blinked, and took a deep breath. "I'm not leaving," I said firmly. "I must speak to the queen. The Kanters are marching across the southlands even as we speak."

"Good," he said. "I hope they eradicate your kind once and for all... Archers!"

He raised a finger and I heard rustling in the branches. Once again, I opened my mind up to the trees, trying to communicate with them. Perhaps, somewhere in the back of my mind, I thought that I could win them over to my cause. As soon as I did this, the man backhanded me.

I stumbled back against the plane and Cinder leapt forward in my defense. She growled and latched onto the man's ankle. There was a slight rustling overhead, and an arrow appeared in Cinder's side. She yelped once and then dropped.

"No!" I screamed. I jumped forward, but an arrow struck me in the shoulder and something hard hit me in the back of the head. I had just enough time to feel the burning sensation of that arrow twisting through my body before I lost consciousness. My thoughts went wild, reaching out to Cinder and to the trees, but the only response I received was darkness.

Chapter 32

I thought I had been alone before. I thought my life had been painful and solitary. I didn't realize until I woke in the Tal'mar dungeon that I had never truly been alone. Nothing I had ever experienced could have prepared me for that.

It was dark. Only the barest light from a distant torch cast shadows on the stone walls of my cage. I tried to reach out with my mind, first to find Cinder and then to study the structure of the cell, and both times I met resistance. It was almost physical, this invisible force that pushed against me, refusing my every attempt. The harder I pushed, the more firm the resistance became. I fought a wave of panic as I realized that I was locked entirely inside myself. Any effort to reach out to the world around me was denied.

I panicked and began to hyperventilate. Locked. Alone. I couldn't understand a world like that. I couldn't reach out, couldn't touch or sense anything. Was this what it was like to be human? Was this what it meant to have no bond with the world, other than one's outward senses? To touch, smell, and hear, but to never truly *feel* anything? It was awful. Sickeningly awful.

I was so distraught that at first I didn't even notice my wound had been healed. All I could think about was that pressure, that force pressing in against me. The more I thought about it, the worse it became, until I felt like I could hardly breathe.

I never realized until that moment how much I had been using my Tal'mar senses all along. It was second nature to me, reaching out to touch things with my mind even as I laid hands on them. I had never even thought about what I was doing. Now I had to think about everything. I had to control that instinct, to force it back.

There was a cot in the cell, and I had to lie down and force myself to take deep, steady breaths. This went on for some time, until I eventually calmed down enough to reassess my situation. I had to force myself not to use my powers, lest I invoke the same response as before. Instead, I used my eyes, and my sense of feeling. I reached out with my hands and touched the smooth stone walls and the heavy wooden door. I studied them in the dim light, looking for some weakness or flaw that I might exploit.

I found no means of escape, and I was too exhausted to persist for long. Eventually, I lay back down on the cot and drifted into a restless sleep. I knew in the back of my mind that I shouldn't, that I needed to stay awake and find a way out of there, but I didn't have the strength. All I could do was pray that something would happen before it was too late.

As luck would have it, something did happen. But it was the last thing I ever would have expected.

I woke to the sound of voices outside my door. I couldn't understand the low murmuring, but I recognized the fact that one of the voices was female. A few moments passed, and then I heard shuffling noises and the door opened. A shadowy figure in a long robe appeared in the doorway.

"Who are you?" I said.

"I am Malina. I healed your wound." The door closed behind her, and she pulled back her hood. She had the delicate features of all Tal'mar, with high cheekbones and a sharp, proud chin. Her face was framed by dark curls, and her eyes were hidden in the shadows. As she approached I saw that the woman's face was stern but kind, and I couldn't detect any animosity in her. She settled onto the cot next to me and began to examine my shoulder. I decided to pry for some information.

"What's wrong with this place?" I said.

"What do you mean?"

"I mean it's... it's all *closed off*. There's something wrong."

"You can sense that?"

I looked into her face and saw that her eyes were a deep violet color. My vision was slowly adjusting to the changing light, and my night vision was trying to work with my normal vision. Her hair seemed to be violet as well, with a reddish hue to it.

"Of course I can sense it," I said. "It's like someone poking their finger in my eye. It's driving me crazy."

"Ignore it," she said. "Do not dwell on what you cannot change. What is your name?"

"Breeze," I said. "Breeze Tinkerman. I had papers, but the guards took them."

"I see." She looked at me for a while... No, she *stared* at me. It was like her eyes were boring holes into my skull. I couldn't even guess as to what the woman might be thinking. Finally, she spoke: "Are you hungry?"

"A little, I guess." I hadn't really thought about food. How long had it been since I'd eaten? A day? Two days? I should have been hungry, but so much had been happening that it was the furthest thought from my mind. She rose from the cot and went to the door.

"I'll see that some food is brought to you. In the meanwhile, try to rest."

"What happened to Cinder?" I said, but she turned away and the guard pulled the door closed behind her. I ran over and started pounding on it. "What happened to my dog?" I shouted. "What did you do to her?"

They didn't respond. They knew that eventually I would tire and go back to my cot, and they were right.

I was lying there in the darkness, still trying to plot an escape when my food came. The guard opened a narrow slit in the door and pushed through a tray of fruit, meat, and cheese. I wanted to refuse it, or at least throw the tray at the wall and make some sort of racket, but as soon as I smelled it my willpower melted. My stomach groaned, and I realized just how hungry I was.

I snatched the tray and started shoveling food into my mouth as fast as I could eat. I didn't stop until it was gone, and then I wished I had more even though my belly was already starting to ache.

A short while later the door opened and one of the guards came in. He appeared to be middle-aged, though for a Tal'mar that may well have meant he was a hundred and fifty. Their average lifespan is three hundred years, and some have been known to live for a thousand.

"Follow me," he said.

Chapter 33

The Tal'mar dungeon was a circular room with cells shooting off from the center. I stepped into this room and blinked against the light of the torches. There were no desks, chairs, or tables. It was simply an empty space with doors lining the outside wall. The guard closed my cell and led me to another door across the room. He waved his hand in front of it and I heard a click on the outside. The door swung open, revealing a steep stone stairway. He gestured me forward.

It was morning, and the sunlight came cascading down the stairwell as I climbed out of the dungeon. It hurt my eyes at first, especially when we reached the top and stepped out into the palace courtyard. I stood there for a moment, blinking against the light.

The courtyard was huge, easily the size of the entire town of Riverfork. It was encircled by a tall stone wall, the surface of which had been carved in fantastical relief. Great trees climbed the smooth stone, their likeness so realistic that I would have believed them real if it weren't for their smooth gray texture. Vines dangled from the branches, bursting with glorious life in the form of leaves and flowers and enticing bulbous fruits. The faces of Tal'mar children peered out from behind the foliage, their likenesses frozen forever in that living stone. Unicorns grazed on the lush ground below the branches.

The guard nudged me, and I realized that I'd been standing there with my jaw hanging open. I swung my gaze upwards and saw the palace towers rising to dizzying heights in front of me. I stood like a fool staring up at them, until the guard bumped me again and I started stumbling forward.

I threw my head around, trying to take in everything at once. A stream emerged from the woods on the eastern side of the palace, where it flowed under a small bridge and through the courtyard, ending in a small pond at the center of the lawn. A path beyond the bridge led into the woods. On the far side of the lawn, to my left, I saw Tal'mar children training. Most of them seemed to be my age, or a few years older at most, and they were both male and female. They were organized into small groups, some practicing archery and other fighting with sticks and wooden swords. Two more groups were engaged in some sort of meditation, and I could tell that they were using magic.

I suddenly realized that my powers had returned. I had been so overwhelmed by everything around me, that I hadn't even realized it until that moment. Immediately I started to reach out with my mind, searching for Cinder. The guard swung around and put a hand on the hilt of his sword.

"Don't do that," he said.

I reined myself in. I had forgotten that they could sense it when I used my powers. The peacekeeper had hit me for it. "Why?" I said.

"It is forbidden. Your kind is forbidden. Do not make pretenses that you are greater than you are."

"Pretenses?" It dawned on me then why they didn't want me to use my abilities. It wasn't because they thought I might escape, it was because I was human to them, and I wasn't worthy of the magic I possessed. "I don't pretend to be anything but what I am!" I snapped. "And I will use all that I was born with!"

"No doubt you will." I spun around as I heard a familiar female voice. It was Malina, the woman who had healed me. Only now she wasn't wearing a simple robe. She was dressed in a long elegant gown. It was made from some sort of green, shimmering fabric, and the cuffs and front were decorated with silver vines.

"Your highness," the guard bowed low, and she nodded in his direction. I stood there with my mouth hanging open as I witnessed this. It appeared that Malina was more than the simple, kind healer she had pretended to be.

"Leave us alone, Chauce." I saw a glimmer of protest in his eyes, but he clamped his mouth shut and scurried off towards the gate. Malina turned aside. "Let us walk, Breeze." She started to drift across the lawn, and I fell in at her side.

"Are you the queen?" I asked.

She smiled and shook her head gracefully... everything about her was graceful. She was the most beautiful woman I had ever seen. "I am not the queen, I am her daughter. You'll forgive my deceit. I needed to find answers, and it seemed the most prudent way. I hope you understand. Sometimes nothing else is adequate."

I wasn't sure what she meant, but I didn't argue. I was trying to figure out what she wanted with me, and why she had come to see me at all. Had the guards told her about me?

"Your name isn't Malina," I said. "It's Brisha, right?" I knew that much from my reading.

"That is correct."

"I have a message for the queen, your highness." I just barely remembered to tack that last part on. If it hadn't been for the guard, I probably wouldn't have. I didn't make a very good ambassador. "The peacekeeper took it..."

The princess produced the treaty, seemingly out of nowhere. "I believe this was what you were delivering?" She handed it to me, and I glanced it over.

"Yes, your highness."

"Hold your thoughts for the moment. We will discuss this in a more private setting."

I followed her across the lawn and into the palace. I was again awestricken as we climbed the stairs and I got to see the structure up close. The stairs, the columns, and the walls all appeared to be some sort of marble, but the surfaces were highly polished and treated with that silvery glass. When glancing across the surface I could see the texture of the stone, yet when the light hit it just right, it looked like polished metal.

We passed through the entrance and into the main hall. There was no ceiling in this room, but rather an open view of the staircase spiraling ever higher into one of the spires. The walls were white, carved in the same brilliant relief as the outer palace wall, and accentuated with dark wooden trim. I saw a few Tal'mar servants hustling around inside the palace, but none of them took any note of me. They were busy with their duties.

Brisha led me across the main hall and through a doorway at the far end. The brilliance faded, and I found myself walking down a long, dark hallway that was barely lit by flickering candles. The floor here was wood, and covered by long rugs. The walls were smooth polished wood, decorated with trim that bore carvings of flowers and vines. Doors sprouted out in both directions the entire length of the hallway, until it turned off in some other direction in the distance.

She paused at one of the doors, and opened it with a simple gesture. I felt the spark of magic as it happened, and realized for the first time how powerful she was. The tiny, thoughtless action on her part sent a shockwave through me. It was nothing to her, but to me it was like feeling a slight burn and looking up to see the sun falling down. Her power was like that; like a huge ball of fire, the size and strength of which I couldn't begin to imagine.

I entered the room with a bit more apprehension now that I understood just how powerful the princess was. It didn't matter if I was younger or faster. I couldn't outrun that kind of power. The instant the door closed, she threw her arms around me. "Oh Breeze, is it really you?"

Chapter 34

I was speechless. She held me for a few seconds and then pulled back, putting her hands on my cheeks and staring into my eyes. "I can hardly believe it," she said. "I didn't dare hope!"

"What... do you mean?" I stammered. My mind flashed over everything we'd discussed, but none of it made sense of this. Then I remembered... my father had been a diplomat. He must have known the princess. In fact, he may have discussed treaties with her. "Did you know my father?"

She threw her head back and laughed. "Yes, of course! Of course I knew your father!" Then the smile faded. "Oh Breeze, I'm so sorry about your father. It was not my wish to have him recalled into duty. General Corsan did that. He wanted your father back because of his past diplomatic relations with the Tal'mar. I believe your father may have been the only human with the courage still to come here."

I saw a great sadness in her face, and I didn't know if it was for my father or for the lives he couldn't save when the treaty had failed. It was obvious that she had been a friend to him, so I suspected she was truly saddened by his death. That was reason for me to care about what she thought. She became something more in my mind -more than a Tal'mar, more than a princess. She had been a friend to my father, and so I considered her to be my friend as well.

185

"It wasn't bandits," I said. "The Kanters did it. They have been sabotaging your treaties all along."

"I know that now," the princess said. "I should have known it before. It seems so obvious now, doesn't it? There have been far too many coincidences..." she glanced down at the treaty.

"Then you believe me?" I said. "Will the queen sign the treaty?"

She nodded. "Yes, it's already done, but I don't know what good it will do. We will send a regiment of three hundred to supplement your forces, but I fear it will take days for them to catch up. By then, the damage will be done."

I was flabbergasted. "You're going to send troops?"

"The order has already been given. Don't be so surprised. It was hard enough to convince my commanders that it was safe to pull away from the Borderlands. At least this way they have some guarantee that the threat is real, and that we are not simply lowering our defenses. They will march south, and fight alongside men. This hasn't happened in a thousand years."

"Thank you," I said. I forgot myself for a moment, and threw my arms around her. A great weight seemed to have fallen from my shoulders. Somehow, incredibly, I was actually succeeding. All I had to do was get that treaty back to the general.

I thought of my plane, and immediately thought of Cinder. "I had a dog with me," I said. "Your guards shot her."

"Ah, yes," the princess said. Her eyes went distant, and I felt her reaching out. I felt that tingle of magic again, that tiny spark of untapped power

Somewhere across the building, I heard a yelp. A few seconds later, Cinder came tearing into the room. She leapt into my arms and started licking my face, almost knocking me over in the process. I heard the princess laughing, and I shot her a smile.

Eventually I got Cinder settled down and I gave her the command to lie still. "So you'll let me go, then?" I said. "The guards won't do anything?"

"The guards won't harm you," she said. "I must apologize for the way they behaved. The Tal'mar think rather highly of themselves and one such as you..." Her voice trailed off, and I finished the sentence for her.

"A half-breed?" The princess gave me a pained look, but I shrugged it off. "I've heard it before," I said. "I'm not Tal'mar and I'm not human. But that's okay, because I'm better."

Her eyebrows shot up. "Is that so?"

"Yes. I can use magic and touch iron at the same time!"

Her face fell in disbelief. "This is not possible. I've never heard of such a thing."

"It's true," I said. "Have you seen my plane? I helped Tinker make it."

The princess bent over and took my chin in her hands, pulling my gaze upwards. "Breeze, you are as remarkable as your father."

I had another thought as I looked into her eyes, though I hardly dared voice it. Somehow, I found the courage. "You knew my father," I said apprehensively, "did you know my mother as well?"

Brisha's face grew distant and sad. "Yes, Breeze, I knew your mother. She would have been so proud. She cared very much about you. She and your father... they did everything they could for you. Don't be angry with them."

"I understand," I said. "I know why they were together."

"You do?"

"Yes. They were in love. And it didn't matter to them what anyone else thought, because love is more important."

"You are right," she said. She smiled, but her voice was sad. "Stay here, Breeze. Stay and see our city with me, and I will tell you everything about your parents."

"I can't," I whispered. I didn't want to say it, for fear of offending her, but it was necessary. "I have to get this treaty back. I have to go."

"Let my couriers deliver it," she said. "They can have it there before the sun sets tomorrow."

"That's not fast enough. The general won't move his troops until he sees the queen's signature on this treaty. Even now, people are dying."

"The same people who call you 'half-breed'?"

"Some of them. Would I be any better if I turned my back on them?"

"You truly are your father's daughter, Breeze. When we have time, I must tell you about him."

"I'd like that," I said.

"At least promise you will return to me. Deliver the treaty and come straight back here."

My heart was jumping at the invitation, but thoughts of Tinker tempered my answer. I was worried about him. I needed to get back to the valley and make sure he and the Traders were safe. "I'll come back as soon as I can," I promised.

"Then we'd best not tarry," she said.

Chapter 35

When Brisha and I left the palace, we found my plane in the center of the courtyard surrounded by a dozen guards. At least a hundred citizens stood nearby, gawking and whispering. I caught bits of words in the common language, "Strange... abomination... machine." It seems my plane was as much an abomination as me.

Two of the younger Tal'mar, a girl and two boys, approached me. "This is your machine?" one of the boys said.

"Yes."

"It's true then, that it flies? Like a bird?" I glanced at them, surprised. They were wholly fascinated. I'd expected them to start mocking and ridiculing me.

"Yes, it flies. The fan on the front slices through the air, pulling the plane forward. The wings plane across the air, giving it lift." I made gestures with my hands as I spoke, trying to visually show them how it was capable of flight.

"Incredible," the boy said.

One of the girls spoke up. "How do you fly it?"

I looked them over suspiciously. Were they trying to learn the secrets of my plane so they could steal it? No, the Tal'mar didn't want anything to do with my plane. I decided it was safe to tell them.

"It's quite easy to control. You sit in the seat, and control the speed with this throttle like so..." I demonstrated as I spoke. I revved up the fan just a little, to their delight. "Pull it back to release the full power of the springs, or push it forward to slow down." I reached over and moved the controls for the ailerons. "You can turn right or left by twisting these in the opposite directions, creating drag in the air current. Or pull both controls back to climb and push forward to descend."

Several more Tal'mar youths came forward as we spoke. They were enrapt, and they all started questioning me at once. The elders had fallen silent. They were listening intently and watching us, but made no move to interfere.

I now realized that I had an audience. I did my best to answer their questions as simply and directly as possible. There didn't seem to be any point in trying to deceive them. They asked about the springs, and I confirmed that they were metal.

"I'm half human," I said proudly. "The metal doesn't affect me." I pulled open the stow at the back of the plane, so that they could see the internal workings. To my surprise, the boy stepped forward and touched it.

"This is amazing! Can I fly it?" My eyebrows arched and I scanned the rest of their faces. I saw two or three disapproving stares, and a lot of expectant looks.

"It doesn't bother you?" I said. "The metal, I mean?" The boy shrugged.

"I don't have to touch it, do I?" he said. "Besides, I'd give up all my powers to be able to fly like you do."

I heard a few gasps among the crowd, and the elders raised their eyebrows and set to whispering amongst themselves. I saw the same look in their eyes that I had seen in Prince Sheldon's. They wanted my plane. Despite the fact that it disgusted them, despite the fact that it contained metal, they wanted it. They saw as clearly as anyone that my machine had important military applications.

Still, there was an irony in the fact that I was no longer a half-breed to these people. I was just the person who owned the thing that they wanted. They seemed to have forgotten my race in the same manner that the humans had, once they realized the potential of my plane. It was a fascinating psychological turn, and it set my mind to working. Humans hated me for being Tal'mar, while Tal'mar hated me for being human... and yet they both entirely forgot that I was anything but a person when they were looking at my plane.

I also saw a notable difference between the younger Tal'mar and their elders. The elders still had that prejudice within them, and it flashed in their eyes when they looked at me. The children were different. They just saw a girl who could fly. They didn't care about who or what I was, because they had been captured by something else... by a dream.

I stepped away from the group, and approached the princess. She was instructing the guards to return my possessions and move the plane back to the road. "Your highness," I said respectfully. I knew it was important that our relationship look official to the Tal'mar. We couldn't be friends in public.

"Yes, Breeze?"

"Do you think your woodworkers could make something like this?" She laughed.

"I suspect they're already trying."

"Good." She raised her eyebrows.

"It doesn't bother you, the fact that they'll try to copy you? That they might steal your invention?" It was my turn to laugh. The thought hadn't even occurred to me.

"No, that doesn't bother me at all. I'm just wondering how good your woodworkers are?" I saw her glance stray to the wonderful architecture around us. I corrected myself: "I mean, *how fast* are they?"

"What are you trying to do here, Breeze?"

I stepped a little closer, and lowered my voice almost to a whisper. "Did you see their reactions? They forgot that I was a half-breed. They didn't care about anything except the plane. They are so in love with the possibilities that they forgot to hate me." Her eyes brightened as I spoke.

"So what are you proposing?"

"I had the same experience with the humans. They wanted my plane so bad that they didn't even care about anything else. It captured their imaginations, and their dreams. Suddenly all they were thinking about was the future.

"What I'm thinking is, why don't we give it to them? We will make a team, a group of pilots, half of them human and half Tal'mar..."

Her jaw fell open. "Ingenious! Such a cooperative would not only ease the tension and distrust among our people, it would also give us something in which to have an equal share of pride. And it would also give us an equal interest in this new type of military technology..."

"And more," I said. "We can deliver messages and packages. With bigger planes, we could even carry people back and forth over great distances, ten times as fast as riding!" In her eyes, I could see my vision taking hold as I spoke. She listened and thought about it for several moments before she responded.

"We can expect a certain reluctance to place a foreigner in control of such a force," She said. "The humans wouldn't trust a Tal'mar, nor the Tal'mar a human."

"That's why I will lead them," I said. "I'm both. For once, I'm going to use that to my advantage." A broad smile crept over her face.

"Your father would be proud of you... Go to your General Corsan and tell him of this plan. Tell him he has my full cooperation, as long as you are the leader. I will accept no less. If he tries to dissuade you, assure him that we're already building planes. He will see the wisdom of this course. Go now, and deliver your message! I'll see to it that when you return, we'll be ready."

"Tell your woodworkers I will be bringing help," I said. "I will be back by the end of the week with springs and gearboxes."

She gave me a bright but clueless smile. "I don't know what those things are," she said, "but I'll tell them." I laughed, and then jogged down to my plane, which was now almost through the city gates.

I jumped up on the wing and settled into the seat, and Cinder hopped in with me. The boy who wanted to fly was still there, and he gave me an expectant look. "Remember everything I told you," I said. "In a few days, you'll be flying with me." His face broke into a grin so huge that it was silly, and I laughed aloud as I pulled my hat and goggles on.

"Hang on, Cinder," I said as I grabbed the throttle.

Chapter 36

My return seemed quicker than the first flight. Perhaps it was because I was familiar with the territory. More likely, it was due to the fact that my mind was overwhelmed with concerns about which I could do nothing.

I had a lot to think about, not the least of which was the risk the princess had taken for me. She had released me from jail and sent me on my way with a signed treaty. That was almost certainly going to be an issue of debate among the Tal'mar. Then she had agreed to establish an aerial force, a joint unit under my command. Would the queen agree? Would the people agree? I could tell that the princess was very powerful, but I also knew that she had taken a risk. Enough of a risk perhaps, to put her in danger.

I tried to push these things to the back of my mind. I focused on all of the things I had to do, and tried to lay out a sensible approach that would make the best use of what little time I had. First, I had to deliver the treaty. While there, I would outline my plan for an air force to General Corsan. It was my hope that this would dissuade him from attempting to commandeer my plane

If it worked, that would buy the time I needed to get the force assembled and train a handful of pilots. Then of course, a much needed visit to Tinker. It would do wonders for my peace of mind to know that he was safe, and that Daran had healed from his wounds.

Even without all of these thoughts bouncing through my mind, I never would have guessed what was waiting for me upon my arrival. It was early evening and the sky was growing dark, but the encampment was lit from one end to the other by torches and bonfires. I could clearly see that the tent city had been split right down the middle, and the soldiers were building a long road paved with smooth stones. One end terminated in an open field, the other into what appeared to be a wide, open-fronted building. The outer walls were about half-constructed and I had a clear view of the work going on inside. Obviously, the road was meant to accommodate aircraft landings and takeoffs. It was clear from the size of the building that the general didn't just want my plane. He wanted to build a dozen of them.

I had very little time to think about this as I brought the plane in for a landing. The general's plans were clear, but how would those plans interact with my own? He wanted an air force, and I had already taken the initiative of starting one. How would he react? It could either go very well or very, very badly.

Armed guards were waiting to escort me to the keep after I landed. I climbed out of the plane and followed them without resistance. "You've been busy," I said.

One of the guards snorted. The other kept his eyes straight ahead as he spoke. "The general and the prince have reached an agreement. Your machine is going to change everything." I entered the keep with those prophetic words ringing in my ears. Corsan was waiting for me in his office.

"Breeze!" he said cheerfully as I entered. "I assume you remember Prince Sheldon?" He gestured towards the corner, and I glanced over to see the nobleman half-buried in shadows. I hadn't even seen him as I entered. The man was even creepier when he was sober. I almost wished he was drunk again.

He nodded solemnly, and I gave him a little bow, uncertain as to the proper etiquette in that situation. A sharp sneer curled up the corners of his mouth. I stifled a chill and jerked my gaze back to the general.

"Do you have my treaty?" he said.

I reached into my jacket and handed it over. He gave me a pleased smile as he saw the Queen's signature. "Well done! Are you ready for your next assignment?" He shot the prince a glance as he said this. Prince Sheldon was watching me with a cold, unblinking stare. His eyes were dark, his skin pale and taut. I tried not to look at him.

"About that, General..." he shot me a look of warning, but I didn't dare hesitate. "I have secured an agreement with the Tal'mar for the creation of a jointly manned air force. We will choose an equal number of human and Tal'mar pilots." The general's eyebrows shot up, and he looked at the prince.

"Preposterous," Sheldon said. "They're trying to steal our technology. They know that we have the upper hand."

"That's not true," I said. "The princess wants this to heal the divide between our peoples. She wants us all to share in this honor."

"Ridiculous. I won't hear of it," said Prince Sheldon. "General, I order you to commandeer that plane this minute. Disassemble it and reproduce it. I want ten more completed by the end of the month!"

"General, wait!" I said. Corsan gave me an exhausted look. So far he'd been standing there listening to the two of us, but unable to get a word in edgewise. I felt sympathy for him, but I couldn't stop arguing. I couldn't give an inch, or I'd lose everything. "The queen's woodworkers are already building planes. They will have the first batch done by the end of the week! I expect at least five."

"The week?" the prince said. "That's impossible. No one could build a single machine like that in a week, much less five of them."

"I've seen the Tal'mar's work," the general argued. "You forget, they have a gift."

Sheldon's eyes narrowed as he digested that. A moment later, he smiled. "Ah, I see. If we enter into this... compromise, we can have an entire force in the air within a few days."

"It would appear so," said the general. The prince slapped his hand down on his armrest.

"So be it then, General. We'll use their skills to our advantage. Very clever. Tell them we'll accept the agreement, but that we insist all the pilots be human." The general turned his gaze on me.

"That's not the deal they've offered, sir. The Tal'mar insist that my team will be half human, half Tal'mar."

"*Your* team?" the prince said.

"Yes, sir. As I am neither human nor Tal'mar, I will lead the team. Besides, I'm the only person who can fly. The engineers will need guidance, and the pilots will need training. If you want my team in the air by the end of the week, then I'd best get to work."

Sheldon looked me over for a moment. Then he rose from his chair and tossed a floppy, black hat over his head. "You have your chance, girl. But we will revisit this." He nodded at the general, and disappeared through the door. Corsan shot me a broad grin.

"Where did you learn to speak like that?" he said.

"Like what? I was only trying to get my point across." The general laughed aloud.

"You're every bit your father's daughter. Tell me, can you really do this? Can you have these planes in the air within the week?"

"Yes," I said firmly. It was a gamble, of course. I was hoping that the Tal'mar would live up to my promise, and I knew what could happen if I was wrong. The humans would see it as another betrayal. They would steal my plane and probably put me in prison, and the war would go on at full tilt. And in the meanwhile, the Kanters would sweep all the way into the Borderlands, decimating our army and probably destroying Astatia.

I knew the risks I was taking, and yet I knew that if I managed to walk that fine line and succeed, the world of tomorrow would be a totally different place. A better place. "Will you move your men south now, General? The Tal'mar are already making preparations. The Queen is sending a regiment to assist you."

"Is that so?" His eyebrows arched. "Well in that case, I'd best get my men moving. We wouldn't want to look lazy in front of the Tal'mar, now would we?"

"No, sir."

"I'll give the order tonight. If the weather's on our side we might get to Anora before the Kanters do."

"Thank you general."

"There's something else. Something I need you to do."

"I have to get those planes flying..." I started, but he cut me off with a gesture.

"This won't interfere with that. All I ask is that you take a compass with you, and outline the Kanters' positions on a map. You can locate them for me and be back here in a few hours. Those hours will save my men days of marching and scouting."

"I'll do it," I said. "But I need you to do something for me."

It was the general's turn to give me a skeptical look. "And what would that be?"

"I need springs and gearboxes for the planes. Tinker can't make them fast enough by himself. We need your smiths to help."

"That would be easy enough, if any of my smiths could do it. Unfortunately, those men are used to hammering swords and horseshoes. They don't know anything about gearboxes. They're smiths, not engineers. They're not tinkerers."

"They will be," I said. I turned away and left him standing there with his jaw hanging open, stricken speechless by the very audacity of the half-breed girl who wouldn't take "no" for an answer. From that moment on, my reputation was sealed. I was my father's daughter, and then some.

Chapter 37

I wasn't sure what to expect as I headed south. The Kanters had been in considerable disarray the last time I saw them, after I'd bombed their wagons and war machines into nonexistence. I wondered if they had stopped to rebuild everything, or simply pressed on. I also had to wonder how fast they had moved since then.

I finally found them about fifty miles north of the place I'd originally attacked them. It was satisfying to realize that I had in fact slowed their progress dramatically. I was also pleased to see that they didn't have any more wagons full of bodies. That meant that the humans had had time to flee before them, leaving the Kanters less resistance but also less food.

Regrettably, they had managed to rebuild their war machines. There were seven or eight cannons now, and only one catapult, but that was still too much. I suddenly found myself wishing I had more bombs to drop on them.

I had been making a wide circle over their heads as I studied the Kanters. I studied their wagons and machines but I took little note of what they were actually doing. This proved to be a disastrous mistake. I was already turning back to the south when I heard the distant thud of an explosion, and instantaneously felt the jarring impact of a cannonball against my plane.

It couldn't have been very large, but the effect was devastating. The cannonball ripped through the fuselage and exploded out the other side, bringing chunks of springs and metal along with it. The plane shuddered under the impact, and I immediately lost power. As I plunged towards the earth, it was all I could do to steer the plane towards the west, hoping to make it to the shelter of the woods.

I glanced over my shoulder as I spiraled in and saw the Kanters shouting and cheering. They had been expecting my return, and they were ready. Their revenge was far from complete. I knew what they would do if they got their hands on me, and that knowledge fueled my strength.

"Come on," I said, helplessly urging my plane to keep flying. "Just a few more miles..." I fought against the controls, desperate to make it to shelter. I didn't have a chance. I was only halfway there and already the ground was rushing up. At that point, all I could hope for was a smooth landing, and enough time to run ahead of the Kanters.

Even with my head start, it wouldn't be easy to outrun them. Their legs were longer than I was tall.

Then the wheels hit the ground with a jolt, and the back half of the airframe tore apart. What was left of the plane spun around in the air and I felt myself thrown free. I did several somersaults, and the gravitational forces dragged the breath right out of me.

Sky and earth melted into darkness as I lost consciousness. I didn't even feel it when a shard of wood from the wreckage tore through my rib cage and into my guts.

Chapter 38

I lapsed in and out of consciousness for the next several hours. Those moments of lucidity were thankfully brief, because they were filled with mind-racking spasms of pain. I remember waking at one point, gazing up at the churning sky. I felt a tugging on the shoulder of my jacket, and realized it was Cinder. I reached out to her, my thoughts full of appreciation and concern, but she ignored me.

I woke again some time later and saw the canopy of trees overhead. I was mystified for a moment, until I remembered the way that Cinder had pulled me out of the field. I noticed her warmth next to me and went to touch her, but pain shot through my body. I cried out once, and slipped back into the darkness.

Even Cinder's heroic act would not have saved me, were it not for the trees' intervention. I still don't know exactly what they did, or how the decision was made. All I know is that I woke the next day in a tent deep in the mountains.

"Shh," said a familiar voice as I stirred. "Just rest. You need to heal."

I fought against the wave of nausea and the delirium of pain-killing drugs as I pulled my eyelids open. I was lying on a makeshift cot made from two long poles with animal hides stretched between. I was covered in blankets. Analyn Trader was sitting on a stool next to me.

"What happened?" I mumbled. My tongue was thick, and my mouth dry as dirt. My voice cracked as I spoke.

"That's an excellent question," she replied. "We found you lying under the trees at the edge of our camp this morning. We probably wouldn't have seen you until it was too late, except that dog of yours was standing over you barking and howling."

"Cinder?" I said. I heard a stirring beneath me.

"She's right next to you, dear. She wouldn't leave your side."

Analyn tipped a cup of water into my lips, and I sipped from it. It splashed across my cheeks and went running down the back of my neck, but it was cool and it felt good. "They shot me down," I said after a few moments.

"What's that?"

"The Kanters. They were expecting me. They shot my plane with some sort of cannon."

"I see. Well that explains... your wound."

I reached down and winced as I felt the swollen, moist flesh and the thick stitches. "Who did this?"

"If you're talking about the sewing, that would be me," she said. "Unfortunately the only doctor in Riverfork was killed when the Kanters attacked. Tinkerman pulled a rather large shaft of wood out of you, and treated the wound. I sewed you up, and we've mostly been praying ever since."

I closed my eyes, and let my mind drift through my body. I could see the wound, the slight infection at the surface, and the stitches holding my flesh together. I probed deeper, and saw where the wood had penetrated my guts, ripping the outer membrane and exposing my entire body to the toxins therein. These wounds were healing now, but even so I was incredibly lucky to be alive.

Then I saw the slivers. There were several of them; tiny shards of wood that had penetrated the outer layers of my internal organs. Infections were festering around them, and I knew immediately that they would kill me if I didn't do something. I started to move them, and it felt like a knife in my guts. I took a deep breath.

"Open it up," I said.

Analyn's eyes narrowed. "Don't be ridiculous, it's healing up nicely."

"No, it's not. Please Analyn, take the stitches out!"

"All right, all right." She fumbled around the tent for a few minutes and then returned to my side with a pair of scissors. I heard the snipping sound, and felt the cool metal against my skin. "There you go, but I'm afraid it won't help. The wound has already closed."

I groaned, and clenched my teeth against the pain. "Cut. It. Open."

Analyn gasped. "Breeze, I don't think..."

"Just do it!" I was in an extraordinary amount of pain, despite the medications I had been given, and it was all I could do to stay awake.

I worked the slivers out of my body towards that now closed wound, every movement excruciating. I hardly even noticed as Analyn brought Tinker in, and he re-opened my wound with a sterile knife. I only noticed the release of pressure and the warmth of the infectious goo trickling down my side. Analyn rushed to grab a rag, and started cleaning the bloody mess.

She held up a sliver of wood about an inch long. "Now I understand," she said. "And this wasn't the worst of them." Tinker stepped forward to brush my hair from my eyes

"Are you all right, Breeze?"

I nodded and smiled weakly. "I'm going to sleep now," I said. He was smiling as my eyes closed.

When I woke, the stitches were back. I was alone in the tent, and I could feel the warmth of the afternoon sun beating down through the canvas. It felt good, and I wanted to roll over and go back to sleep, but curiosity forbade it. Instead, I turned my attention back to the wound, and set to work getting everything properly mended. Analyn returned at some point during this process, but I think she sensed what I was doing. Either that, or she assumed I was still asleep. Either way, she watched over me for a few minutes and then left once she was satisfied that I was well. She returned a while later with a tray of food.

"I assume you're hungry?" she said. "Tinker tells me that the healing process leaves you feeling starved as a black bear in spring."

"You have no idea," I said, propping myself up. I snatched up a biscuit and took a bite. "What is this place?"

"It's a refugee camp. The people of Riverfork and the surrounding villages escaped into the mountains when the Kanters attacked. They found us last night, and brought us here."

"Daran?" I said. "Is he okay?"

"He's healing quite well. We're still confining him to a bed, but he's been chatting like a schoolgirl all day long."

I sighed. Knowing that he was going to be okay lifted a huge weight from my shoulders. I laid into my food with a newfound strength.

I ate three biscuits, a bowl of soup, and two thick slabs of meat. By the time I was done my body was begging me to go back to sleep, but I fought it. Tinker had come in while I was eating, and I needed to talk to him.

"You're looking much better," he said as I settled back onto the pillows. I let one arm dangle over the edge so I could rub Cinder's ears and stroke her soft fur.

"And feeling better, thanks to you," I said.

"I did what I could, but obviously it wasn't enough. It was just lucky that we found you. Your arrival was quite a shock to us."

"I don't think it was luck," I said.

"What do you mean?"

"I wasn't anywhere near here, Tinker. I don't even know where *here* is for sure. Last thing I knew, I had crashed about a hundred miles north of Riverfork. The Kanters shot me down."

Tinker's eyes widened. "Analyn mentioned something about that. She thought you were feverish, because it didn't make sense."

"I know. It was my own fault." I went on to describe everything that had happened over the last two days, particularly about how I had bombed the Kanters, and about how they'd been expecting my return.

"Don't be so careless next time," he warned me. "You need to stay at a much higher altitude."

"I know that," I said. "But I don't think there will be a next time. The plane was destroyed."

Tinker thought that over for a few moments. "This project you discussed with the princess and the general, is it what you really want?"

"You mean my team of pilots?" I said. "Of course! It's the only way to bring our people together. I'm surer of it now than ever."

Tinker rubbed his hands together. "Then we'd best get to work. Can you ride?"

I was baffled. "In your steamwagon?"

Tinker laughed aloud. "No, I don't have the steamwagon here. But if we take a horse we can be there by midnight."

"Be where?"

"Home. We still have the other plane back in the barn, remember? I'll make a few modifications to it, and you'll be flying by morning. But first, we'll need to salvage what we can from the crash."

I threw off my blankets. "Let's go."

Tinker went to get a horse saddled while I got dressed. It was a long, painful process. Thankfully, Analyn helped out. "You've saved me again," I joked as she tugged on my bootlaces.

"Nonsense. It's the least I can do, considering all you've done." She paused to look at me with bright, round eyes. "You don't know how much it means, the way you saved Daran."

"You're welcome." It was nice to have her look at me like that. I wasn't a Tal'mar to her anymore, I was just a person. More than that, I was a friend.

I felt a bond growing between us, and I suddenly wanted to spend long nights talking to her about all the things I'd seen and done, and exploring her vast knowledge of the world. The thought sparked a question. "I gave the general your seal," I said. "He recognized it, and he recognized your name. Is he a friend of yours?"

Analyn finished tying my laces, and stood back. She took a deep breath. "Well, I suppose it can't hurt for you to know. At this point, everyone's going to know everything soon enough."

"What do you mean?"

"Well, I do know the general, but only in passing. We used to cross paths every now and then, especially when I was with my brother, Prince Sheldon."

Chapter 39

My jaw dropped open. Only now did I notice the similarities between the two of them. The broad foreheads and dark, stringy hair; the strong chins and narrow set eyes. "Sheldon is your brother?" I almost shouted it. Only after the words were out did I realize how loud I had been. Analyn winced.

"Half-brother actually. King Ryshan has three wives. Each of those wives bore him several children. The eldest, Prince Talanar will inherit the throne, and I am third in line. Thankfully, I'll never see the throne. Most of my siblings feel the same way. None of us want to be leaders. We just want normal lives."

"Sheldon does," I said. I could tell that much about him from my previous encounters. The man was already drunk on what power he had. It made me shiver to think of what he would have been like as king. I realized after I said it that this may have been disrespectful, but Analyn didn't seem to notice. She was in full agreement with me.

"True, unfortunately. Which is one reason that he is as far from the capital as possible. His ambitions make him dangerous to our older brother."

"Talanar believes Sheldon would kill him?" I could hardly believe a family could behave in this way. I'd never had a family, and if I did I would treasure them above all else. I was shocked.

"He believes it because it's true. Sheldon would stop at nothing."

I was aghast. It took a few moments before I picked up on my previous train of thought. "Why did you leave? How did you end up in Riverfork?"

"Not without a fight!" Analyn laughed. "As a member of the royal family, I traveled often. The princes and princesses were expected to take an active role in the politics and relations of the kingdom, and part of this was to visit the provinces regularly. Naturally, I met many interesting people during my travels. None so interesting as a young merchant named Daran Trader, though.

"We eloped, fully without the King's consent. It was possible that my father would have allowed the marriage, but it was also standard practice when I was young to arrange the marriages between the children of noble families. Rather than face this possibility, I took a false name and married Daran in one of the outlying provinces of the borderlands, where I knew no one would recognize me.

"We lived there for a few years before the King found us. He had Daran arrested and I was taken back to court. Of course, it didn't take long for my father to realize that there was little he could do. Our marriage was legal, after all, and no self-respecting nobleman would have considered me eligible for one of his sons.

"After it was all over, my father released Daran and invited us to stay in the capital, but I declined. I have no taste for the royal life. I hate the politics of court; the facetiousness of it all. I'd rather live a simple, honest life in the country with the man I love."

"So you became a teacher..."

"Yes, it seemed logical. I did have extensive knowledge of our kingdom and the rest of the frontier."

Tinker walked in at that moment. "I hope I'm not interrupting," he said, "but we really need to get going."

"Not at all," said Analyn. "I was just entertaining Breeze with old stories of my youth. I'm sure she's glad for the chance to escape."

I rose to my feet and gave Analyn a hug. "You'll have to tell me the rest when I get back," I said. She smiled and then shooed me out the door.

I found myself standing on a narrow mountain plateau. I was surrounded by makeshift tents, and I was surprised to recognize many of the faces around me. "Where exactly are we, Tinker?" His answer surprised me.

"Actually, we are not far from the area where you bombed the Kanters. The refugees have been talking about it ever since."

I spun around, scanning the landscape at the base of the mountain. Dense trees blocked most of the view, but I could still see some of the devastation that the Kanters had left behind them. I could also see some of the wreckage. I immediately thought of the bodies that the Kanters had been taking with them. "There were two wagons..."

"They're buried, now," he said. "You did the right thing. It would have been wrong to let the Kanters have them like that."

I felt sickness welling up in the pit of my stomach. "How could they do it, Tinker?"

He stepped around the horse and motioned for me to climb up behind the saddle. He helped me up, and I moaned as my insides twisted up. My wounds were mostly healed now, but there was a certain amount of pain that would be with me for some time.

"They're evil," he said. "They consume human flesh and worship demons. Do they need any more reason for their madness?"

"I suppose not."

He climbed into the saddle and guided the horse through the camp, towards a deer trail that led down the south side of the mountain. We were at the edge of the woods when I heard a voice calling out my name. Tinker pulled back on the reins, and I twisted in the saddle. A moan escaped my lips as my body absorbed the strain.

"Breeze! Breeze!"

I almost laughed aloud as I saw Robie come flying out of the tents and down the hill. Shue, Jesha, and several other children from school were following him. He ran up to us and breathlessly started talking, all in one long gasping sentence:

"I saw you the other day when you flew your... plane... and you were throwing the cannon charges... down on the Kanters... It was amazing... We all saw it... Where are you going? Can I fly your plane when you get back?"

The other children swarmed up behind him. They were all smiles and waves. Very different from the last time that I had seen them. I wanted to feel happy, but I had to keep control of my emotions. I knew better than to put too much trust in anyone too quickly. "You want to fly?" I said. Robie nodded emphatically and I heard a few of the other children murmuring in agreement. "I'll be back in a few days. I'm going to need pilots. They'll need to be strong and healthy and smart. You think you can do that?"

"Yes!" Robie said. "Anything you want. I'll do anything!" Again, several others were agreeing.

"Good. I'll need no less than three but no more than five to start with. You'll have to prove yourselves. Go to Mrs. Trader and ask her about geography... Oh, and ask about engineering too."

"When will you be back?" he said

I glanced over the group, wondering if any of them could live up to my expectations. The last few days had been hard on them for certain, but prior to that they'd been simple-minded fools in my opinion. Of course, it didn't help that they'd accused me of being a spy and an assassin.

"Soon," I said. "Just be ready."

Chapter 40

Robie saluted me, and the other children followed his example. I have no idea what inspired them to do it, and I had to force myself not to break out in laughter. Thankfully, Tinker heeled the horse and we vanished into the shadows of the forest.

"You've got some powerful admirers," he said once we were down the hill a bit.

I chuckled. "So I noticed. How exactly did that happen?"

He twisted in the saddle and gave me a sideways glance. "You've changed, Breeze. I noticed it as soon as I heard you speak. You don't sound like a shy little girl anymore."

"I guess I'm not," I said. "I'm not really sure what happened. I was just trying to get things done. I found myself getting more forceful out of frustration. I found myself talking to nobles and generals as if they were children."

"Sounds about right," he murmured.

"What do you mean?"

"One thing I've learned over the years is that authority has to be taken just as much as its earned. People who get ahead in this world don't just wait around for somebody to promote them. Sure, they might work hard, but for the most part they pretty much just take what they want."

"That doesn't sound like a good thing." I was thinking of Prince Sheldon and his ambitions.

"Often it's not," he said. "But sometimes it can be a very good thing. Take General Corsan, for example. Do you know where he came from? He was a farm boy in South Bronwyr. He wanted more than a life of feeding chickens and milking cows, so he joined the army.

"He grabbed every opportunity that came along; even when he was afraid he might not be up to it. Usually, he managed to pull it off. Now he's one of the most powerful men in the kingdom, and he's right where he should be."

"How do you know so much about him?" Tinker shrugged.

"I came from South Bronwyr, too. We went to the same school for a few years. Then he took off and became a living legend. Meanwhile I finished school and grew up to be a crazy old hermit."

I laughed. "You're not crazy, Tinker. When was the last time you saw him?"

"About five years ago, shortly after I invented my black powder charges. I sold a few charges to Baron Par'Tishan so his servants could clear out some old tree stumps. He spread the word, and pretty soon the general showed up asking for a demonstration.

"I showed him how they worked and he placed a standing order. He wanted the recipe, of course, but I wouldn't give it to him. A man's got to see to his own fortune, you know." He gave me a wry smile and I laughed aloud.

"Tinker, just how much does the army pay you?"

"Well, lets just say I live in my little valley because I find palaces to be pretentious." We both laughed until my stomach started to hurt and I had to force myself to take deep, slow breaths.

I spoke to the trees a little as we descended the mountain, and they confirmed what I had suspected, that Cinder had brought me to them. She had dragged me into an irrigation ditch, and then pulled me out of danger with my body floating gently in the water. Not only had the fresh water helped to cleanse my wound, but it saved me from additional injuries I might have sustained by being dragged across the rough ground. It also kept me safely out of the Kanters' view.

Upon reaching the woods, the trees had recognized me and carried me from limb to limb across the many miles to the refugee camp. I thanked them for saving my life. The trees, as always, were quiet and gracious.

We passed a small graveyard at the base of the mountain. Actually, it wasn't so much a graveyard as a mass grave. It was in a shady grove, overlooking a small pond. It seemed a nice enough final resting place for the people who otherwise would have been food for the Kanters.

It was a sad testament to what the Kanters had done, and I felt hatred welling up inside of me. I knew the suffering that they had caused, the pain of children who no longer had parents. It served to remind me of the importance of my mission.

I was anxious as we left the shelter of the trees, but Tinker assured me that all the Kanters had moved on. "They didn't stay to defend the defeated provinces," he explained. "I guess they assumed that there weren't enough humans left to threaten them."

"That doesn't seem very smart," I said.

"It's not. There's a good chance the angry farmers who escaped their initial attack will rally, and attack the Kanters from behind. If that happens, the Kanters will be trapped between the angry mobs and the army. Personally I'd rather face the army." We both laughed at that.

It took about an hour to get to the crash site. We found the wreckage of my plane easily enough. I looked out across the plain, knowing that the Kanters were out there somewhere. Suddenly something was bothering me.

"Tinker, everyone seems to think the Kanters are mindless barbarians. Judging from how they live and fight, it seems like it's probably true."

"You'll get no argument from me."

"So how did they get smart enough to build cannons and riverboats and catapults? How did they figure out that they could put an army together with archers and footmen, or that they could disguise themselves by traveling at night and painting their swords?"

Tinker shot me a look. "What are you saying, Breeze?"

"I don't know. It just seems like... like maybe they had some help."

Tinker surveyed the damaged machines around us, and paused to scratch the stubble on his chin. "Now that you mention it, it does seem awfully sophisticated for that bunch."

"What if they had help?" I mused. "I mean, you already said you didn't think the Tal'mar were helping them, but what if somebody else did? Maybe someone who wanted to overthrow the king?"

Tinker's eyebrows narrowed and he spoke to me in calculated words. "I don't follow the intrigues of court and state, but I'm sure there are any number of people who would like to place themselves on the throne, if that's what you're getting at. I can think of a *very small number* of people with the resources to do that. Be very careful about what you say, and who you say it to, Breeze. This line of reasoning borders on treasonous, and the penalty for treason is death."

"I understand." I wanted to push the subject, but Tinker was clearly uncomfortable with it. Even out there, with scarcely a living thing around us, he was afraid someone might overhear our conversation. It gave me a chill.

The more I thought about it, the more certain I was that someone had put the Kanters up to it. It just made sense. They were too primitive to have the technology that they were using, and I couldn't imagine what would have motivated them. They didn't seem to be the nation-conquering type.

Unfortunately, even making the accusation was enough to get me killed. In fact, being a half-breed Tal'mar had almost been enough to get me killed. I didn't want to think of what tortures might lie in store for a genuine Tal'mar traitor.

I forced the problem to the back of my mind. For now I had more immediate problems. Like getting the gearboxes, controls, and cables out of my old plane. Tinker and I set to work on gathering what we could and discarding those parts that were damaged beyond repair. The gearboxes were intact, but one of the springs had been destroyed by the cannonball. Tinker used leather thongs to compress the remaining springs and then he tied them to the saddle.

I also found my old sword among the wreckage. I never had used that thing. I unsheathed it and held it for a moment, remembering the day I'd found it up in the rafters of Tinker's barn, buried in a box of old weapons. It was a good memory. A simpler time.

"You still have that thing?" Tinker said.

I smiled. I shoved the blade home and tucked it under my belt. I didn't care if I wouldn't ever use it; I wanted it with me. I wanted to keep that memory.

I turned back to the work. Within an hour, we were back on our way.

Chapter 41

Tinker spent the entire night modifying the plane. I helped him throughout the evening, until I finally became so exhausted that I fell asleep on a stool in the barn with my head resting on the table. Tinker must have taken pity on me, because I woke the next morning in the windmill, curled up on that dusty old bench.

The rest had done me good. I could feel the changes in my body; that I had healed considerably since my accident. In fact, I was quite ready to go on another mission.

I wandered back to the barn, and found Tinker there, still working. He had been up all night.

"It looks great!" I said. The barn doors were thrown wide to make room to remove the plane, and the morning sun splashed across the fresh paint.

"As you can see I've given it the same paint scheme as the last. I'm not sure if it ever helped or not, considering that you were shot down…"

"It helps," I assured him. "That never would have happened if I hadn't been flying so low. How did you manage to fit two seats in there?" I didn't notice it until I got up close. Tinker had cut open the top of the fuselage, just like before, only now there were two seats. They looked a little out of place on the smaller plane, and I was a bit worried about whether it could actually carry the extra weight.

"The opening is slightly larger," he said. "And unfortunately, the seats are smaller. But I figured you'd need to carry passengers while you were getting your pilots around. At least until you have your new planes."

"I suppose I will." I hadn't even thought about that. Once again, Tinker did what he did best.

He went to the rear of the fuselage and opened the stow compartment. "If you look here, you'll see that I've modified the spring assembly slightly. I've replaced one with a slightly heavier version."

"What will that do?"

He shot me an exhausted smile. "That remains to be seen. The concept however, is to allow you longer flights. If my theory is correct, you'll be able to double your distance by dropping into the highest gear once you reach altitude."

"That's fantastic!"

"Yes, well that's the good news. It seemed prudent, considering what lies between us and the Borderlands. I didn't want you making any unnecessary landings. The bad news is that you will fly slower. The overall flight will probably take about twenty-five percent longer."

I listened carefully as he spoke, and I began to circle the plane. "How much weight can it carry?"

"That remains to be seen. You may be able to carry more than before because you have a smaller, lighter fuselage. On the other hand, the wingspan of this plane is smaller."

"All right, we'd better not push it too much. This is going to take a few trips..."

And it did. I started by flying a stack of three gearboxes and a set of springs up to the airbase at Relian Keep. While I was there, I apologized to General

Corsan for not having his maps. After I explained the situation, he was more than understanding. It helped that I had a firm grasp of geography, and I was able to point out the Kanters' most recent locations.

"How fast are they moving?" he said.

"Faster, now that they've got the cannons repaired. But I still don't think they'll cover twenty miles a day."

"Excellent. If you're right, we'll beat them to Anora, and they'll have a bit of a surprise waiting for them. When will your planes be ready?"

"By the end of the week. But not if I sit here all day chatting." The general laughed and shooed me off.

On the return trip I took a small collection of Tinker's tools and two more springs, the last of them. The third and most interesting trip was when I brought Tinker himself. It was the next morning. He protested at first, trying to say that the smiths should be able to finish the work without him.

"Not a chance," I said. "All they know how to make is horseshoes. Besides, I'll also need your help for the assembly process. The Tal'mar are making the fuselages but they won't touch the steel."

He wandered into the barn mumbling something to himself, and returned with his heavy leather jacket, a flight cap, and a pair of goggles. It was then, as I saw him eyeing the plane uncomfortably, that I realized he had developed a phobia.

It must have happened when he first crashed the glider and broke his leg. When that happened, I think it reminded Tinker of his mortality, or made him conscious of it. I remembered how I had insisted on flying after the crash. I wondered now if that had been a mistake. Perhaps if Tinker had gotten right back in the air, this new fear wouldn't have developed. I felt sad and partly responsible for the look of dread he wore.

I could almost feel the anxiety emanating off him as we towed the plane down to the field, and guilt welled up inside of me. "It's okay to be afraid," I said as we drove out onto the field. He shot me a nervous glance.

What do you mean?"

"I mean that I know how you feel."

He set his jaw and mumbled, "I'll be fine. Let's just get this over with."

The seats were considerably smaller than the comfy one in my old plane, but they were still better than sitting on the floor. I hopped in the front and grabbed the controls, and then waited patiently as Tinker lumbered into the back. I felt him tense up as I increased the throttle and we went bouncing across the field. Then I heard him moan as the plane lifted off the ground. I tried not to laugh.

I headed northwest, building up the altitude I needed to pass over the mountains. I'd found that it was worth the extra turbulence flying in this direction, because it cut my flight time by more than a third. So despite the fact that this plane was slower than the last, I was actually making the trip more quickly. That made it possible to check up on the Kanters and see how they were progressing, but I wasn't eager to get too close to them.

Tinker wasn't happy about the turbulence, though. The first time we started to drop, I feared he might just jump out of the plane. Then we bounced back up and he groaned like a sick child. A bit later, when we passed over the mountains, the icy cold wind took his mind off his fear.

"Is it always like this?" he said. I glanced back at him and saw ice crystals forming on his beard stubble.

"It's a lot colder over the mountains," I yelled. "But it's a lot faster."

"Keep going then."

Chapter 42

Tinker was amazed when he saw the landing strip that General Corsan had built. "They really did want the plane, didn't they?"

"You have no idea."

We touched down on the smooth runway and parked in front of the hangar. I had gotten to know several soldiers in the process of transporting parts back and forth, and I brought Tinker into the hangar and made a few introductions. While we were talking, General Corsan showed up. He offered Tinker a handshake.

"It's been a long time," he said grimly. "I'm glad you're here."

"Me too," said Tinker. "Sorry that last shipment was late. I was a little distracted."

The general laughed. "I suppose you were." He put a hand on my shoulder. "Now that we all know about Breeze, I think we understand. When you're ready, the smiths are on the west side of the building. Just a word of warning though, you've got your work cut out for you... Breeze, I need a word with you in private."

Tinker wandered off to find the blacksmiths, and I followed the general back to the keep. As we entered his planning room, he gestured for me to sit. He dropped into his own chair and shot me an indecipherable glare.

"What's the matter?" I said. He'd been unusually quiet, and I had an apprehensive feeling growing inside of me.

He reached into a drawer and produced an envelope. "Do you know what this is?" he said.

I accepted the envelope and pulled out a pile of papers. They were covered in some strange foreign script. "I can't read it," I said. "What language is that?"

"It's Kantrayan."

My heart stammered as I stared at the awkward scrawls. "Are you sure?"

"Without a doubt."

"What does it mean?"

He grinned mirthfully. "The Kanters don't write. Their language is crude, barbaric. Their alphabet consists of thirteen letters, which makes it easy to scratch their lunatic ravings onto cave walls. But to my knowledge, the Kanters never developed the ability to make paper and pens."

As I examined the paper, it occurred to me that the writing looked quite flowing, not at all the way I would expect a Kanter to write. The letters may have been correct, but they weren't crude. They were written by a hand accustomed to the use of pen and paper. "Then who wrote this?"

"That's the other problem. One of my men found that letter among Prince Sheldon's personal things."

I met the general's stare with a confounded look. "You've been spying on him?"

"I didn't get this far in life without knowing my enemies. I knew the prince was up to something from the way he'd been behaving the last few months. His behavior was getting more paranoid and erratic by the day. And his frequent trips... Until now, I had assumed he was preparing a legal case against me. I thought he was going to have me removed from command. I didn't think he might be involved in something like this."

"Treason, you mean?" I said. "I did."

The general raised an eyebrow. "Really?"

"Yes. Yesterday, when I spoke to Analyn she said the reason he was posted at Relian Keep was because he was a danger to Prince Talanar. He has ambitions for the throne. Of course, I'd already seen the way he acted, and I didn't trust him.

"Then I thought about the way the Kanters have been behaving. The way they had built riverboats and catapults... it seemed beyond their ability. Almost like they had help."

"Agreed. What else?"

I pursed my lips. I'd had another thought, but I hadn't had much time to consider it. "The Kanters went straight towards Anora and the Borderlands. They've gone right through the countryside. They haven't even left guards behind. They're completely exposed from the rear. It's like they're working towards a goal, something specific."

"I thought as much myself. I believe Sheldon's plan is to cripple my army here and then move towards the capital. So here's what it comes down to: I need two things from you. First, deliver a letter to the king. In it, I explain everything. Second, I need evidence. I need you to go south, into the Badlands, and find proof."

Chapter 43

So there it was. Despite my best efforts and my illusions of being in control, the general was still going to use me like a tool. Instead of rising above his intrigues, I was about to become part of them. I wasn't sure how I felt about that.

"Where's the prince now?" I said.

"On one of his trips. He said he was traveling to the capital, to personally inform the king about our treaty with the Tal'mar."

"You don't believe him?"

Corsan settled back in his chair and laced his fingers behind his head. "I don't believe anything Sheldon says. That doesn't mean it isn't true. He could quite possibly be on his way to the capital. He could also be conniving with the Kanters right now."

"How can I get the proof that you want?"

He pointed to a spot on his map. It was about five hundred miles south of Riverfork. "The Kanters' leader is a warlord named Keng'Sun. His tribe is based here, among these cliffs. I don't know if he's with the army or not, so you'll have to be careful. You'll need to get into his home, and find more papers like this letter."

"How do you know all this?"

The general winked. "I wouldn't be a very good general if I didn't." He rose from his desk, and for the first time since I'd arrived, offered me a genuine smile. "The Tal'mar will be expecting a delivery of parts by tomorrow, or the next day at the latest. You've got a lot of flying to do between now and then."

"Suddenly I'm exhausted," I said. He laughed.

"You're in good company. Don't worry, I have faith in you." Somehow, that made me feel even more tired. I started towards the door, but then paused as I saw the general throwing on his jacket and cap. It was the first time I'd ever seen him wearing a full uniform.

"Why are you all dressed up?" I said.

"I'm leaving. As much as I'd love to stay here and twiddle my thumbs, I've got a war to attend. My men are almost in position, and the Tal'mar have been streaming across the channel for the last two days. We're confronting the Kanters on the field south of Anora."

That was a sobering thought. I suddenly realized that this could be the last time we'd meet. "Be careful," I said.

"Don't worry about me. You just get those planes in the air. I'll be looking for you, day after tomorrow."

"I'll be there," I promised.

I found Tinker at the smithy. He was instructing several men at once, apparently giving them a crash course in foundry. "Tinker, I have to go."

"Just a moment gentlemen." He came over next to me and whispered, "What's going on? I thought we had a couple of days to deliver these parts."

"We do. It's something else." His eyes narrowed as I said this. I spoke carefully, in a hushed whisper: "It's what we spoke about yesterday, at the crash site. Remember my suspicions about the Kanters? I was right."

229

Tinker's face grew very serious, and he leaned in close. "This is dangerous business, Breeze. Can't someone else do this?"

I shook my head. "You know I'm the only one Tinker. I'll be okay. Just focus on getting those parts made." He gave me a big hug and, before turning back to the men said:

"You be careful, Breeze."

I took to the air with the intent of flying straight to the capital and delivering the general's message to King Ryshan, but I soon thought better of it. First came the realization that Prince Sheldon might actually be there. If he saw me, it would be difficult to explain my presence to him, and if the King didn't take the general's message well, then I might be headed straight for the gallows.

That thought sparked the memory of my previous experiences, particularly when the Tal'mar had jailed me as soon as I'd landed. It was quite possible that the king's guards would do the same, and there was no guarantee that he'd get around to hearing my case any time soon, or that he'd ever see that letter.

With that thought firmly in mind, I turned south and headed straight for Kantraya. I hated to do that to the general, but I figured I'd better follow the more important course. If he wanted to toss me in the dungeon for it, he'd have to catch me first.

It was a mind-numbingly long flight, made interesting only by my occasional stops to rewind the plane's springs. It was already dusk by the time I passed over the southern border of Astatia and entered Kantraya.

The landscape had long since become a barren plain, marked only by plateaus and occasional oases. There was a certain simple beauty to the land, despite the fact that I knew the Kanters were down there. Fortunately, I was at a high enough altitude that I couldn't see the piles of skulls and human bones. Soon enough I would see them all too well.

As night crawled across the land, navigation became exceedingly difficult. Using my maps while flying –and in the dark- was a haphazard endeavor at best. Especially considering that the maps of this territory were nearly a hundred years old, and were almost void of significant landmarks

It was about ten o'clock when I finally found what I was looking for. On the map, it appeared to be an especially large plateau, but in reality it was a volcano. A partially active volcano.

There was a full moon but I had little concern that the Kanters would spot my plane in the darkness. I circled over their village a few times from a high altitude, getting a feel for the layout of the place, and then landed about a mile away. It was an incredibly smooth touchdown. The dry desert soil was hard as stone, and almost perfectly flat. Even the paved road that the general had built wasn't as smooth as that barren land.

After landing, I waited in the plane for a while. I wanted to be sure that I hadn't been seen. I was ready for a quick take-off in case anyone appeared.

I got a new appreciation for the desert landscape while I sat there. The horizon was like the edge of a giant ball, perfectly smooth and slightly curved. The stars flashed overhead like radiant jewels, and the moon cast pale, silver light across the foreign terrain.

Plateaus and tall, smooth spires appeared at random, and in the dark they looked like the ruins of some ancient alien civilization.

I observed this strange beauty for several minutes, until I was certain that I could safely leave the plane. Then I gave Cinder a firm command to wait for me, and I headed towards the village.

The light of torches and bonfires were clearly visible in the distance, and I made a conscious effort to hide myself in the shadows as I crept closer. It wasn't long before I heard the voices and saw the huge, lumbering shapes of the Kanters moving up ahead.

The village was a mish-mash of strange, rudimentary construction. Lean-to tents lined the outer perimeter, facing in towards a group of small buildings. Some of these buildings were made from stone and adobe while others appeared to be made from animal hides stitched together and stretched tight over poles.

The buildings formed a half-circle that faced a pyramid at the base of the volcano. The entire thing was carved from the stone face of the mountain. The walls were of smooth stone, but a row of steps in the front climbed up to the sacrificial altar at the top. Even in the darkness, I could see bloodstained stones. They were blackened from centuries of human sacrifice.

I could feel power emanating from that altar, though at first it was just a nervous tingle in my chest. As I got closer, I realized that it was more than nerves. The altar had absorbed the life of those sacrifices, the energy of human souls, and had become a strange epicenter of dark magical energies. It was like a demonic presence, like an entity staring at me with eyes of cold stone. I shuddered as I look at it, and a chill crawled down my spine. I knew exactly how I'd end up, if I got caught.

Chapter 44

I snuck around the outside perimeter of the village and crept closer to the pyramid. I could feel the energy growing, pressing against me like an invisible force. I felt my guts twisting up with sickness. I couldn't explain it, but it was evil. It was as if the pyramid had stored up all those years of suffering and madness, and now projected it outwards. I had to wonder how many people had been sacrificed there over the centuries.

I watched the Kanters eat their meals and begin to settle in for the night, and I waited patiently for the right moment. As I watched, my eyes adjusted to the flickering light of their camp, and I began to take note of things. Their campfires were not lined with stones, they were surrounded by human skulls. Their buildings and tents were decorated similarly, with the bones and skulls of their victims dangling from leather thongs or nailed into wooden posts. I realized with a sickening certainty that the skins used to make their tents were likely *not* the skins of animals. I had to force the bile down my throat.

I had a powerful urge to get back in my plane and go get some of Tinker's cannon charges. I wanted to level that place to the ground. I managed to keep that emotion in check by focusing on my mission. Somewhere, in one of those buildings, I had to find proof that Sheldon had been working with the Kanters. I had no idea what I might be looking for, but I knew I had to find *something*.

The moon slid down towards the horizon, and one by one, the Kanters began to slip into the dream world. I was growing anxious. I could feel my opportunity approaching. Then, to my surprise, I suddenly heard the ringing *clip-clop* of horseshoes against stone.

The Kanters were almost all asleep by then, but as soon as they heard that sound they leapt to their feet and went careening into their tents and homes. The males emerged carrying long spears and knives made from sharpened bone. The women and children slipped inside their dwellings and stayed there.

The warriors gathered at the far side of the village and then made a commotion as their visitors arrived. To my surprise, I heard the sound of cheering. The oddness of the situation struck me at once. I knew already that the Kanters didn't ride horses. I'd never even seen a horse that could have carried a full-grown Kanter.

Tal'mar didn't ride horses either. They preferred the quick stealth of traveling among the tree branches. That left only one possibility. Humans had arrived.

I bent forward and stared unblinking into that crowd, straining for a glimpse of the humans. Eventually, when the Kanters settled down and started walking back into the village, I saw them. I was not surprised. Prince Sheldon was there, with a dozen guards. He spoke to the Kanters in their growling, guttural language for several minutes. They questioned him and listened expectantly to his answers, and several times, they all broke into laughter. Then I heard a shout and everyone turned towards one of the buildings. The Kanter who emerged could only have been the Warlord Keng'Sun.

He stooped as he exited the tall doorway, and I heard the clinking of the dried skulls he wore on his necklace. Once outside, he stood erect and I almost gasped. He was easily fifteen feet tall. His body rippled with muscles, and his skin glistened with sweat. The tattoos that covered his body seemed to dance in the firelight. He stretched, and his bones cracked like hammers against anvils. Then he turned to face Sheldon, and bellowed out a deep, guttural laugh. I cringed as I saw the sharp, yellow teeth that lined his mouth.

Sheldon strode forward, and bowed down before the giant. His guards stepped into the clearing behind him, following his lead. The prince said something in Kanter, but the Warlord responded in the common tongue.

"At last you return," he bellowed. "Have you come to reward us for a great victory?"

"Indeed I have," Sheldon said. "The land itself quakes beneath the strength of your army."

Keng'Sun's laughter was like a drum. "Come, human. Let us discuss these matters." He turned away from the crowd and went strolling towards the pyramid. Sheldon and his men followed. I caught my breath and slipped back into the shadows, making myself as small as possible.

I know they couldn't see me down there in the corner, but I swear the warlord paused and looked right at me as he started climbing those stairs. I cast my eyes down, fearful that they might reflect the light and give me away. Keng'Sun grunted, and resumed his climb.

Most everyone in the village looked on as the group climbed up towards the altar. I heard the scraping sound of stone against stone, and their voices disappeared inside the mountain. The villagers returned to their campfires and began to speak amongst themselves. I started looking for an alternate path up the pyramid.

The stones were smooth on the outside walls, but they weren't flawless. I found that they were riddled with cracks large enough to accommodate my fingers. The mountainside at the edge of the pyramid was also quite rough, and easily allowed me to begin making my way up. I had to move slowly of course, taking great care not to make a sound. I moved a few inches at a time, pausing often to survey the village below and make sure that no one was looking in my direction.

I was breathless by the time I reached the top, but I forced myself to keep moving. There was a tall stone door behind the altar, and it stood partially open. There was no clever engineering that allowed the door to open; it required brute force. I doubted any of the humans inside could have opened that door without a Kanter's help.

I crept up behind the altar, ignoring the wild magic that disrupted my senses and the nausea that twisted at my guts. I took a good look at my surroundings. Once I was certain that it was safe, I slipped inside.

The doorway opened into a steep tunnel that twisted down into the mountain. Sheldon and his men had brought torches with them, but I had to rely on my night vision. Fortunately, my vision was quite functional in this dark environment. Even the pale starlight that streamed down from the entrance was enough to light my way.

Where the path became too steep to accommodate easy passage, the Kanters had carved stairs into the floor. This allowed for a quick descent, and within a few moments, I had reached the end of the tunnel.

I approached the opening cautiously, my senses trained on the voices in the room beyond. As I got closer, I realized that the room was in fact the crater of the volcano itself. I crept up to the doorway, kneeling in the shadows, to spy on the men. I saw them standing in a group about ten yards away. They were surrounded by pools and streams of lava. Waves of heat radiated out of the volcanic core, sucking a constant stream of cool air in through the tunnel as the warmer air rose into the night.

Sheldon and the warlord were talking –mostly in common language now- about how the war had been going. "The troops ran into some trouble with the cannons," he explained, "but they were easily replaced. Unfortunately, it did leave us a few days behind schedule. The Borderlands have not yet been attacked, and even now the general is preparing to confront your army."

"The general knows we are coming?"

"Yes. You understand that this changes things?"

The warlord made a grand gesture, throwing his hands in the air. "This is not my FAULT! We did everything you said!"

"Nonetheless, your men have failed." It was clear from the prince's tone that something was going on. I got the impression that Sheldon was somehow trying to alter their agreement. Keng'Sun pointed a long finger at Sheldon.

"You promised us land! You promised us food!" I could see some of the men drawing their swords, and

Keng'Sun noticed it too. "Betrayer!" he shouted. He rushed forward, swinging a massive fist at Sheldon, but the guards leapt between the two, brandishing their swords. The warlord stopped in his tracks, and Sheldon backed up a few steps.

"You didn't really think I'd turn over half of my kingdom to an animal like you, did you?"

The warlord's eyes went wild with rage. As if proving Sheldon's statement true, he threw his head back and roared. "I'll kill you human!" he shouted.

Sheldon's men started swinging their swords, but killing Keng'Sun was about to prove harder then they'd expected. He moved, and his limbs became a blur.

Two of the closest men thrust out their swords, trying to stab him in the gut. Keng'Sun twisted sideways, displaying surprising agility as he picked the first man up by the head and threw him. The warlord caught the second man with a backhand as he spun around, and I heard the unmistakable sound of the guard's neck breaking.

Chapter 45

The rest of the men fell back. It was obvious that none of them could take the warlord down individually. They needed to attack him as a unit. Unfortunately, they couldn't get close enough to hit him without getting in each other's way. This compounded the problem that Keng'Sun had turned out to be a much better fighter than they had expected. I saw a look in their eyes, and it was terror. Sheldon however, was too stupid to realize it. He continued taunting the warlord.

"Your army will rush in to attack Anora tomorrow, and the general will be waiting for them. In the meanwhile, the reinforcements I have requested from King Ryshan will fall in to cut off their retreat. Your army will be slaughtered."

Keng'Sun laughed when he heard that. "Your plan is falling apart, little man. You might defeat me, but you'll never gain the throne."

Sheldon threw his head back and gave the warlord a haughty stare. "Not so. While the King's personal guard is busy cutting off your army's retreat, the King will be assassinated -by one of your men, of course. And then, after I assume the throne, I'll come back here and crush you. You've left your entire country unguarded you fool. When I'm done this land will be scoured clean, and your entire filthy race will be eradicated."

Keng'Sun flew into a rage. He started kicking and swinging, and all the men around him had to jump out of his way. A few tried to rush in behind him, but the warlord was far too quick for that. He spun around and caught one of them by the arm. He ripped the man's arm out of the socket and tossed it aside. The man dropped to the ground, screaming. Two fell back but another rushed in and managed to stab Keng'Sun in the back of the leg. The warlord threw his arm back, slamming it into the soldier's chest. The volcano echoed with the sound of breaking bones as the man's rib cage was crushed. He died instantly.

It was then that I noticed a change in Sheldon's face. I think he was starting to realize that his men weren't doing so well. "Kill him!" he shouted. "Kill the dog!"

The guards went mad, cutting and slashing wildly. The Warlord anticipated their moves, and danced just out of reach. I heard screams as men fell, their bodies broken. The warlord let out an occasional howl as one of the blades struck him, but never more than a glancing blow.

It was beginning to look like everyone in the room was going to die. Except Sheldon, of course. He was slowly but surely backing towards the tunnel... towards me! Unfortunately, by the time I realized this, it was already too late.

Sheldon spun around and plunged headlong towards the tunnel, and I had no choice but to step out of the shadows and start running. There was a split second where our eyes met, and Sheldon almost tripped.

"YOU!" he shouted. I turned and ran.

I heard rather than saw Keng'Sun's reaction as he realized Sheldon was escaping. "SHELDON!" he roared, and the sound of his voice went booming

241

through the tunnel. There was a clash of weapons and a chorus of screams. I glanced back down the tunnel as I ran. I saw Prince Sheldon's shadowy figure running full tilt behind me, and I saw a large, dark shadow appear behind him. I didn't wait to see more. I put on a burst of speed and ran for my life.

Chapter 46

I was already thinking ahead as I ran. In a few seconds, I was going to emerge at the top of the pyramid. Judging by the screams echoing up the tunnel from behind me, my exit would not go unnoticed. Sheldon was hot on my tail, and my best guess was that Keng'Sun was right behind him. The odds of any of us escaping alive were getting slimmer by the second.

The only consolation I had was that if they caught me, they were certainly going to catch Sheldon too. Which meant his plan to assassinate King Ryshan and steal the throne was as good as dead. I hadn't planned on this turning into a suicide mission, but if it turned out that way, at least I could die knowing I had saved the people I cared about.

The first thing I noticed as I plunged through the doorway was that the moon had set. The land was very dark now, which was going to work to my advantage, if I could get past the Kanters. The bad news was that the Kanters had grouped up at the base of the pyramid, and they were waiting for us with spears and torches.

I heard Sheldon's heavy footsteps behind me and I stepped aside, pressing myself back up against the wall next to the door. He plowed out of the doorway and came to a screeching halt as he saw the angry crowd of giants waiting at the base of the stairs. He spun around and saw me standing next to the doorway. And he joined me

Time seemed to stop as we stood there shoulder to shoulder, with our backs pressed up against the cold stone. He was breathing heavily and he held a short sword tightly in his right hand. His clothes were soaked with sweat, and I cringed at his touch.

I looked away from him, and was again awed by the natural splendor of that place. That brilliant starry sky spanned the horizon in front of us, and it seemed such an ironic contrast, not only to what the place was, but to what I had just witnessed. Out of the corner of my eye, I saw Sheldon watching me.

All I could think to say was, "Beautiful night, huh?"

Sheldon looked at me like I was stark raving mad. Then he followed my gaze across the desert. He shrugged and nodded weakly. "Yes."

I heard the heavy *thud, thud* of Keng'Sun's boots coming up the tunnel. Then, a half-second later, he burst through the door. He didn't even pause as he went plunging headlong down the stairs. He was halfway down before he realized what the frantic screams of his subservients were telling him. By that time, Sheldon's guards were piling out of the doorway, providing a buffer between us and the warlord. As they squared off for battle, Sheldon decided to take advantage of the opportunity. The next thing I knew, his sword was at my throat.

"Where is it?" he hissed.

"What?"

"The airplane. That flying contraption of yours. Where is it?"

My eyes rolled to the south, and he followed my gaze. "All right, then. Let's go." He grabbed me by the back of the neck and shoved me off the side of the pyramid. My feet went out from underneath me, and suddenly I was on my back, sliding down that smooth stone wall. I flung my arms out wildly, trying to stabilize myself as I plummeted towards the ground.

Sheldon was right behind me. I realized that if I didn't get out of his way, he'd crush me at the bottom. I could think of only one thing to do. A split-second before hitting the ground, I pushed my weight up onto my feet, and launched myself out of the way. I somersaulted forward through the air and came down on my feet about ten feet away from the base of the pyramid. Behind me, Sheldon slammed into the ground so hard it knocked his breath out.

I can credit my Tal'mar ancestry for the grace that allowed me to come out of that on my feet. I didn't waste a second. I spun around and started running, not towards my plane but towards the far side of the village. Sheldon and his guards had arrived on horseback. I now reached out to those horses with my mind and sent them a command: "HOME!" I filled their minds with images of lush green pastures and blue, flowing streams. This was all the permission they needed. The horses had been trained to stand immobile when saddled and riderless, but they now ignored that training, and headed for home at full speed. I was right behind them as they broke into a gallop across the desert. That was when I heard Sheldon scream behind me.

"NO! What are you doing?"

I glanced back at Sheldon and saw several Kanters bearing down on him. I didn't wait to see how it turned out. I ran.

My heart was exploding in my chest by the time I got to the plane. I breathlessly greeted Cinder and leapt into the pilot's seat. All around me I could hear screams in the night, the sound of both humans and Kanters spilling their blood on the thirsty desert.

The fight wasn't over yet, but I wasn't going to stay for the rest of it. I had a pretty good idea of how it was going to end, and I had no desire to share the fate that awaited Prince Sheldon. I hit the throttle and took to the sky.

I thought long and hard about what I'd tell the general when I got back. After all, he'd sent me to find evidence of Sheldon's betrayal. I had done that, but not in any tangible form. I had nothing concrete to offer. No letters, no plans, just what I had witnessed with my own eyes.

I couldn't imagine the general going to King Ryshan with no more than the word of a half-breed. But I was also relatively certain that Sheldon wasn't going to be returning. I hoped that would be enough.

Chapter 47

I got back to the keep in the middle of the night. Tinker was busy training his engineers when I parked in front of the hangar. They had constructed a work area along the western side of the building, close to the existing smithy. They now had a large smelting furnace. The heat radiated off and hit me in a wave as I walked around the building.

Tinker was dressed in a long leather apron and wearing his heavy gloves and welding goggles. One of his trainees was assisting him in removing a jar of melted iron from the oven. Tinker shot me a smile when he saw me, and I waved. I watched from a safe distance as they twisted the long rods, turning the jar over into the molds. When it was done, Tinker threw off his gloves and ran over to greet me.

He threw his arms around me. He smelled like iron and sulfur and old sweaty leather, and suddenly I felt like I was right back at home. "Making gears?" I said as he pulled away.

"You remember! This is the same process we used when I trained you."

"I remember," I said with a grin. "How's it going?"

Tinker walked over to one of the tables under the canopy, and gestured at several rows of gears. "That's the last batch, the one we just poured. We'll be able to start assembling the boxes in a few hours."

"Excellent. What about the springs?"

"We're progressing slower on that front. I've got five smiths, but teaching them a correct temper is like teaching a pig to fly."

"Well you never know what might happen," I said. Tinker laughed.

"I was worried about you, Breeze. Did you find what you were looking for?"

"More or less. I think the situation has been taken care of." I think he guessed from my tone that it wasn't something we could talk about. Not at the moment, anyway. "When will the springs be ready?"

"Tomorrow."

"I need them tonight Tinker. We still have to do final assembly on those planes, and the general is expecting them in the air tomorrow. They *have* to be in the air tomorrow."

He wiped the sweat from his brow with the back of his sleeve. "In that case, they'll be ready tonight."

I smiled. "Thanks, Tinker. I'm going to need you in Tal'mar for the assembly."

"I'll get packed." I spun around and started walking towards my plane on the runway.

"Where are you going now?" Tinker shouted.

"To get some pilots!"

I flew south over the mountains until midmorning, and then landed near the base of the mountain below the refugee camp. It was a bit of a hike up the hill to the camp, but I was too excited to notice. I practically ran halfway up the mountain. Robie saw me coming. He had a group of five children, including himself, lined up and waiting for me.

They saluted me as I approached and I had to hide my smile. I had almost forgotten Robie's attitude. It had been funny at first, but now it occurred to me that this might actually be useful. With humans and Tal'mar living and working together for the first time in thousands of years, there were bound to be some rough spots. A militaristic sort of discipline might be just what we'd need to hold our group together.

"Welcome back, Sir!" he said. I didn't bother to point out that I was in fact a ma'am. I knew what he meant.

"Are these our recruits?" I said.

"Yessir!"

I walked along the line, and paused at the end. The last recruit was a ten-year-old girl. I bent over to look her in the face. "You want to be a pilot?" I said.

"Yessir!" she said, imitating Robie the best she could. I smiled.

"What's your name?"

"Angela."

"I see. Well Angela, I admire your guts. The problem is, you're a bit short for our planes. Too short to be a pilot. If I come back next summer, do you think you can grow between now and then?"

"I will, I promise!"

"Good. Run along, then. Tell your parents you need some good hard work and a good dinner so you can grow up to be a pilot."

"Yessir!"

She turned and ran back to the camp. The rest of the pilots were grinning broadly as I brought my attention back to them. "Are you all packed?"

"We weren't expecting you so soon," Robie said apologetically.

"That's fine. I only have room for two at a time. Decide who's first and meet me at the bottom of the mountain. That'll give the rest of you time to pack."

"Kalen, Jesha, MOVE OUT!" Robie shouted. They took off at a full run.

"You don't want to be first?" I said, surprised.

"I do want to be first," Robie said. "But I can't make sure they've all packed right unless I'm here."

Before leaving, I found Daran and Analyn in their tent. Daran was still bedridden, but more out of caution than necessity. I understood, considering the man had suffered a broken neck. Analyn invited me in and we exchanged a hug.

"You've grown!" Daran said.

I hadn't even thought about it, but I suddenly realized I was slightly taller than Analyn. I had put on several inches of height since the night he was injured a week ago. Perhaps when I had to heal my own injury, I had somehow stimulated my growth... I shrugged, not wanting to make a big deal of it.

"Tal'mar children grow up fast," I said.

"Very fast," he agreed. "I never knew that. I wonder what else we don't know?"

"You'll find out soon," I said.

"Is it finally over, then?" Analyn said. "Is the war over?"

"The Tal'mar and humans are allies now, if that's what you mean. Kanters are pressing the Borderlands now. I'm doing my best to get these planes in the air because General Corsan is leading his men into battle tomorrow, and they're going to need air support."

"That's a lot of responsibility," she said. There wasn't any way to respond to that. It was true, of course. It was so true that I didn't even want to think about it. Even if the alliance of Tal'mar and humans was successful, it would not be without cost. The sooner I had those planes in the air, the fewer lives would be lost.

"I've got to go," I said sadly. "There's too much to be done still." Analyn embraced me.

"Don't take it all on those young shoulders," she said. "You didn't start this war." I looked in her eyes when she pulled back, and I wanted desperately to tell her what had happened to Prince Sheldon, but the time wasn't right. Instead, I just smiled and said "Goodbye."

Chapter 48

As I wandered down to my plane I thought about the way Robie had been acting, and I had to wonder if he was being ambitious or if he fell into that leadership role naturally. I thought back to the time I'd spent with him in school. He'd always been the largest boy, and in my opinion had been kind of a bully. The girls seemed to adore him, but I was convinced that it was as much about his nobility as anything else. Now I wasn't so sure. He actually did seem to have a certain charisma. I shook my head. It must have been a human thing.

Kalen and Jesha arrived a few minutes later, and I helped them stow their bags. Jesha wasn't thrilled about having to share a seat with Kalen, but she forgot all about it as soon as I hit the throttle.

With all the extra weight it took almost twice the usual distance to get in the air, and my overall speed was considerably slower. It was immediately clear that this version of our plane was going to have to be temporary. I could already feel stresses building in the airframe. The thought of retiring the plane saddened me, but I was also anxious to see what the Tal'mar had waiting. Of course, somewhere in the back of my mind was the deep fear that the Tal'mar planes would be completely useless. I knew that their woodworking was beyond excellent, but building an aircraft was a whole different thing.

It was just after noon when we got back to the airfield. We went straight to the hangar. We were all starved, so we fixed plates of cold meat and bread from the food Kalen and Jesha had packed. Tinker wandered in while we were eating. He cast a glance at the two of them.

"Only two?" he mused.

"The first two," I said. "I expect seven or eight by tomorrow. Tinker, meet Jesha and Kalen." Tinker shook their hands. I stuffed the last chunk of bread into my mouth and rose from the table. "I've got to get back in the air," I said. "Tinker, maybe you can show them what you've been working on?"

"With pleasure. Be careful, Breeze." I smiled and tossed my leather jacket over my shoulder. As I taxied to the landing strip I saw Jesha and Kalen helping Tinker assemble gear boxes. I waved at him. He was grinning from ear to ear. His work had never gotten so much attention before. Now it seemed everyone was interested in tinkering.

The rest of the evening was a flurry. I made my return flight with Robie and an older boy named Danil. That took about four hours altogether. Then I set out for Tal'mar with Robie and a collection of gearboxes.

It was well after dark when we reached Silverspire, but the Tal'mar had a lit runway waiting for me. The queen had ordered lamps installed along the main road that led right into the city gates, so that even in the worst weather, pilots could always find their way home. The reception I received was considerably different than it had been the first time.

As soon as I'd landed, two soldiers came running up to me. I recognized one of them from my previous visit. "We've been waiting for you, Breeze!" he said cheerfully. "Your planes are almost done."

I felt a light catch in my throat as he used my name. I didn't even know the man, but he greeted me like we were old friends. "Excellent," I said. I hopped down and opened up the tail stow. "I have a batch of gear boxes..."

"Allow us," he gestured for me to move aside, and started piling the boxes up in his partner's arms. Then, once they were both loaded, he gestured with a nod to follow. "Your planes are just around the corner. I'm sure you'll want a look at them."

Robie and I followed him through the gate. We took a sharp right turn, and there they were. The planes were located in a park at the edge of the city, scattered amongst the scenery like garden statues. And beautiful they were. I gasped as I saw them.

I forgot everything else, and approached with a certain disbelieving awe. At a distance, they look very similar to my old plane, but as I got closer, I realized they were much more. The Tal'mar design was sleeker, much more refined. The wingspan was slightly larger, and yet the construction looked lighter. The pilot's seat was more spacious, and there was room for the flight controls and gauges to be mounted directly in front of the pilot.

The overall design was much friendlier, both in aerodynamics and comfort. The word *perfected* came to mind. When Tinker had built my plane, it had been a natural progression. It was a long process of finding out what worked and what didn't, and then altering the design accordingly. The result was something that was very functional, but nothing spectacular to look it.

These planes addressed that issue and then some. I could hardly believe they were made from wood.

Robie and I strolled among them for about ten minutes, in awe of the perfect craftsmanship. There were seven airframes in total. Five were standard one-man craft. Another was a two-seater, something like my current hybrid. The last was for cargo, and it was twice the size of the rest of them. It had a wide belly with a large door that opened out of the back. I peered inside and caught my breath.

"This thing could haul a dozen men," Robie mumbled.

"Or a handful of cannons," I added.

Finally, I had to pull myself away. I returned to the guards and told them I would be back in a few hours. "Tell the princess I'll have the rest of my recruits and supplies here before dawn. I'll need the Tal'mar pilots ready to fly tomorrow morning."

"As you wish," the guard said. He motioned for Robie to follow him. Two minutes later, I was back in the air.

From that point on, it all became a blur. On the next trip I brought Tinker, along with a load of springs and some of his tools so that he could go straight to work assembling the planes. I left him to it, and returned for my remaining pilots.

As promised, I returned from my last trip right at dawn. When I got there, my Tal'mar recruits were waiting with the rest of the pilots. There were five of them, ten of us in total. I instantly recognized the three who had shown such interest in my plane when I'd first arrived. They greeted me by name as I approached, and then introduced me to their companions.

"So you all want to be pilots?" I asked. They all pronounced loudly that they did. "And you all understand that these planes will have metal in them?"

"We understand," the boy said. "We don't care." They all seemed to share his sentiment.

"All right, then. Let's take a look at our planes." We walked over to the park, and a small crowd started to form behind us. I think everyone around us knew that we were making history, except perhaps my pilots. They were just kids who wanted to do something exciting, something different.

I located Tinker and asked him about his progress. The two guards who'd been on duty when I arrived were now assisting him. The woodworkers who had actually built the planes were nowhere to be seen. I suppose that shouldn't have surprised me. They must have been horrified to learn that metal was going inside of them.

"We've got four," Tinker said. His eyes were dull from exhaustion, and he looked older than he ever had before. "We've had to make a few modifications to fit the gearboxes and controls. The Tal'mar didn't quite understand how it was all going to fit together."

"All that matters is that they work," I said.

"They do. But as I said, we've only got four. I'm still working on number five, and the last two will require extensive fabrications."

"Then four will have to be enough." I spun around to face my pilots. "There will be four of us on this first mission. Robie, Shea, and Thala... come with me. The rest of you, help Tinker get these other planes finished."

There were a few sighs from the pilots who had been excluded, but I gave them an encouraging smile.

"Don't worry, by the time I'm done with you, you'll be sick of flying."

"I doubt that," Kalen said.

I led my small group back outside the city wall. "We don't have much time," I told them. "Our troops are fighting today, maybe even right now. The faster we get to Anora with air support, the more soldiers go home tonight. So this is what's going to happen: each of you is getting a lesson. We will take off, circle the island, and land. That's it. You get this one flight, you do it right, and you're a pilot."

"What if we don't get it right?" said Robie.

"What do I care? If you don't get it right, I'll be dead. Robie, you're first." He gulped as I motioned for him to climb into the pilot's seat.

Robie had already seen me fly, and he was familiar with the controls. I instructed him through the takeoff, and moments later we were in the air. Robie let out a triumphant shout as we climbed up through the treetops and the landscape shrank below.

"Nice job, Robie. Circle around to the west. When you see the coast come back around. Keep an eye on your gauges."

"Yes, sir!"

Robie did fine. His landing was a bit rough, but he already had a good grasp of the fundamentals and I was confident he was going to make a great pilot. It wasn't so easy with Shea and Thala. Shea was one of the Tal'mar boys who had first asked me about flying, and he was eager to learn. His hand was unsteady, which I partially attribute to the fact that he was surrounded by steel. I could also sense his apprehension, and I did my best to keep him calm as I walked him through it.

It was a rough and uncomfortable flight. It seemed the more I told him to calm down and focus on his flying, the more nervous he became. Ultimately, we survived and that was good enough for me. I was confident that he would settle into it after some practice.

Thala was a whole different situation. She was older, about twenty in human years which made her considerably older than me. And she had a chip on her shoulder. She was an aggressive flyer, to say the least. I couldn't tell if she was trying to prove something or if she just had a very wild personality. When we took off, she jammed the throttle wide open and shot us into the air like a rocket. Instead of making long, sweeping turns, she tended to yank on the controls and shoot us off at a ninety degree angle. Several times she did this, and each time it left my stomach hanging somewhere out there in space behind us. I tried to explain the stresses this was creating on the airframe, but it seemed to pass in one ear and out the other.

I was glad when we landed. I was reluctant to let Thala fly again, but at the same time, I knew she must have had some bottled up emotions that she needed to work through. Flying perhaps, was a way to do that. Besides, I had promised. So, with my pilots chosen and trained −at least as well as they could be - we returned to the park to collect our planes.

The streets were crowded now, mostly with Tal'mar citizens eager to get a look at this exciting new invention and the pilots who would be taking it into war. They cheered as we walked through the gate, and my pilots took to their newfound celebrity like fish to water. They smiled, waved, and shook hands as we entered the city and crossed into the park. My reaction was more reserved. I was too focused on our mission to let the elation of the moment take me. I kept my eyes ahead and my face straight. Inside however, I was dancing. Now we just had to complete our mission, and come out of it alive. I should have known I was hoping for too much.

Chapter 49

I've already described the absolute mastery that went into those planes. The real test however, was in the air. I was not disappointed. With their sleeker, lighter design and longer wingspans, the Tal'mar planes flew almost twice as fast as mine did. Thala was the first to test the planes' aerobatic abilities, almost as soon as we were in the air. She was a fearless pilot, and I turned into a nervous wreck as I saw her somersaulting, diving, and spinning through the clouds. I allowed this to go on for a few minutes. Despite my anxiety, I too, wanted to see what the planes could do. Then I set a course for Relian Keep and thankfully, the others fell in line behind me.

In my other planes, the flight from Silverspire to the airfield had taken about three hours. This time it took less than two. Cinder spent the entire flight curled up at my feet, enjoying a considerably more comfortable space than in our old plane. The cockpits in these new planes were almost completely enclosed, and much larger than anything we'd had previously. It was a good thing, too. Cinder had grown over the weeks, and I don't think she would have fit in the old one for much longer.

We landed single file, and stayed just long enough to load a box of cannon charges into each plane. I took a few moments to warn them about the Kanters' anti-aircraft gun, and then to describe the use of the cannon charges.

"They don't fall straight down when you drop them," I warned. "The inertia carries them forward at the speed your plane is traveling. Pay careful attention to this, because if you drop a charge on one of our men, your career is over." The pilots exchanged nervous glances.

"I'll drop the first charges," I continued. "Watch how I time it. Then you'll have a better idea of how it works." Three minutes later, we were back in the air and headed towards Anora.

It was just after noon when we located the battlefield on the plain south of Anora. It was the first time I'd had a chance to get a good look at the city. From the sky it looked more or less like Riverfork, except that it was ten times the size. The city was backed up against dense forest to the north and west, and pushed up against a river along the eastern and southern sides. There was no wall around Anora, but its location made it a difficult target to attack. The only direct access was over a bridge on the southern side. This, I saw as I flew over, was heavily guarded.

A broad plain stretched from the south side of the river to the northern edge of Riverwood, a dense and swampy forest. It was here that the human and Tal'mar armies chose to make their stand against the Kanters. I circled the area once, taking careful notice of the layout of the battlefield.

The human infantry clashed with the Kanters in the middle of the field, and it was not going well. Bodies lay scattered across the ground. A few Kanters had fallen, but very few. Several dozen humans lay dead or wounded in the midst of the chaos.

The Tal'mar detachment was comprised largely of archers, and they stayed on the fringes of the battle, taking careful aim at the Kanter foot soldiers. As accurate as the archers were, their arrows were no match for the Kanters. I saw one tattooed giant pluck half a dozen arrows from his flesh and give no sign of injury other than a trickle of blood.

I knew the Tal'mar archers could have taken the Kanters down if they were deeper in the battle, but they were afraid. Their small, lithe bodies were made for life among the branches, not for the press of combat. Even their human allies could have accidentally crushed them.

Further south, I saw the Kanters firing their cannons randomly into the enemy formations. Each one of these shots killed or injured a handful of men. I made the cannons my first target. I circled around behind them and came in for the attack, with the other planes trailing me. I had the advantage of surprise, and I used it. I counted ten cannons as I started dropping bombs. I was halfway across the battlefield by the time the first charges started to explode, and the dull, thudding booms echoed up from below.

When I made my second pass, less than half of the cannons still appeared functional. As I came around, something the Kanters were doing caught my eye. They had gathered around one of the cannons, and I realized that it was the special one... the one that had shot me down.

They were shouting and pointing, but not at me. I was in the lead, and the other planes were still circling around the battle behind me. Suddenly I realized that the slowest of the planes, the one at the end of the line, was a clear target for the Kanters.

I watched helplessly as they trained their gun on Robie's plane as he circled over the western woods. I screamed, but he couldn't hear me of course. Even if he could have, there wouldn't have been anything he could do. The Kanters methodically lined up their shot, and then fired. Robie's plane went down in a spray of shrapnel and black smoke.

Then the bombs started going off. The other pilots took heed of my lesson, and they aimed well. They destroyed the last of the cannons in a hail of explosive charges, and then set upon the Kanter infantry. The Kanters observed this with dismay. Then they looked up and saw three planes bearing down on them, and they broke ranks.

The Tal'mar and human soldiers cheered as their enemies started to fall back. A few of the Kantrayan commanders tried to force their men back into the battle, but the Kanters turned on them and killed them on the spot.

A dozen humans mounted up to pursue them as they fled into Riverwood, but for the most part the battle was over. The soldiers waved at us and cheered as we passed overhead. I knew at that moment that our place was secured in history, but it was a bittersweet moment. We had lost too many lives, and the one that pained me most was the young bully who'd once had a crush on me. I knew that even if he survived the crash, a cruel death at the hands of the Kanters was inescapable.

I wept for Robie as we turned to the north and headed for home.

Chapter 50

We celebrated that night, toasting to Robie with elderberry wine and feasting on roasted pheasant. We did our best to offer him a cheerful wake and share his memories with each other, until exhaustion and despair overtook us, and we collapsed in our bunks.

It was the first full night of sleep I'd had in recent memory, and I slept so deeply that I didn't even hear my companions leave the next morning. I woke to find the mid-morning sun splashing across the floor of my hangar. Cinder was curled up in a ball at my feet. Everyone else was gone.

I stretched, and then casually made my way over to the table for a breakfast of cold pheasant and dry, crusty bread. I'd just taken my first bite when General Corsan strolled in.

"Ah, the spoils of war," he joked, gesturing at the remnants of our dinner.

"It's good," I said. "I was too tired to taste it last night."

The general threw his head back and laughed. "At least you came back in one piece. I think you forgot something, though. You left this in your plane."

He reached into his jacket and produced an envelope. My face fell as I realized what it was. It was the message he'd asked me to deliver to King Ryshan.

"I'm sorry," I said. "I didn't have time. And I was afraid that if the king didn't believe me..." My voice trailed off. I stood there nervously as he studied me.

"I could have you court-martialed," he said. "Even hanged."

I hung my head. "I'm sorry, General. I let you down."

"No, you didn't." He surprised me with a smile. He put his hand on my shoulder. "I asked more of you than I had any right, Breeze. And you did more than anyone else could have. I dispatched messengers to the king last night to tell him of our victory. It won't be long before everything comes to light. Thanks for all you did, Breeze, and for all the lives you saved."

That jingled my memory. "I couldn't save Robie though," I said sullenly.

"Nonsense, Robie's just fine."

"What do you mean? We were all sure he had died!"

Corsan smiled broadly, and gestured towards the door. "Take a look." I trotted over to the hangar door and peered outside. Robie was in the field left of the runway. He wasn't alone. My hand strayed to the hilt of my sword as I saw the tattooed giant lumbering across the field towards him. Kanter!

The general stayed me with a hand to my arm. "Wait," he said. "Watch."

I frowned. Robie let out a shout and rushed towards the giant. He made a sudden, deft movement to the right and I saw... I saw a leather ball bouncing across the field. The giant laughed. He turned and ran after it. They appeared to be playing kickball.

"Are you kidding me?" I said breathlessly.

"Do you know who he is?" the general said with a smile. I shook my head, and realized that my jaw had been hanging open. I clamped it shut.

"I have no idea."

"His name is Keng'Chen. He is Keng'Sun's cousin." I stared at him.

"What does that mean?"

"It means we have a revolution on our hands. The Kanters are tired of Keng'Sun's leadership. They've seen our towns and cities, and some of them are beginning to understand that life can be... different. They want change."

"And I suppose you're going to give it to them?"

I wasn't sure how I felt about all of this just yet. What the general spoke of sounded to me like another war. We had just finally reached a peaceful accord with the Tal'mar after a thousand years of hatred. We'd lost good men, including my father, because of that. Everything I had done had been to stop the war. Not to start another one.

"It's not our problem at the moment," Corsan said with a shrug. "Not yet anyway. Chen is going to return to his people and try to overthrow Sun. In the meanwhile, he's already signed a treaty with us. Keng'Chen is now our ally."

I could hardly believe what I was hearing. "You honestly made a pact with *them*? You don't understand, general. I've seen what they do. The skulls, the bodies... They eat people. They're animals!"

He cocked an eyebrow at me. "Wasn't so long ago that some people might have said the same about you."

I bit my lip as his words struck home. He was right. Regardless of what I'd seen, and regardless of what they had done in the past, there was no reason not to give the Kanters a chance to change. We had everything to gain and nothing to lose, if they could do it.

"When will you need us ready?" I said.

He winked with his good eye, and put his arm across my shoulders. "Now that's the Breeze I know and love."

Chapter 51

My pilots were absent that morning because the general had sent them out to spread word of our victory. I was anxious to get back to Tal'mar, but with all three planes gone, I had no choice but to wait the day out. If that weren't enough, Corsan gave me specific orders to relax. Naturally, I did the exact opposite.

After breakfast, I walked through the encampment and quickly realized that we had an overwhelming number of injured soldiers. Though the physicians were doing their best to keep these poor men alive, even with my limited healing skills I could do more.

During the course of the day I saved two men from becoming amputees, and a half dozen more would certainly have died without my intervention. In addition, there were a good fifty more with serious injuries that I set on the path to a quick recovery.

Some of the men were reluctant to let a Tal'mar lay hands on them at first, until they realized who I was. My fame was apparently beginning to spread. *Breeze Tinkerman*, the humans began to say, *is no Tal'mar. She is half-human.*

By the end of the day, they were all lined up waiting to see me. Of course, the act of healing even a small wound requires intense concentration, and by sunset, I could hardly focus my eyes. General Corsan personally took me back to the hangar and brought me a warm plate of dinner. He smiled as he watched me devour it.

"Are you laughing at me?" I asked.

"Not at all. I just find this whole situation incredible."

"Why?"

He slapped his hands down on the table and threw his head back, his face a mask of wonder. "Don't you see what's been going on around you? The men have been talking about you all day: *It's a good thing that girl showed up when she did. Have you heard, she's a healer too! Does anyone know where I can find Breeze? I have a splinter!*"

I burst into laughter as I listened to him mock the soldiers. "What's wrong with that?" I said.

He slumped back in his chair, shaking his head. "Nothing. Nothing wrong, it's just difficult to believe. It seems like Tal'mar and humans have been fighting since the dawn of time. Then you come along and, within a week, the entire world is changed."

"It's not just me," I said. "This is what they all wanted. No one wanted to fight anymore. I just happened to come along at the right time. And it didn't hurt that I had Tinker's plane."

"Yes, there is that," he said with a distant look. "The world's never going to be the same, is it?"

"No." I could almost hear his thoughts. "I'm sure there will always be a need for good soldiers."

"I suppose you're right. To be honest though, it won't hurt my feelings if we spend most of our time building roads and landing strips. That wouldn't be a bad future."

We sat there in silence for a few minutes. The general's mood was contagious, and I found myself wondering what the future might bring. He was right. Everything was going to be different. *With peace comes prosperity,* or so they say. If it's true, then the future looked awfully inviting.

I glanced at Corsan, and suddenly found that I had the nerve to ask him a question I'd always wanted to. "General, how did you lose your eye?" I took a sip of water after asking this, and waited expectantly for his answer.

He smiled wickedly. "I had a terrible fishing accident." I laughed so hard that water came out of my nose.

In truth, he'd lost his eye in battle. His shield had broken, and a Tal'mar arrow had nearly found its way into his skull. It was one of those things that he could have been bitter about; something that could have driven a wedge between the general and his new allies. But he was a better man than that.

The general was always first in line to greet Tal'mar dignitaries and offer them a handshake, and from that day forward I hardly ever saw him without a smile on his face. "War," he used to say, "is at times an unfortunate necessity. But peace is a blessing that all people should have the luxury of taking for granted."

Chapter 52

I finally made it back to Tal'mar, two days later. By that time, word of our success had already spread across the kingdom. The streets were filled with celebration and festivities. As I arrived, a throng of admirers surrounded me. I stepped onto the wing of my plane and they lifted me up on their shoulders and carried me through the streets.

Revelers danced alongside us as the crowd moved through the city. It became a parade as onlookers shouted and waved at me, and I waved back at them. It was both incredible and hugely embarrassing at once. I never was the type to enjoy being the center of attention. On that day however, I managed to live with it.

We made a full circuit around the palace walls twice before I asked my bearers to take me to Tinker. They happily complied, and within a few minutes, I was back at the park near the city gates. Tinker rushed up to greet me, along with my pilots who'd not yet had a chance to fly. Naturally, they were all eager to learn, and I promised that their lessons would begin the next morning.

Some of the Tal'mar woodworkers were there as well. To my surprise, they had decided that Tinker and his devices of steel and iron weren't so bad after all. They had been advising him on the process of modifying the planes for power. The large plane that was designed for hauling cargo was especially going to present challenges. We were discussing this when the royal coach rolled up onto the lawn.

The guards leapt to the door and Princess Bresha appeared. She looked incredible, dressed in a lavender gown and wearing a jeweled tiara. One of the guards supported her hand as she stepped down to the lawn. She rushed over and threw her arms around me. That earned her a few raised eyebrows from the elder Tal'mar, but she didn't seem to mind.

"Breeze, you must come with me to the palace at once!" she said. She smiled broadly and put her arm around me, guiding me to the coach.

During the brief ride that followed, Bresha questioned me about every aspect of everything that had happened. I could barely answer each question before she asked the next. Then the coach came to a shuddering halt. I followed Bresha up the palace stairs and across the main hall.

"Where are we going?" I asked as the princess led me down a long hall.

"We're going to meet the queen," she said. I licked my lips nervously. In the time I'd spent with the princess, she'd never even once offered to introduce me to the queen. That left me with a sense of inferiority, a feeling that the Tal'mar queen considered herself too superior to allow me in her presence. I was, after all, a half-breed.

"Are you sure we should?" I said breathlessly.

"Of course we should, don't be silly."

We passed through a guarded doorway and into the throne room. The queen was there, alone except for the guards at the entrance. We crossed the room and stopped a short distance in front of the throne. Bresha bowed slightly, and I followed her lead.

"Is this her?" the queen said. I glanced at her apprehensively. She looked a lot like Bresha, except that her hair was lighter, almost red. She looked very young to be Bresha's mother. But then I remembered that Tal'mar didn't age the same as humans. She may very well have been hundreds of years old.

"This is her, mother," Bresha said.

The queen rose from the throne and cautiously made her way down the stairs to stand in front of us. "This is the girl who built the flying machine? The girl who brought us a treaty and then exposed the conspiracy of Prince Sheldon?"

"This is the girl, mother."

"Then this is my granddaughter?"

"Yes, mother." Bresha smiled slightly -a careful and guarded look.

My jaw went slack. Their words became a buzz as I looked back and forth between them. "I... I don't understand." My voice was breathless, my heart drumming in my chest.

"I'm sorry Breeze," Bresha turned to me and said. "I wanted to tell you sooner."

I felt my legs giving out beneath me, and the princess guided me over to a sofa. I felt dizzy as I settled onto that delicate fabric. She continued.

"We had to be sure it was really you, and not some sort of deceit. And of course, I was afraid. Not for myself, I mean, but for you. The Tal'mar may have let a child like you live, but not as a member of the royal family. Not the daughter of their princess. But you see, all that has changed now-"

"You're my mother?"

273

She nodded, her face apprehensive. "Breeze, please don't be angry."

I tried to push myself up, but found I didn't have the strength. "I should go," I muttered. "I'm putting you in danger."

"Nonsense," said the queen. "One thousand years of nonsense, and it ends today. The war is over, and so is the nonsense."

Bresha stroked my hair back from my face, and wiped the tears from my cheeks. I didn't know I had been crying. I looked up into her face and saw that she was as well. "I'm proud of you Breeze. You have proven yourself a hundred times over. You are more than human and more than Tal'mar. You will be remembered as this land's greatest hero. And you are my daughter."

"My granddaughter," the Queen added in a proud voice. "And soon the world will know it!"

Robie and the other pilots arrived that afternoon. The queen called for a feast, and she declared the entire week to be a holiday. She said that the land of Tal'mar would celebrate the holiday every year, for all eternity, in gratitude of what I had done. And then she announced to the entire world that I was her granddaughter. She brought me out in front of the whole city, standing hand in hand with her and my mother, and made the declaration to thousands of shocked Tal'mar citizens. And then, as one, they began to cheer.

I felt something that I can't quite explain. My heart pounded inside my chest, and my emotions ran from fear and exhilaration to pure undiluted joy. I looked out over the city and saw a collage of brilliant smiling faces. Tal'mar faces. Human faces. They stood next to each other, shouting and cheering as one, united by a dream and a belief in something greater for their combined futures. This was something that had never happened before. Tears of joy slid down my cheeks, and I wasn't the only one.

After the excitement died down, my mother insisted that Tinker and I accompany her back to the palace for the feast. The rest of the pilots joined us, of course.

The Tal'mar were quite excited to spend time talking with Tinker about his inventions. Now that they had a good idea of how the airplanes worked, they wanted to know what else Tinker could build. Naturally, they were working to find ways of building all of these devices without metal. That was one area where humans and Tal'mar would always differ.

Chapter 53

Over the months that followed, I trained my pilots, and in their own ways, they trained me. We got to know each with an intimacy that I had never imagined. In essence, we became brothers and sisters, and in time, we could almost read each other's minds.

Years later I would often look back on those days and wonder what might have happened if I had done things differently. There were a dozen times that I could have turned aside from my quest, moments that I could have taken the prudent course instead of the dangerous one. And I can say with the utmost certainty that if I had done this even once, the world would not have been the same. I'm not bragging or being arrogant, I'm simply stating it the way that I believe it happened.

I faced my fears and I refused to accept my fate. I chased my dream despite obstacles that seemed to be insurmountable. Eventually, I succeeded, and in the process, I changed the world. I'm proud of that fact.

The End

Epilogue

1,000 years of war had ended. As the rebuilding process began, the world around us began to take shape in wonderful and exciting new ways. General Corsan spent the next two years planning and building a bridge to connect the Isle of Tal'mar with the mainland. Meanwhile, I managed my fleet and pilots to both military and civilian ends. At times we were spies, at other times destroyers, but most often we were simply delivering mail.

For my part, I often met and accompanied members of royalty and dignitaries from city to city and country to country. I helped these people form alliances, treaties, and business partnerships. As these agreements came to fruition, the world around us blossomed. I watched as small towns like Riverfork grew into prosperous cities, and technologies like Tinker's steamwagons and airplanes brought us all closer together.

Analyn never gave up teaching, though with my encouragement, she and Daran healed their relationship with King Ryshan. A few years later when the king died and Analyn's older brother succeeded him, she thanked me for helping to bring them back together.

Tinker returned to his little valley, the only place he could ever call home, but I visited him there frequently. He also made annual trips with me to Tal'mar to visit with my mother during the solstice. We always exchanged gifts, as was their tradition, and Tinker's gifts were always well received.

My mother and the Tal'mar nobles –especially their children- spent all year looking forward to the night that Tinker would arrive in his old airplane and deliver dozens of wrapped gifts containing the most incredible mechanical toys and devices.

In time, Tinker too became a legend.

*

Thanks for reading "The Tinkerer's Daughter." Please take a moment to post a review at Amazon.com, and while you're there look at my other exciting titles! Keep reading for a free sample of Book Two in the series, "Tinker's War!"

Free Sample

TINKER'S WAR

Prologue

I was a fool in the company of fools, and I was the greatest fool of all. I was naive to believe the world could change so quickly. I wanted to believe - *I needed to believe*- because it meant so much to me. I was so desperate to have those narrow-minded fools who meant so much to me accept me into their fold. I was foolish enough to believe that they could, and that if they did, I would be happy there. But it was only one small way in which I misunderstood the world, and there were so many more. Yes, we were all foolish, and for that, we would pay a terrible price.

After a thousand years of bloodshed, men and elves had found peace. We were building roads and bridges, sharing our wildly different technologies with no expectations other than a better life for all. Our understanding of the world and the sciences grew exponentially. For a time, it truly was a golden age. But the Kanters, the cannibalistic giants from the Badlands to the south, were reluctant to abandon their old superstitious ways. The small tribe of Kanters that integrated into our society came alone. Meanwhile, their brethren fell into a civil war that King Ryshan fueled as he gifted weapons and machines to help the sympathizers overthrow their tribal leaders. Soon the

Kanters knew how to use bombs, cannons, and blunderbusses, and they did so with great efficiency.

The newfound peace we had achieved in the north lulled us into a sense of complacency. As the Kanters poisoned the ground with the blood of their kinsmen, many of the tribes began to foster a deep resentment towards both the humans and the Tal'mar. Trouble was brewing. In the end, it was not the Kanters that would bring us to ruin. It was something entirely different.

We had long since become aware of the special properties of the steel made from ore mined in the Blackrock Mountains. It possessed a unique quality, the ability to store energy at an incredible rate of efficiency. In fact, the simple act of heating and forging steel made from Blackrock ore appeared to imbue it with even greater capacity, so that when done correctly, the steel almost seemed to possess an energy all its own. Some metallurgists speculated that the energy contained in Blackrock Steel was the same energy that gave the Tal'mar our magical abilities, though our science was far too primitive to prove this theory.

Regardless, it wasn't long before word of our special steel spread beyond our borders and eventually, even beyond the seas. It was the lure of this powerful ore and the machines and weapons it could create that enticed the Vangars from their icebound continent in the west, across the Frigid Sea.

Nothing could have prepared us for the onslaught. We had fallen back into our petty ways, bickering over territories, coinage, and power. We were unprepared. We were fools, and for that we would pay in blood.

Tinker used to have a saying: *"A revolution may take centuries to happen, but when it does, it happens overnight."*

I always thought I knew what he was talking about. After all, I had lived through many of the same experiences he had. I had seen the centuries of bitter warfare and intolerance give way to a new, peaceful society. That change had happened seemingly overnight, and I thought Tinker's words had referred to this. What I didn't understand was that Tinker's proverb wasn't a recollection of history, but rather a vision of the future.

Little did I imagine how prophetic Tinker's words would prove to be, or how quickly we would fall under the wave of black dragon ships that stormed our shores that fateful summer.

Chapter 1

Robie asked me to marry him on a breezy summer afternoon under the shade of an old elm tree on a hill overlooking the Riverfork Midsummer Faire. It was not the first time he had asked, though he had grown increasingly persistent in recent years. I said "No," of course, as I had so many times before.

Ten years had passed since the death of Prince Sheldon and the end of his ambitious coup attempt; ten years since the end of the war between the humans and the Tal'mar, and the destruction of my home town of Riverfork. In the years that followed the war, the humans rebuilt the town and eventually Riverfork grew into a small but bustling city. Brick walls and tile roofs replaced the thatched-roof, split-log construction of the old village. Tall buildings grew up in place of the rustic cabins and frontier homes, and muddy paths became wide cobbled streets with boardwalks and intricately wrought gas lamps. The streets were lined with bakeries, shops, restaurants, and inns.

Docks sprang up along river. Barges made regular trips back and forth between Riverfork and Anora, the large city to the north. Commerce thrived. Families grew. Young men and women left their family farms in increasing numbers to move into the city where they could work and earn money to buy the wonderful things that industrialization had provided for us.

In the center of Riverfork, the residents built a park as a memorial to the brave souls who had died during the war. It was a lovely, sprawling piece of land with a wide grassy meadow and trees scattered throughout, and a dense old growth forest along the western edge. It was there, beneath the shade of an ancient elm that I found myself cornered by my would-be mate.

It had been an exhausting morning filled with faces both familiar and half-remembered. I had seen farmers and storeowners I had known in my childhood, as well as many of the children that I had gone to school with, now grown and raising children of their own. Among them was Terra Cooper, a farm girl I'd met while living with Tinker. I had never known Terra very well but I remembered her family fondly, especially for the dog that Tinker had bought from her father to protect me when the Kanters invaded. That dog, a flame-coated heeler I named Cinder had been my constant companion for years, until the inevitable creep of age and an especially cold winter took her from me. I missed her terribly. I had considered finding a new companion many times, but I knew that no other animal could ever replace Cinder.

That afternoon, Tinker and I left the faire to have a picnic up on the hill overlooking the park. Tinker's fans followed us, and it wasn't long before he wandered off surrounded by a flock of admirers - mostly elderly women who had outlived their husbands and were now reveling in the glow of a true hero. They took great pleasure in catching the attention of the wily old adventurer, and he took great pleasure in giving it to them.

I watched Tinker's highly animated movements as he described some old battle that he'd probably never even witnessed, much less fought in, with the gaggle of old women hanging onto his every word. He soaked up their adoration like a sponge. Honest man that Tinker was, he wasn't beyond exaggeration from time to time, especially in the company of admirers. I didn't want to deprive the old man of his simple pleasures so I smiled and let him enjoy the attention as I watched him from the shade of the elm tree. And that was where Robie found me.

"Can I sit with you?" he said as his long shadow fell over the blanket that I had spread out on the ground. I glanced up at him sideways, squinting against the sun. He was dressed in a fine white shirt with a long-tailed coat and tall knee-high boots that he'd folded halfway down. He wore a cutlass on his side –not an expensive one, but a quality weapon that a man could trust with his life- and a long brown cloak with the hood pulled back. He hardly looked like the young pilot I had known all those years. He was more like a buccaneer out of some storybook.

"Of course," I said, as congenially as I could manage.

He happily joined me on the blanket, leaning back against the tree and ran his fingers through his thick black hair, brushing long bangs away from his face. "It's a nice park," he said matter-of-factly.

"Yes, it is."

"It doesn't look anything like it did before."

"No," I agreed, nodding slightly. I was purposefully curt. I had been sitting alone, watching Tinker and enjoying the blissful weather. I found Robie ruining my mood. I had a feeling that I knew where the conversation was headed, so instead of helping it get there, I just kept quiet.

"I hear General Corsan retired last year."

"He was getting old," I acknowledged.

"Not as old as Tinker," Robie said with a chuckle. He was watching Tinker with a wide grin. The old man shouted something and waved his arms in the air, reenacting some battle between our air force and the Kanters, or perhaps Sheldon's loyal foot soldiers. "I wonder when Tinker will retire."

"Tinker will never retire," I said. "What would he retire from? All he does is build things and he certainly won't quit that until he's dead. The man's mind never stops."

"Good for him," Robie said. "I hope I have half that man's energy when I'm his age."

I watched Robie as he watched Tinker. There was no arguing the fact that Robie had grown into a fine young man, but somehow I still saw the boy I'd known in his face. Perhaps it was because I had matured so quickly in my youth, my years advancing well beyond those of my peers. Though he was my senior by several years, I had attained physical maturity years ahead of Robie. Such is the nature of the Tal'mar. Even as a half-breed, I'm no exception.

"He has a farm north of Anora now," I said. "General Corsan, that is. I was there last spring. He has a vineyard. He makes excellent wine."

"Is that so?" Robie said. "I'd like to try it some time. Good wine is hard to find."

He had been gazing across the field, watching Tinker, but now he turned to look me in the eyes. "Breeze, don't you think it's time to stop all this?"

I narrowed my eyes. "Stop what, Robie?"

"The planes, the air force. You don't have to do it anymore. I don't even know why you bother. Your entire life these days is delivering packages and shuttling ambassadors back and forth. How can you stand it? How can you stand to be in the same plane with those people?"

"I'm not with them," I said. "I'm with the sky."

He sighed, exasperated. "Is that all that matters to you then? The sky?"

I rolled my eyes. "Don't be foolish."

He twisted slightly and slid closer to me, taking my hands. He folded his own large, rough-skinned hands around them. "Breeze, marry me. Let's put all of this behind us and get on with life! We can buy a farm, and you can have children-"

"What are you talking about?" I said, interrupting him.

"A family, Breeze. A life!"

"I already have a life."

"This?" he said cynically. "Shuttling fat diplomats back and forth so they can feed each other greasy food and buy each other fancy clothes with our taxes? This is no life you have, Breeze. You're not living, you're hiding."

I pulled my hands away from him and placed them in my lap. "I'm doing exactly what I want to do, Robie. Look at me. Look at my face, my ears. Do you think I'm one of your farm girls? Do you envision me standing at a cook stove all day, my belly swollen with child, our house full of chaos and noise? Is that what you want?"

A mystified look swept across his face. "Cook stove? I don't know... you do cook, don't you?"

I snorted, pushing away from him, and rose to my feet. My skirts caught in a root as I did, and I tugged them free, causing a small tear in the fabric. "I hate these things," I snapped.

"You hate trees?"

"No, fool! I hate skirts. I've half a mind to throw them all away and buy a drawer full of breeches like yours."

"That's ridiculous," he said, laughing. "Women don't wear breeches."

I stared at him furiously, and the smile vanished from his face. "Do you mean to say that after all I've gone through, you'd refuse to let me wear comfortable clothes because I'm a woman?" I pressed my fists to my sides. "Do you think *you could stop me, Robie?*"

His face reddened. "I, uh... no, of course not. It's just that-"

"I know. *Women don't wear breeches.*"

He stared at me, suddenly speechless.

Perhaps he was right. Perhaps I was being foolish. After all, it was tradition -not only for the humans, but also for the Tal'mar- that the womenfolk wore skirts and dresses. It didn't matter so much for children, but when young girls grew into women they were expected to wear the right clothes and to cook and work in the garden, and to have children. That was simply the way things had always been.

Why did it suddenly bother me so? After all the things I had accomplished, how had I been reduced to hating my skirts? Was it simply that there was nothing else to worry about? Was I so safe and comfortable in with my life that the little things seemed more important than ever before? Or was it something else? Was it really about skirts at all, or was it because I was hiding, as Robie had said?

I didn't have time to examine the thought more closely because a plane whooshed over the park and sent ribbons and streamers spinning across the grass.

The faire-goers froze, turning their faces skyward and stared frightfully at the aircraft.

"What's that idiot doing?" Robie said next to me. "It's illegal to fly over cities!"

I watched quietly as the plane circled around the north end of town and swooped in for a landing right in the middle of the park. The citizens broke into a screaming panic as they raced out of the landing path. I glanced at Robie and saw a snarl creeping across his features. He flexed his hands into fists.

"I'm going to beat some sense into that rookie, whoever he is!" With that, he went stalking down the hill towards the plane. I threw caution to the wind and ran after him.

Robie rushed up to the plane just as it pulled to a stop. "What's the matter with you, pilot?" he shouted.

The pilot looked down at him, his face shielded by his flying cap and goggles. "Who's flying that thing?" Robie demanded. "What's your name, pilot?"

The pilot climbed out of the cockpit and dropped to the ground. He pulled off the helmet and goggles and we both suddenly realized that *"he"* was in fact a *she*. Her name was Becca. She was one of the younger pilots from the squadron located at Avenston, the capital city. She had tucked her long blonde hair inside her flight jacket. From the ground, it had been impossible to tell she was female.

Becca looked right past Robie towards me, ignoring him entirely. "Commander Breeze, the kingdom has been invaded. The King is dead."

I hardly knew what to think at first. The words were such a shock to me that my instinctive reaction was to believe this some sort of elaborate joke. But I knew from the look on her face that it was not. My breath caught in my chest. "Attacked? Who was it, the Kanters?"

"No. I don't know who they are, ma'am. They came in the night with no warning. The dragon ships swept in from the west and we were completely unprepared. It was all we could do to escape. A few of us, anyway."

"Dragon ships?" I said. "The attackers came by sea?"

"No, by air. They fly in massive boats unlike anything I've ever seen. They look like ships sure enough, but they're held aloft by great balloons and a vicious black smoke follows in their wake everywhere they go. They're armed with flamethrowers and cannons larger than anything we've ever built. One shot could level an entire house."

I took a deep breath, steadying myself. "The King, you said?"

"Yes, ma'am. Their first volley all but decimated the royal palace in Avenston. The entire royal family is..." she stopped as her voice broke. She took a breath and blinked away the tears. "The King and his family are all dead."